The Hero's Call

Alex McGilvery

Hero's Call
Alex McGilvery

ISBN 978-1-989092-60-6

Cover Illustration by Victorine Lieske

CHAPTER 1

Robin danced away from Hal's training sword. He was bigger, faster, and more experienced than her. That's why she liked sparring with him.

The yard clattered with the wooden training swords; laughter echoed from the walls. There were twenty of them, the most Sir Garraik would allow in training at a time. Hal and a few others wore colours on their right sleeves marking them as squires. Plague it, but Robin wanted her colours. She was one of the oldest trainees at fifteen winters, but not yet chosen to squire a knight. She had to prove herself, even more so because she was the smallest trainee.

The sword met Robin's breastplate which stopped the blow as it should, but Hal followed up by closing the distance and grappling her to the ground while she was still trying to breathe. His wooden sword lay across her throat.

"You're improving." Hal rolled to his feet and gave Robin a hand to pull her up.

"Doesn't feel like it." Robin snapped her mouth closed on the complaint then coughed out the dust from the ground. A cloud crossed the sun, sending a chill down her spine.

"That's because you're training with people bigger and stronger than you. You don't pick safe partners like the other girls." Hal bowed slightly. "Don't give up hope."

"Thanks, Hal." Robin gave him a smile, hiding the wince. The breastplate stopped the blow, but it was only leather over mail and she would have a new bruise to add to her collection.

"What are Hal's weaknesses?" Sir Garraik stepped up beside her. His face carried the same neutral expression it always did. Out of his hearing, the trainees joked it was carved from stone.

"He over commits." Robin wracked her brain for something else to add to what she'd answered every other time she'd lost. "And he's quick to grapple because he's bigger than most."

"Now you know how to beat him." Sir Garraik stalked off to torment some other trainee.

Sword was her weakest weapon, but it was the knight's honour. Robin grit her teeth. *How is grappling a weakness?*

"Mooning again?" Crispin smiled to take the sting from his words.

"Trying to think how to beat Hal." Robin pushed the gloom out of her head. As long as she was a trainee, there was a chance.

"If you figure it out, let me know."

"You will be the second to know." Robin's lips quirked.

"Second? I'm hurt." He dramatically put his hand on his heart. "Who's the lucky gent who will be the first?"

"Hal."

"That calls for a duel." Crispin drew his sword with a flourish.

Robin scanned the area to be sure they had space and marked an X in the sand with her heel. "Three paces."

"I truly wish this place had at least one set of stairs."

"Half of the trainees would break a leg on the first day." Robin lifted her sword and buckler to the ready.

"Have at you, rogue." Crispin leapt to the attack. If Hal was a bull, Crispin was a cat. Robin focused on her defence while she waited for the opening. Crispin prided himself on his flamboyant style. Sir Garraik's jaw clenched at the unnecessary movement, but Crispin was the best trainee not a squire yet, and he'd beat all the squires, except for Hal.

She concentrated on deep breaths; fighting Crispin meant outwaiting him. It was good stamina training.

Crispin's cut came too far forward, and Robin bashed it aside with her buckler. He tried to step farther in and grapple. Robin had been waiting for that. Unlike Hal who towered head and shoulders above her, Crispin only had a few fingers advantage and not nearly the bulk. Robin tilted her sword to claim his attention then slammed the buckler into his training helmet, only pulling the blow at the last second. Head blows were the only ones Sir Garraik insisted they not strike full force.

Even if she hadn't pulled it, the attack would have barely brushed Crispin. He recovered and leapt back with unbelievable speed. Robin lunged forward to stay in measure. A slash to his throat clashed against his buckler. As Crispin responded with his own cut, Robin kicked him on the thigh. Since he was still moving backward, it unbalanced him enough to send him staggering to the three-pace distance from the X. He made an impossible sideways leap and lunge to catch her under the arm. *Another bruise.*

Crispin saluted. "Should try that kick thing with Hal."

"When was the last time you kicked a tree? It only works if the opponent is moving backward." Her neck hairs lifted. Someone was watching her.

He laughed and moved to ready again. "That was a nice move with the buckler; almost got me."

She pushed the feeling away. "I will get you eventually!" Robin shouted and lunged to the attack.

***

Sir Garraik stood straight as an arrow but relaxed, like he could keep that position all day.

"Lord Huddroc from up north is visiting to have a word with the king. I'm not allowed to tell you what that word is." Sir Garraik frowned, then visibly shifted his thoughts away from the lord's purpose. "He may try to steal one of you away as a squire. Keep in mind you need my permission to accept any offer." The knight didn't move, but Robin felt her face burn under his gaze. She kept hoping he'd forgotten that incident. This was her last year of training unless she became a squire. Then it would be back to town running errands for the neighbours. She'd stopped growing soon after starting training. who'd want a runt for a squire? Robin was sure the only reason she hadn't been sent home already was Sir Garraik's sense of duty. He'd chosen her but had to have since regretted it.

***

In the equipment shed, Robin hung up her equipment after checking it for damage. Someone had put a stool near her spot years ago, and she decided to take it as being helpful. Even the new trainees, years younger than she, were taller and heavier. Once that chore was done, she took one more breath of the mixed scents of metal, oil, and wood that made the shed one of her favourite places, then jogged away toward the bath house.

"I don't know how you can face Hal." Jalliet shuddered dramatically as she dropped her towel on a bench and tiptoed into the steaming water. "He terrifies me."

"That's why you'll never beat him." Tamlyn spoke without opening her eyes, already in place and motionless as a stone. Her long hair floated in a halo around her. Robin quashed a flash of envy, long hair in battle was dangerous, but…

"What are you thinking?" Jalliet asked, then splashed Robin. "Letting the fae take you away again?"

"Only wishing I could lengthen my hair as quickly as shortening it."

"Your hair is cute; it suits you." Jalliet pushed a stray lock of blonde curls under the towel on her head. "You have a dancer's body, and that cap of raven black makes you look like something out of a grandma's story."

"She's right you know." Tamlyn rinsed her hair and sighed. "Still mouse brown. I keep hoping it will get darker."

Jalliet shook her blonde curls, splashing Robin and Tamlyn. "Maybe you should want it lighter, use your women's wiles to distract the enemy."

"Jalliet, you can't guarantee that someone who accosts you in an alley will be younger than you and besotted by your beauty." Robin sank deeper, hissing as bruises contacted the hot water.

"Whoever won't expect me to know anything. I'll smile coquettishly at them, then stab 'em in the eye." Jalliet shook her blonde curls, then poked Robin in the ribs with her finger. "I will never be a knight."

"Nope, our families want us to be able to defend our honour and know enough not to get in the way of our bodyguards." Tamlyn splashed Jalliet. "They'd be upset if we visited home bruised like our senior here."

Robin rolled her eyes; both the girls were older than her fifteen years. "If I'm your senior, why don't you ever listen to me? A little work and you'd be twice as strong."

"I know, learn more than three attacks and use them in different orders." Tamlyn nudged Robin with a toe. "But neither I nor Jalliet will be knights. All we need to learn is to survive long enough for the people who can fight to do their job."

"I think it's wonderful that you work so hard." Jalliet glanced over at Robin, "but our worlds are different. When Lord Huddroc returns north, I will travel with him."

They were the daughters of nobility, and Robin was the youngest of a brood of merchant brats. "I'd better get out before I fall asleep." Robin climbed out of the bath and snagged her towel to dry off.

"We'll see you tomorrow." Tamlyn waved, eyes still closed.

Robin dressed quickly in the plain grey of a trainee. She pulled the weighted vest on over her wool blouse and wrinkled her nose at the musty smell. Wearing the vest had started as a punishment, a knight had asked her to squire him. Sir Garraik had found out and stopped it. Robin didn't see the knight again. After three months of the extra weight, she decided to keep it on in her quest to get stronger. That was three years ago.

Outside, Hal was heading toward the hall, light shirt unlaced. *Not that he needs weight training.* He served Sir Garraik as the junior squire. Robin wasn't sure if that was a privilege or a punishment.

Like the other trainees, Robin served a section of the hall assigned by the chief steward. The delicious odours made her stomach rumble, but she ignored it. She and the other trainees would eat at the end of the meal, but it did mean she could fill her plate as she wanted.

She picked up her tray. It was the heaviest one, more weight training, and the kitchen staff loaded it down with plates of cut meat. Robin had mastered the technique of balancing the tray with one hand, removing a plate with the other, all while adjusting to the new balance of the tray.

"You want to change sections?" Crispin asked as he picked up his tray.

"Why would you ask that?" Robin frowned. "I don't want to run punishment laps tomorrow."

"You already run more laps than you'd get for punishment."

"Then maybe I don't want to have to run less." Robin glanced over at the son of the lord visiting from the north, the one Sir Garraik might have hinted was looking for a squire. The boy had to be younger than her, but he acted like a lecherous grandfa. Perhaps he got away with it in his home, but after dodging him all last meal, Robin was more than ready to bash him with her tray. *That would convince the lord of my worth.* "Thanks, but I need to find a way to deal with this myself."

"It's not weakness to ask for help."

"It won't be the last time I have to deal with someone like him. Better to learn now than later."

Crispin frowned but headed away to his section without responding.

Conversations ebbed and flowed as she passed, pausing as the men and women served themselves and tucked in. The king was a generous man to work for. Most of the people were the King's Guard and had no interest in the trainees. She could have been a dog carrying the tray, and as long as the meat didn't run out, they wouldn't notice.

Robin came to the table with the lecherous boy sitting in the middle, where she'd be forced to move close to do her job and not have space to dodge. If he wasn't such a nuisance, she might almost admire his tactics.

A long breath in through her nose and out her mouth centred her for battle. Robin walked along the table putting plates in front of the diners. Like the night before, the boy was surrounded by fawning followers even younger than him.

"Whew, why would a little, young thing like you feel the need to wear that uniform?" The lecherous boy got the twitter of approval from his friends. "I've not walked out with a girl so fae-touched. Is *all* your hair so raven black? I'm Lencely. What's your name?"

What gives him the right to talk like I'm a plaything? Protocol forbade her responding in the way her mouth wanted to, but at least she wasn't required to answer. Fae-touched, no one had called her that since she'd arrived as a trainee. Sir Garraik had stared at them and listed the reasons they could be sent home in disgrace. Interfering with another trainee was one; inability to get along with everyone was another.

In her distraction, she left a chance for the youngster to try to catch her, but Robin spun away, just avoided bumping into the guests at the next table. She finished the table and the next.

"More meat over here, girl!" The lord's son yelled. Robin nodded in acknowledgement. She went through her section putting platters of meat on the table. When she reached the boy's table, he leered at her and patted his knee. "Take a break."

Robin bit her cheek and turned to put a platter on the other table.

Someone yanked on the shoulder of her tunic, unbalancing her. The tray slipped and fell behind her as she fought to not end up sitting on the boy's knee. The squeal of outrage might have come from Jalliet, and Robin giggled as she recovered and turned to face the boy to apologize. The northern lord's son snarled as his knife thudded against the tray. Robin bumped into something as she backed up and kicked it out of her way. A yelp of protest made her frown. As if she wasn't already in enough trouble.

"Hold." Sir Garraik barely raised his voice, but all the sound in the hall stopped. Robin's face burned as all the attention focused on her.

"She dumped the meat on me deliberately. Look what it did to my clothes," Lencely squeaked and made a face as he picked meat off his robes. Robin pushed her estimate of his age lower.

"Trainee?" Sir Garraik looked at her.

"I wouldn't waste good food that way." Robin told her white-knuckled fingers to relax. They refused and clutched tighter on the tray as a wave of laughter swept through the hall.

"I want her punished!" Lencely shrilled, pointing at her. "No servant can be allowed to humiliate a noble."

"You are operating on wrong assumptions, boy." Sir Garraik's tone didn't change, but experience told Robin the boy had made a bad mistake. "First, you aren't a noble; you are a noble's son. I will request your father to explain the difference to you. Second, she is not a servant. Waiting tables is part of the training all my trainees undertake."

"I would never wait on others."

"That is your choice, but you will never train with me."

"What about her punishment?" The boy waved his hand, and Robin reflexively moved the tray between them.

Sir Garraik plucked the knife from the boy's grasp, scowled at it, then tossed it on the table. "Carrying weapons in the hall is forbidden."

The boy paled. "Tis but a knife."

"It became a weapon as soon as you used it to mark the tray. Be glad for her training and reflexes. If you had wounded her, you would be facing trial." The knight folded his arms and glared at the boy. "As for punishment, show up at the training yard in the morning. Wear training gear."

Robin muffled a gasp, but she wasn't about to argue with her training master. It wouldn't have been the first time she'd faced his punishments, but she didn't know what he was thinking and that, somehow, was worse.

Sir Garraik spun and walked away. Robin followed him as his hand sign commanded.

"Trainee, report."

"He has been a bother, but I didn't expect him to pull one of the others into his antics. The meat truly was an accident." Robin stood at alert and waited for her punishment, gut clenched with a mix of fear and rage.

Sir Garraik glowered at her while the blood thudded in her ears. "At least you didn't kill him. You will serve at the head table tomorrow. Wear your dress uniform and no extra weight. I will have no more such incidents. There is a knight who may be suitable to squire you, if you can stay out trouble for the next few months."

"Yes, sir." Robin's palms sweated more than when she'd faced Hal.

"Dismissed." Sir Garraik walked away to speak to another knight.

Robin returned the tray and filled a plate. Her stomach insisted it wasn't hungry, but she needed the fuel. She wanted to be angry with Sir Garraik but didn't dare, so she directed it at the brat.

"Eat in the servant's hall." The head of the hall staff pointed with his chin. "Out of sight, out of mind."

"Good idea." Robin carried her meal to the plain room. She nodded to the scattering of men and women wearing royal livery, then picked a seat at the end of a table where her trembling wouldn't be noticeable. She'd dumped a tray on a noble's son, and Sir Garraik thought having him show up for training would be his punishment? Maybe he would be there to watch Sir Garraik thrash her. A mistake was worked out on the training ground as Sir Garraik demonstrated why they were training with him.

"You showed admirable restraint." A man sat across from her. "Geoff, sommelier in the king's service."

"Robin, trainee in the king's service." Her voice hardly trembled, though her heart skipped a beat. She had to stop letting herself get distracted.

"Well, well." Geoff smiled. "You continue to delight. There are those who would view eating with servants as a punishment."

"We all serve in our own way." Robin stuck her chin out. "With a slightly different story, I would be wearing livery beside you."

Geoff nodded and tucked into his dinner. Robin followed his example. When the sommelier finished, he stood and nodded to her, then paused as if debating something internally.

"You look like the type who will listen to advice. Don't make the child look a complete fool when you're thrashing him tomorrow."

Robin sat in shock as he left. She would spar with that brat? Her mind couldn't come up with a reason, but Geoff was clearly higher up in the hierarchy of the castle, no matter what his title. He'd seen something she'd missed. Robin finished up without paying attention to her meal, put her plate on the tray on the sideboard then headed for her room. She had a great deal of thinking to do. Her lips turned up as she imagined matching swords against the boy. Then her stomach rebelled as she imagined his father watching the match.

CHAPTER 2

The early morning air chilled her as Robin woke and stretched. Dressing quickly, she jogged down the many flights of stairs from the trainee's barracks to the backdoor of the main barracks. The soldiers at their breakfast ignored her. The odours of the meal followed her out into the clear morning air. Though they lived under the same roof, these soldiers had little to do with the trainees who were destined for command.

She'd be wishing for the cool, but she'd wish for it once her training gear was in place. Robin removed the weighted vest to don the gambeson, then put the mail over it. The leather pieces went on top of that. They formed a simpler version of the plate mail the knights wore. On top of that, Robin slung the pack she'd weighted down to feel like steel plate armour. Then she picked up her sword and buckler and was ready to warm up. The vest she hung on her hook.

Once burdened down, she jogged outside and around the training yard. By the tenth lap, all the rest of the trainees had joined her. As they did every morning, Jalliet and Tamlyn rolled their eyes at the extra weight Robin carried.

Sir Garraik entered the yard and the trainees formed up, the five squires in front, the rest in columns behind them.

"We will be welcoming a guest," he announced. "I expect morning for him means something different than for us. You will demonstrate the full extent of your skills. Squire Hal, lead the drills."

Hal stepped forward and settled into the position for unarmed combat. By the time they'd run through punches, blocks, and kicks, sweat poured down Robin's back.

Everything they did, Robin carried the extra weight, except for placing the wood sword and her buckler on the ground.

When they'd finished the jumping, rolling, and other agility work, she had a fierce grin on her face. While she might be one of the smallest trainees, only the squires and Crispin came matched close to her ability to move.

"I don't know if you're mad or terrifying." John, one of the next most likely to make squire, grinned at her.

"My mother would tell you this is nothing. She was a dancer before marrying, and she would have done all this on her toes and gracefully." Robin pirouetted, then did a jump she'd learned as a child.

"Terrifying," John laughed as he tried to spin. "Definitely terrifying."

"Pair up, light sparring, two paces," Sir Garraik called out.

"I'll wait for you to get rid of the extra weight." John nodded toward the equipment room. She dashed over, replaced the weighted gear where it belonged, put her training helmet on, then sprinted back to where John waited, pretending impatience.

She picked up the sword and buckler and barely had them in hand before John lunged. Robin had expected it and stepped aside, making her own cut which he deflected with his buckler. They sparred until Sir Garraik called a halt. She'd forgotten about their visitor as she fought.

Switching partners, they sparred until Sir Garraik called a halt

"Archery now."

The trainees fetched traded their swords and bucklers for bows and training arrows and lined up, facing the human-shaped straw targets hanging on a wood wall.

"First row, to the line."

When Robin stepped to the line, she strung her bow and waited for the order.

"Looks like a child's bow." The comment was accompanied by laughter behind her, but not from the trainees. They treated her and the other two women with the same informal courtesy as all the other trainees. Robin's mother had warned about bullying and worse, but from the beginning, they'd been nothing but respectful.

Robin's gut tightened as she breathed to center herself. The brat wouldn't rattle her.

"Fire at will."

She plucked an arrow from her quiver, had it nocked on the string and drawn before the others had the first arrow in hand. *Don't rush.* Robin paused to focus properly, then released the arrow, it struck the target's right hand. Part of her registered laughter behind her. Her second arrow found its mark in the left hand. Two she sent into the knees, one into the groin, and the last into the head.

Robin unstrung her bow and stood at ease waiting for the others to finish. They were grouping arrows in the torso of the targets, tightly enough for the fletching to touch.

"I swear you do that one shot just to put us off." Crispin spoke from behind her.

"I heard you fellows carry something important there." Robin grinned. "It would never get through the armour, but I'm sure it would put him off his pace."

"I'm getting a stronger codpiece."

"Retrieve," Sir Garraik ordered.

Robin laid her bow down and jogged to fetch her arrows. When she returned to the line, Sir Garraik gave her the hand sign to follow as Hal took over running the range. He led her over to where Lencely waited in full plate armour.

"I said training gear." Sir Garraik glared at Lencely. "And you're late."

"I didn't bring any here, and I will have to train in armour soon enough." Lencely

"Sir, I've never sparred against armour. It might be educational." Robin felt a tight grin on her face. She was looking forward to this. The glare Sir Garraik levelled at her could have turned her to ash.

"I could educate you about all kinds of things." The kid leered at her, and Robin rolled her eyes. He reddened and put a hand on his sword.

"Set the blade aside and choose a training sword."

"I will fight with steel." The hand didn't move from the hilt. Robin couldn't hide her snort of derision.

"Only fools spar with steel." Sir Garraik's voice became like grinding rocks. "Put it aside or forfeit."

"My father..." the boy sputtered.

"I trained with your father." Sir Garraik's gaze should have set the kid aflame.

One of the followers took the sword and scabbard from the boy and another ran to the equipment room and came back with an armful of wood swords. The kid rejected one after another before finally settling on one.

"Would you like time to warm up?" Robin asked. "I know it is hard to adjust to a new weight in the hand."

The kid didn't answer but tromped past her to the center of the yard and ran through a few drills using the sword two-handed.

Surely, he can't really be that slow. Robin shook her head and jogged over to the equipment shed to fetch her sword.

The brat's hanger-on who'd fetched the swords had grabbed them at random from the trainee's hooks. One of the missing ones was hers. Robin ground her teeth, then went through the spare swords to find one. She'd spent candles working on her sword to balance it exactly as she wanted. The closest one to tolerable was a span longer than she was used to. She stuffed the helmet on her head, still muttering.

She walked back out with the sword in hand but no buckler since she hadn't seen the kid carrying one.

"As the one accepting the challenge, trainee Robin will choose the arena."

The kid looked confused.

"No limits."

"Very well." Sir Garraik lifted a hand. "Take your place and introduce yourselves."

"I am Lencely Huddroc, third son of Lord Huddroc of Vilscape."

"Robin Fastheart, first daughter of Milend and Chomas of Kingstown."

"You're a commoner?" Lencely sneered and pushed his visor down.

Robin shrugged and stood ready. He didn't look capable of beating her, but he was a lord's son, so who knows what training he had. She sweated under her gambeson. The honour of the trainees was on her shoulders, or maybe being trounced by the brat would be her punishment.

"You have the attack," Robin said.

Lencely leapt forward with a hard cut at her head. Robin almost blocked it with her arm, but she had no buckler. *Got distracted by thinking about the wrong things, stupid.* She felt unbalanced without it. When she jumped back out of measure Lencely started yattering at her. Some of the other trainees were the same, trying to distract with words.

"I could teach you a lot about the sword." Lencely's voice carried the leer past his closed visor. Robin shook her head and focused on her opponent. His words couldn't lose her the match.

"Seems a pity to put bruises on such delicate skin." He took up the attack again hammering at her. The boy did have speed but not much finesse.

"You're overextending on your cuts." He wasn't the only one who could natter. Robin took up a commentary on his style, offering advice, congratulating him on a good attack that pierced her defence and gained a point from Sir Garraik. She danced out of range and examined him. The armour fit him like a skin. He probably did his agility warms ups in it. She would.

"Enough blathering, fight!" Lencely yelled at her. Other voices yelled from the side. If the trainees weren't still at the range, she'd have given all the boys bruises to carry away for their impertinence.

"Very well." Robin slipped past his lunge and tapped him on the chest. "Don't worry, trust your armour."

He picked up his speed but grew sloppier. Robin took to tapping on his armour letting each blow land harder than the last. She kept her commentary, now more directed to his defence.

"Blast it, wench, come at me with whatever you have, no more games." Lencely snarled through his visor.

"Since you asked so nicely." Robin put her second hand on the sword, it was crowded even for a hand and half, but for once she blessed her small hands. Her first cut blew past his counter to clang on his shoulder, then she kept up the barrage landing strikes at will. Though to give the kid credit, he never stopped trying.

He backpedalled valiantly trying to slow her down. Robin's teeth were bared, and she wanted to laugh, only it would embarrass him more. The catcalls from his followers had died down.

Lencely growled and let her sword clang off his breastplate and cut at her face. Robin stepped aside taking the blow on her shoulder pauldron. She nodded in delight as she drew her sword back lifting his over her head, then charged into him, bowling him over. She had her foot on his sword arm and used the point of her sword to flip his visor up, then gripped her blade halfway to the tip to threaten him.

"Match!" Sir Garraik called.

Robin stepped back and offered a hand to Lencely. "You fought well, almost had me with that last move."

He gripped her hand, and she pulled him up. "My oldest brother would love to spar with you. He's almost ready to be knighted." *He would trounce you* stayed unspoken but glinted in his eyes.

"Maybe I can teach you a few tricks to take home with you."

"Really?" His eyes lit up, then darkened and became calculating. "My lady, I apologize for my behaviour and the insult to your person. Has this duel satisfied your honour?" His voice dripped with fake sincerity, and Robin almost snorted again, but it was the formula, even if he didn't mean it. He couldn't honourably do anything less with Sir Garraik watching.

"It has." Robin clapped him on the shoulder. "How about you meet the rest of the gang before I get back to work?"

His eyes widened, but he didn't say anything but offered his arm. She put her hand on it as she'd seen the noble ladies do, and they walked to the other trainees.

"That was quite the demonstration." Hal nodded at him. Turned out the trainees hadn't been working much on their archery.

"This is Lencely of Vilscape." Robin grinned at him.

The trainees gathered around him chatting about the match. Robin waved over the boys who had come to cheer Lencely on from the other side of the training yard.

"Are you also trained?"

"Some, ma'am, but not as much as Lencely." The boy holding the steel sword spoke while turning red. "I'm sorry 'bout last night." He sounded a bit more real than Lencely.

"Apology accepted." It would be a waste of time to hold grudges. Time enough to find out if they were lying.

Hal had offered to spar with Lencely, so Robin looked over at Sir Garraik who nodded.

"Why don't I get you some gear and see what you've got." The boys' eyes gleamed as they followed her to the equipment room.

CHAPTER 3

Robin called a halt to the training, and the boys slumped their shoulders in the heat of the training yard. It did get hotter later in the day. She didn't bother mopping her face.

"Check your equipment and put it away." Robin followed them into the cool of the equipment shed and watched as swords were examined and hung, then attended to her own gear. Breathing in the scent of wood and steel, the smell of her dreams.

Robin sat on a bench and passed Lencely a waterskin. He drank half and poured some on his face. She finished off the skin and set it aside to refill later.

"Uh, sorry about being so nasty." Lencely looked at his shoes. "I don't get to see many boys my age at home, I guess I was showing off."

"We resolved that with our duel, but apology accepted." She took a deep breath. "You strike me as someone who will learn from their mistakes."

"I will try."

Robin softened her voice. "Listen, the trainees, we're friends because we share a common goal. We serve the King. Everything we do is to better ourselves for that task. If you really want to impress others, find a common goal with them to strive for."

"What do I have in common with the others?" Lencely for once looked honestly puzzled, brow wrinkled, not haughty.

"You will have to watch and listen." Robin stretched and moaned. "One of the best places to learn about people is the baths. Speaking of which, I'm off to the woman's bath." She emphasized woman and grinned at him. "Do you mind doing me a favour? There is a water barrel at the back there; the funnel is on top. Could you refill the waterskin for me?"

Lencely pushed his chin out but didn't say anything. Robin tensed, she didn't trust his new self, but her pulse had slowed and if she didn't move soon, she'd fall asleep here.

"Never mind." Robin stood with a groan. "See you tomorrow." She picked up the skin and walked back to the barrel, filled by rain from the roof. When she'd started, this had been her responsibility. Now one of the younger boys had that task. The tin funnel was on a string, and she put it in the mouth of the skin. She had to remember he was the son of a noble. They would never be friends, not even comrades like the trainees. Yet he wasn't the only one using the other. Robin wanted to try instructing for a while. It felt like the logical next step. When she replaced the skin, Lencely and the others were gone

***

The heat of the bath didn't do anything to wake Robin up. She'd just got there, so she worked on washing the grime of the day away.

"How are you dealing with the lord's brat?" Jalliet said, secure in her own lineage.

"He seems sincere, but I think it's only because he's learning the sword. The kid has to be bored, stuck here with nothing to do but cause trouble."

"He was kind of cute." Jalliet sank so only her nose and eyes were out of the water.

"I don't think he'd appreciate being called cute." Tamlyn paused in washing out her shoulder-length hair.

"What do you think?" Jalliet said, then splashed Robin. "Letting the fae take you away again?"

"I still don't trust him." Robin wiped her face.

"Of course not, I've met men like that." Jalliet turned serious. "Never let one corner you."

"I thought you were going to stab any attackers in the eye." Tamlyn broke the serious mood.

Jalliet laughed and splashed Tamlyn. Robin joined in the play, shoving the burn in her gut down. It wasn't their fault she was so small. Both her parents were taller, so she couldn't blame them either. It was fickle fate, and there was little she could do about it.

They finished and cleaned up the puddles before dressing and heading over to the barracks. As Robin walked through the ground floor to the stairs, she shivered. Something was different, but she couldn't put a finger on what.

"What's the use of having a bath, then climbing all these stairs and getting sweaty again?" Jalliet shook her head, then grinned and took off up the stairs taking two steps at a time. Robin sprinted after her, leaving Tamlyn's groan to fade away.

Jalliet made it to the top a full flight ahead of Robin and leaned in a deliberately lazy pose on the rail. "What took you so long?"

"I don't know how you do it." Robin stopped at the top and breathed slowly until her racing heart returned to normal.

"That's me. If something needs running away from, I'm your girl." Jalliet waved and sauntered over to the door of the room she shared with Tamlyn.

Robin's quarters were at the far end of the hall, only slightly larger than the pantry at her home, but it had a window and a bed. That was enough.

She'd laughed as hard as Jalliet at Tamlyn's wish her hair would magically change colour. Yet she stood at the wall where she'd driven a peg into the plaster at exactly her height. Just as every other day, she was no taller.

Before she could give into the bed's siren call, Robin changed into her dress uniform and backtracked to the stairs, waving at Tamlyn as the other girl made it to the top.

"Don't know how you can serve in the hall after a day's training," Tamlyn gasped.

"It is another part of training." Robin ran down the stairs, taking each flight in two bounds.

At the bottom, she almost crashed into a soldier with grizzled hair and cold blue eyes.

"My apologies." The man wasn't someone she'd seen before, and his uniform was different. Must have come from the north.

"An apology is worthless words unless you back it up with action." His accent made the words shorter and sharper. A second look showed his uniform to be finely tailored. Not just a visitor, but an important one.

"You are right." She put her hand over her heart. "I am yours to command for one task I may honourably fulfill."

"What's your name, boy?"

In her uniform, she was easily mistaken for a boy. She lacked the curves both Jalliet and Tamlyn had. "I am Robin Fastheart, trainee with Sir Garraik." Robin kept her voice carefully neutral.

A strange expression flashed across the man's face but vanished before she could read it.

"I will call when you are needed." He stomped up the stairs, and Robin headed off to the hall at the fastest pace she could call a walk.

Whatever chilled her in the barracks hadn't reached the hall. There was no sense of something off. Robin gathered her focus. The trainees never went near the head table. What should she do? The sommelier stood by the door, so she headed over to him.

"I'm supposed to serve the head table." Robin couldn't stop the glance at the table set on the raised dais surrounded by nobles and knights in fine clothes.

Geoff handed her a tray covered in gold leaf. A meal had been set out on it, down to the cutlery and goblet.

"Robin, relax. The king hates people making a fuss. Treat him the same as you would any other knight. Off with you."

Robin walked along the long wall of the hall to the dais where the head table stood. Sir Garraik sat in his usual place, beside the King's empty chair, his bulk blocking her view.

The Chancellor and other advisors chatted as casually as the crowd below. Only when she climbed the steps to the dais did she see the king in his seat at the table. He was only a few years older than her, if that. King only because his parents died of the plague a few years ago, rumour said he was still not comfortable ruling the kingdom.

He hates people making a fuss. So stop fussing, knees.

She carried the tray over to the table. There were seats only on three sides, so she didn't have to go behind the people at the table.

The king looked away from Sir Garraik. "Hello, you're new."

"Yes, sire. I'm Robin Fastheart, trainee under Sir Garraik." Robin slid the tray over. "My apologies, but I've never done this before. If you wish anything done differently, I will endeavour to please you."

"Thank you, Robin." The king leaned forward "I heard the sweet tonight is cream puffs. I'd like an extra one." He winked at her, and Sir Garraik's expression suggested if he was any other man, he'd be rolling his eyes.

"Very well, sire."

Throughout the rest of the evening, Robin spoke to the men and women at the head table. They were all polite, some asked about her training or who her parents were. When she delivered the sweets to the table, one plate held two, which she placed in front of the king before passing out the others. But most of the time they acted as if she wasn't there.

"What do you make of Lord Huddroc's news?" The chancellor asked Sir Garraik.

"He isn't a man to imagine things, even less to needlessly ask for help."

The butterflies had almost left her stomach when she cleared the empty table.

***

The next morning at training, Sir Garraik took her aside.

"The king has requested you continue to serve the head table."

"I would be happy to."

"Some of the conversation at the table is delicate in nature."

Robin put her hand over her heart. "I will keep everything I hear in confidence."

Sir Garraik nodded, and they returned to work. Lencely and his friends showed up to watch and took to cheering during the sparring. A man stood behind them. She couldn't see him well, but his presence chilled her. She looked up again, and he was gone.

At the end of the day, Robin, Hal, Crispin, and a few others stayed behind to work with the boys.

"It isn't enough to swing your sword around." Hal had them standing in a line like the trainees. "You need to strike your opponent, all the strength in the world is useless if you can't touch them."

"So our goal is not to get hit before we land a blow?" Lencely's brow wrinkled as he thought it through."

"That's why we work as hard on defence as on attack." Hal crossed his arms. "Time for drills."

He worked them until they staggered with exhaustion. "Take a break, but don't stop moving, or you'll lock up."

"Robin, you up for a demonstration match?"

"Always." She grinned and hefted her sword.

"Pay attention, we fight with sword and buckler. It lets us defend and attack at the same time."

They went through some simple sparring, keeping the movements slow for the boys to see.

"Have you ever won a match against him?" One of Lencely's friends asked.

"Not yet." Robin grinned.

"You up for it?" Hal raised his sword.

Robin led them a little way from the watchers.

"Stay sharp," Crispin told them. "You never know what will happen in a full-on match."

Crispin kept up a running commentary, making it absurdly dramatic and sending the boys into gales of laughter.

Hal wasn't only big and strong, but also fast. Her arms complained it wasn't fair. *Deal with it.*

She knew her mistake as soon as she made it, as she swung her sword a little too wide. His buckler slammed against it and sent it flying. Robin crouched behind her buckler and drew the wood dagger front the sheath at her back.

Hal's foot stomped on the sand.

Here it comes. I'm dead, again. Robin gritted her teeth. Not yet, I'm not.

He lunged forward with his signature unstoppable thrust. Robin threw her buckler at him and dodged to the side, then jumped forward catching Hal's sword arm and climbed him like a tree. Her left hand wrapped around his helmet where it could have lifted his visor if he wore one. Her right hand held her knife at his eye.

"Yield."

Hal laughed and dropped his sword on the sand. Robin jumped off him.

"Good match." She held out her hand.

"Good match?" Hal grabbed her hand and pulled her into a bear hug. "That was amazing."

The watchers cheered, and Lencely was looking at her as if she were a hero out of legend.

"Luck." Robin's face warmed at the praise.

"Nine-tenths of training is to make us ready to take advantage of what luck comes our way." Hal pulled a woven ribbon from a pocket. "These are the colours I will wear when I'm knighted. I give it to in token of your victory." He handed it to her and bowed.

Robin took the swatch of fabric and tucked it into a pocket.

Lencely and his friends crowded around her. Their babbling washed over her. She'd done it, defeated Hal, and she had not the slightest idea of how to repeat it. Robin grinned; for now she'd take it.

"How did you know to have your colours on you?" Crispin asked.

"I always carry them." Hal shrugged. "On any given day I may be defeated."

"Um," Lencely stood at alert in front of Hal. "Would it be okay to use the trainees' bath?"

"Sure thing, but only after you've earned it by training hard."

Hal led the group to the equipment room to put their gear away. Robin walked over to pick up her sword. A crack ran halfway through the wooden blade. Robin thought about her match with Lencely. *Maybe a proper hand and a half this time.*

***

As she walked into the hall that evening, Robin's knees and stomach were calmer. She'd served the king and survived; she could do it again.

"I hear you were victorious over Hal this afternoon." The king grinned up at Robin as she set out his plates.

"Hardly a glorious win, sire." Robin ducked her head. "I climbed him like a monkey."

The king laughed loud enough for heads to crane at the lower tables to see what was going on.

"I would have loved to have seen that." He brightened up. "Sir Garraik, would it be possible to set up some exhibition matches? It might distract our guests from their worries."

"I will see to it." Sir Garraik replied. The other people around the table looked pleased at the idea.

"And Robin, I expect you to cross swords with me." The king pointed at her.

The tray slipped out of her hands and rattled on the floor. Robin knelt to pick it up. She took the time to try to slow her heart.

"I would be most honoured, sire." Somehow the words came out in the right order.

"And no holding back." He waggled a finger.

"Yes, sire." How can I seriously attack the king? But he'll be mad if I don't. I'm dead.

As Robin backed away, the king leaned over toward Sir Garraik. "And about that other thing..." His hands waved in the air, and Robin sincerely hoped he wasn't pointing at her.

"You dropped the tray." The hall master frowned at Robin.

"The king challenged me to a match," Robin stammered, still having trouble believing it.

"I will forgive you, this time." He nodded at her, then bustled over to instruct some other.

"You do have a habit of dropping things." Geoff stood came up behind her. "It will be a while for the king to eat. Sit with me a few minutes."

They went to the servant's hall and took seats at the corner of a table.

"What may I do for you?" Robin tilted her head.

"I hear you turned that snot-nosed noble brat into something resembling a human being."

"It just happened." Robin thought back, *Was it only two days*? "I think he was putting on an act. I'm not sure he's not still putting on an act."

"Ah," Geoff stared at Robin for a long moment. She shifted uncomfortably. "You were willing to be gracious, more than gracious with him. Lencely is the youngest of Huddroc's three sons. Not just youngest, but younger by ten summers than his middle brother, Vipal; fifteen than his older, Geoffroi. He feels overshadowed and is trying to make his mark on the world. An act may become reality."

"You know a lot for a sommelier." Robin peered at him doubtfully.

"It is my job to understand the people I will serve. How else could I know what wine they would like? That includes guests and their children."

CHAPTER 4

"I will not." Sir Garraik paced around the council chamber. He glared at the king.

"Sir Garraik, it is a matter of the kingdom's survival." The king's face glowed red, whether from embarrassment or anger, Sir Garraik couldn't tell.

The other occupant of the room stood against the wall as if hoping she'd fade into it.

"Are you sure this is necessary?" Sir Garraik snarled at the woman, immediately regretting it. "Sorry, this has us all discomfited."

"All the histories and old stories mention it." The woman looked down. "If we get it wrong, it could kill everyone involved."

"Sir Garraik, ask your page to summon trainee Robin here. Time is growing short."

***

The banging on the door of her tiny room woke her. At first Robin thought it was her father, angry that she'd overslept, but the window was still dark.

"Robin Fastheart!" a voice yelled from the other side of the door, and it was far too young to be her father.

She shook the cobwebs out of her head and climbed out of bed to unbar and open the door.

"You are summoned by the king. Dress quickly and come with me." The page in royal livery was tall enough to look her in the eyes.

"Right away." Robin turned her back and took off her nightgown, then pulled on her dress uniform as fast as possible. She shoved her feet into her boots and did a quick check.

"I'm ready." When Robin turned back the boy stood beet red, eyes wide.

"Uh, right, let's go." The page turned and jogged down the hall, Robin followed him, her own face burning as she realized she'd changed in front of the boy.

They travelled to the hall, then through a door held open by a dour-faced guard. She'd never entered this part of the palace; the halls didn't look much different. *What kind of trouble am I in to be summoned in the middle of the night?* She ran through possibilities but dropping the tray was the worst she'd done lately. The page led her to double doors. He knocked, then pushed a door open.

"He's waiting for you."

Robin took a deep breath. Was that sympathy on the page's face? She walked into the room to see Sir Garraik and the king with thunderous faces. Her knees went weak and she knelt.

"My sword is at your service." *Please don't send me home.*

"Get up." The king growled and pointed at a chair. "Sit." The affable young man of the head table had vanished. Robin sat in the chair, her heart pounding and knees shaking.

"There is something you can help with for the sake of the kingdom." Sir Garraik didn't sound any less angry than the king. "Before we can brief you, we need to ask you a question." He turned red and glared at the king.

"Ask." Robin's voice shook, but all her training was about serving the king and Caldera.

Sir Garraik took a deep breath but didn't say anything.

"Oh, good grief." A woman Robin hadn't noticed came and crouched by the chair. Her robes marked her as a high-ranking mage. "We are planning a very powerful ritual."

The king cleared his throat.

"Right, part of that requires I ask you a question." The woman sent a scowl at the king and Sir Garraik. "Are you a virgin?"

"What?" Robin's heart flipped in her chest as relief and outrage battled.

The woman didn't repeat the question, only held Robin's gaze.

"Yes," Robin whispered and hung her head.

Sir Garraik's words rasped like a sword on the grindstone. "The magic is ancient and can be deadly. You are needed for that ritual. Do what the mages tell you."

"Come with me." The woman took her hand and dragged her from the room.

In the hall, Robin dug in her heels.

"What is going on? The king summons me in the middle of the night to ask if I'm a virgin? Is there that much of a rush?"

"Yes." The women's voice had no give.

"That ritual?" Robin's face burned. "Does it involve…you know?"

"No. I would have nothing to do with such magic." The mage's face soured. "But the ritual isn't without danger."

"Is it really that important?"

"Yes."

The woman walked in silence until she opened a door and ushered Robin in.

"Who is this, Mage Wren?" an older mage asked.

"Our Shield Maiden."

Mage Wren turned to face Robin. "We are trying a summoning magic. Lord Huddroc has reported an army of 30,000 gathering on the far side of the pass. We need a hero who can somehow stop that invasion. You are here so we can explain your part in the ritual."

***

Light poured in through the windows and lit the middle-sized meeting hall, setting dust dancing in the beams. It looked far too peaceful for the reality.

Robin stood on her point of the star that been drawn on the floor. After much discussion, the people in charge of the ritual let her wear her dress uniform. They hadn't been able to find armour to fit her. Mage Wren told her attitude was more important than appearance. Nobles sat in ranks behind her. The king sat on his throne. The room was used for medium gatherings but was already stuffy.

That had been candles ago, now she fought to stay at attention and ignore the tiredness and hunger gnawing away at her stamina. Clenching the muscles in her legs and feet kept the blood flowing, and the spear the Mage Wren had insisted she hold gave her a third point for stability. The shield weighed heavy on her other arm

The mages had been chanting for ages without stopping and looked ready to fall into dust. Her task was easy in comparison. She stared at the center of the sigil and willed herself to stand rock still.

A light formed in the center and Robin let out a gasp of wonder. It was really working, they'd be saved. The Hero would stop the invasion. She straightened out the least bit of softness in her stance. The Hero would not arrive to find her slouching.

The glow brightened until she had to squint to protect her eyes. But Robin didn't want to miss the moment of arrival. Something began to take shape in the light.

***

In the Green Acres Retirement home, Retired Master Sergeant Christopher Severson admired the slickness of his opponent's cheating. Even the aides watching hadn't caught on. Mary had ruled the rummy table since arriving a year ago. Sarge didn't care. It added an extra challenge to the game. He had blasted little of that in his life now.

Mary laid down her cards with a beaming smile of triumph. The others tossed in their hands and mechanically organized them for the next hand.

"Mr. Severson." The woman's colourful scrubs contrasted nicely with her dark skin. "The occupational therapist wants to make sure you didn't forget your appointment."

"I didn't forget." Sarge took control of the deck and shuffled. "I just have no intention of going."

"Please..." The aide was new, only been working a few weeks.

Damn, he didn't want her dragged into the battle between him and the O.T. "Fine." He put the cards down and pushed himself to his feet, balancing by leaning on his chair until he got his cane into position.

The woman smiled and pushed the wheelchair out of his way. *Ha, a win.*

They walked at a tortuously slow pace down the hall. Old ladies with walkers whizzed past him. At the O.T.'s office, she stood in the doorway tapping her foot.

Sarge turned to the aide. "Thank you for your kindness." Only after the woman had smiled and walked away did he turn his attention on his enemy.

"If you had a walker, it would not have taken so long to get here, and you wouldn't have wasted my time."

"It's my time." Sarge tightened his grip on his cane. "Not yours. You and the rest of the staff are here to serve me, not the other way around."

"It's a safety issue…" she tried a different angle.

"If I die because some old biddy runs me down with her walker, it will be a relief."

The O.T. frowned. "The home's regulations…"

"Won't stand up in court. As long as I am competent to make my own decisions, I have the right to refuse a walker." He bared his teeth at her. "I've been spitting in death's eye for so long that I've outlived everyone I knew. A good fight is just what I need."

He turned and walked away from her. He'd just make it to the dining hall in time for supper. His foul mood boiled like acid in his gut. At one time, no one would have dared get in his way. That was longer ago than he liked to remember. They were so worried he'd die in a fall.

His fear was that he wouldn't die, that he'd continue forever falling apart, death passing him by until…

A giant fist reached into his chest and crushed his heart. Sarge toppled to the floor as the world faded into black.

It's damn well about time.

***

The light burst like a bubble and more than one mage slumped to the floor. A wave passed through Robin for a moment she felt…different.

Standing the center of the sigil was a naked old man. He was the oldest person Robin had ever seen and black as charcoal, though his hair was like white moss on his head.

Someone in the gallery of nobles behind her groaned. Sir Garraik leapt forward to wrap his cloak around the old man.

"Forget the cloak." His voice was stones scraping together. "Bring me a damned chair."

Robin shoved her spear and shield into the hands of a noble who had stood to get a better view, then took his chair and carried it to place behind the old man.

"The strength of my arm is yours if you have need." The words of greeting never sounded to proper than at this moment.

"Thank you, lass." The old man leaned on her arm and with great slowness and care lowered himself into the chair. Once settled, he sighed and pulled the cloak tighter around him. Robin swept hers off to cover his legs. Something about this old man compelled her.

"Welcome, sir…?" Sir Garraik knelt gracefully and bowed his head.

"I'm no officer. I work for a living." The man's response sounded as rote as Robin's greeting.

Sir Garraik chuckled "No offence meant." He paused for a second as if leaving space for an unspoken 'sir' "What may we call you?"

"Master Sergeant Christopher Severson, but if you're in a hurry, call me Sarge. Where the hell am I? I'm sure my heart finally quit." The old man's eyes twinkled as he took in the room. He didn't look entirely displeased to be there.

"Master Sergeant Christopher Severson, I bid you welcome. We," he waved his hand, "are the protectors of Caldera. Our apologies for the indignity of your arrival. The council is ready to explain our situation."

"When you get to my age, dignity is a thing of the past." The crinkle around his eyes appeared again. "I'm sorry to be rude, but can the briefing wait? I died on the way to my supper."

Robin glanced at Sir Garraik who scowled and shrugged his shoulders.

"I'm hungry, lass, bring anything that isn't gruel." Sarge winked at her, and she grinned in response before dashing out of the room call for the palace servants, then back to kneel by Sarge's side.

"Master Sergeant—" Sir Garraik's smile had slipped from his face.

"Let him rest." Robin tugged the cloaks more snugly around Sarge as he mumbled something about a walker. Maybe that was a monster in his world.

"Trainee, know your place."

Robin's shoulders hunched as she thought of the punishment to be handed out at training later today.

"Leave her be." Sarge opened his eyes and levelled a glare at Sir Garraik that made him pale, then patted Robin on the head like she was a cat. "You folks dragged me here – wherever *here* is. Do you know how long I've been looking forward to being dead?

"Very well." Sir Garraik clearly struggled to keep the anger from his voice. "She will be your squire. If there is anything you need, it is her responsibility to provide."

"I'm honoured by your trust." She put her hands over Sarge's. "I will serve you faithfully, I give you my oath." Robin's heart banged against her ribs, as she bowed her head to the master sergeant . Sir Garraik meant it as a punishment, but she wanted to dance in excitement. Years she had been training for this moment. She'd become a squire, however irregularly.

"See to the master sergeant," Sir Garraik scowled at Robin. "We will meet in one candle's time.

The servants returned with food and a white robe such as initiates wore before being knighted.

***

Robin walked beside Sarge. She'd never walked so slowly, not even at a funeral march. He leaned heavily on her shoulder. They entered the War Room, Robin all too aware they were late.

The conversation around the table cut off. A few of the older nobles stood, but the rest glowered at Sarge. The king sat at the head of the table rubbing his temples.

"We wanted a hero, not an old man with one foot in the grave," one man said.

"What can he do to stop the invasion?" another sneered, and Robin's stomach sank when she recognized the grizzled man she'd almost run into. A babble of complaints rose.

Robin slapped her hand on the table, and the king winced.

"You will address him as master sergeant." Her voice slashed through the shocked silence. "We summoned him; it is not his fault you expected something different."

"Squire Robin, you forget yourself." Sir Garraik's cold voice poured ice water on the flame in her chest. "Everyone in this room outranks—"

"Sir Garraik," Sarge cut off the knight. "What is a squire's first duty?"

"To serve their king." Sir Garraik's face reddened.

"And their second duty?" The words came out as a growl.

"To serve their knight." The red deepened to purple.

"I would say that Squire Robin is filling her role admirably." Sarge's glare had no give in it. "You made her a squire, effectively making me a knight."

"A squire should not be rude to their betters." Sir Garraik set his chin stubbornly.

"And if those betters are being rude to their master, are they to stand idly by?" The king spoke up in a tone that said he was losing patience.

Sir Garraik paled.

"My apologies, sire."

"It is not me you offended."

Robin feared the knight would faint, he turned so white. Sir Garraik faced Sarge who still stood at the foot of the table and bowed deeply.

"My humblest apologies, Master Sergeant."

"Not me." Sarge thumped his cane on the floor. "My squire."

Sir Garraik clutched at the table, then pushed himself upright and looked at Robin. She wanted to hide behind Sarge.

"Squire Robin, I apologize for my words, and for putting the need to protect your master from your own people on your shoulders."

She couldn't get any words past the lump in her throat, so she bowed. Sir Garraik nodded.

"Allow our guest to sit and be comfortable before you begin the meeting." The king scanned the room.

"I'll not stay in the room with that girl." The grizzled lord pointed at her.

"I'll not stay if she must leave." Sarge leaned on the table and met the lord's gaze.

"Lord Huddroc, you know where the door is." The king tapped a finger on the table.

Lord Huddroc reddened, then slumped down into his seat. Other nobles in the ring outside the table muttered.

"Sire, we have a war to fight. It's no time to coddle old men, no matter how they got here."

"Sonny." Sarge settled into his seat but kept a hand on Robin's arm. "I was fighting wars while your grandfather was still in diapers." His gaze raked the room. "To be honest, I was more than ready to sleep beneath the clay. This is no more my desire than yours, yet it is foolish to reject help because it didn't come in the expected shape."

"Well said." The king signalled to the page at his side. The young boy carried several rolls of paper and laid out one before Sarge. He held one edge and Robin the other.

The map was the finest she'd ever seen.

"Our kingdom is protected by a mountain wall on all sides." Sir Garraik used a stick to point at the features. "The major road in and out is alongside the river cutting through the wall to the west. A handful of passes in the south and east can be taken by small groups. Our problem now is the pass to the north, secured by a fortified town, Vilscape. With the right timing and luck, it would be possible to bring an army through the pass."

"I'm guessing someone is trying their luck. Tell me about them." Sarge gazed at the map.

"The Anca Empire has gathered 30,000 troops on the north side of the mountain wall. They are waiting for the snow to melt enough to allow them passage." Lord Huddroc crossed his arms.

"How did you learn about this?" Sarge leaned on the table.

"We have people who live at the far end of the pass." Sir Huddroc frowned. "They try to ensure those crossing the pass know what they're up against. One of them saw the Ancan camp while they were hunting. The border between their empire and ours is very blurred. Five of them set out to make a late winter crossing. One of them survived to report.

I sent his Majesty a message, then came myself. My eldest, Geoffroi is planning blockades to slow the army."

"Do you have a more detailed map of Vilscape?" Sarge didn't look up.

The page let the map roll up and set out a second one showing the narrow snake of the Vilscape River pass through the mountain wall ending at the town built across the exit before it met the plain.

"How many soldiers can you put on the field?" Sarge might have been talking about what was for supper, not a war.

"10,000 if we pull every available person." The king leaned forward. "A plague went through a couple of years back. For some reason it killed mostly healthy men and women."

"You can't stop them." Sarge leaned back.

"You would have us surrender?" Lord Huddroc pounded the table.

"It's an option. I don't know enough yet to come up with a strategy. I need the best maps you have, someone to explain your tactics to me, and I'll need books of history about you and this empire."

Lord Huddroc's frown deepened.

"Sir Garraik, please aid Squire Robin in gathering all necessary information for our guest. We will meet again when the master sergeant has something to tell us." The king stood and the nobles jumped to their feet. He walked out, and the others filed after him. Lord Huddroc stopped in front of Robin.

"You remember your oath?"

"Of course, my lord," Robin said.

"My youngest son is with me on this trip. The truth is I wanted him well away from Vilscape. I place him in your care." Lord Huddroc glowered at her. "He's my son. Don't forget that. Keep him safe or crawl back into whatever hole you came out of."

"My lord, it will be my pleasure." Robin bowed.

He left without farewell.

"Master Sergeant, I will assign some knights to be your aides." Sir Garraik stood at attention by the table.

"Robin will be fine for now. Send someone familiar with tactics and command tomorrow in the morning."

"Very well, Master Sergeant." Sir Garraik turned to Robin. "You are brave, but you'd be wise to learn tact to go with it."

CHAPTER 5

The servants helped Sarge from the chair, then Robin walked with him back to his rooms. The bed was freshly made. Robin helped Sarge to lie down.

"Rest for a while, and I will organize your things for you."

"Thanks, lass." Sarge closed his eyes and began snoring.

Robin checked the wardrobe. It had been filled with variations on drab green hunter's clothing, though some had decorations in gold thread. She'd need to get the cobbler in to make proper boots and shoes for Sarge. He couldn't walk barefoot in the palace.

The basin and jug for washing were laid out with soap and towels. Writing materials filled the desk, both ink and charcoal. Rolls of paper were copies of the maps from the war room.

No art hung on the walls, nothing decorated any of the tables.

She found a nook with a narrow bed behind a tapestry. Another tapestry could be pulled over the window to block out the light. Robin yawned. What time was it? She hadn't eaten since the night before the ritual. Maybe a quick nap before she ordered food for Sarge, and she'd have to get her gear from her trainee's room. The nook would be her new home.

***

Sarge awoke and sat up. He'd not asked where the toilets were, but likely there was a pot under the bed. He found it and took care of the need that had awakened him. He considered lying down again, but the prospect didn't entice him.

Time to explore. He shuffled around the room poking into corners and found Robin sleeping in a nook. She looked even younger at rest. He couldn't underestimate her. She had to be tough, stronger than she looked. *Let her sleep.* She was his problem now, and he still didn't know what that meant.

He discovered a rope that disappeared into the wall. He gave it an experimental tug. Something moved, later would be soon enough to learn what it was for.

Moments later a soft knock caught his attention.

"Come in."

The servant who'd found the clothes for him entered and bowed.

"You called, Master Sergeant?"

The rope. "I did. Please help me over to the chair." Once seated, Sarge took stock. The servant waited patiently. "First things, first, what do I call you?"

"I would be pleased if you called me Edward." Edward bowed.

"Very good." Sarge moved until he was more comfortable. The chair was heavy leather slings on a wood frame, surprisingly comfortable. "Brief me on the situation."

"Master Sergeant?" Edward's eye's widened.

"Sorry, let me rephase. I know nothing about this world or your customs. I don't wish to offend by accident."

"If I may, Master Sergeant, I will start with the ranks and how they interact…"

By the time Robin sat up and ran her fingers through her hair, Sarge had a basic understanding of the etiquette. It was much like the army, with the king, nobles and knights as the officer ranks, then other who ruled their own specialty and so on. He was pleased to learn that respect in both directions was expected.

"Sarge?" Robin mumbled. "Sarge!" she bolted upright. "I'm sorry, I shouldn't have slept. Tears hung in her eyes.

"Squire Robin," Sarge frowned at her. "I am going to give you my first order. You must not neglect yourself to care for me. Do that and you won't be there when I need you. Maintain your training and other activities as you can. You have a problem, come to me and we'll deal with it."

"Yes, Sarge." Robin sighed. "Do you mind if I wash my face?"

"That's what I mean, you shouldn't have to ask permission to do anything to care for yourself. Never give an unnecessary order, or the men will expect you to give that order every time. Only if you see a conflict between my needs and yours do you need to ask."

"I think I understand." Robin splashed her face and dried with the towel. "Ugh, my uniform is wrinkled. I'll have to go get my things from my room."

Sarge raised his eyebrow.

"A squire lives with their knight." Robin's chin set stubbornly.

"Edward, please arrange to have Squire Robin's possessions brought here at your earliest convenience." Robin's stomach rumbled, and she reddened. "After you bring food for us. What I ate when I arrived will be fine. No ale; that's for a special occasion."

"Yes, Master Sergeant." Edward left as quietly as he'd come in.

"Robin, drag that chair from the desk here and sit down." When she sat across from him, he leaned forward, hands on the crook of his cane. "I have no clue how this squire/knight thing works here. I've some idea from my own world, but I need you to answer my questions. Everything, even things the least child would know."

"Knights form the command structure of the army." Robin furrowed her forehead like she was taking a test. "Below them, the Regulars have their own commanders. The army is broken down into units. We have two legions of 5000 each, though really, they should be 10,000.

"Who is responsible for strategy?"

Sir Garraik is in command of one legion. Sir Kenly commands the other. He's stationed in the west.

Sarge nodded. "Are these legions a standing army?"

"Standing army?" Robin shook her head.

"How many are paid to be soldiers?"

"At any one time, we only have a small number of active soldiers. A thousand here in Kingstown; two hundred live here at the palace in the barracks. There will be active troops in Vilscape and in Fhayden in the west. There are garrisons where the river cuts through the mountain wall to the west."

"We'll look at the map later. You said the knights command. Is that all they do?

"Just as not all soldiers are active, not all knights are, but in time of war, they will be expected to take up their duties." Robin looked at him as if waiting for a response.

"So far it isn't much different from what I expected. Go on. Tell me more about these knights. I don't want to put my foot in my mouth too much."

"Physical prowess is only part of who they must be. One day in three, we read books of history or listen to knights or regular commanders."

"How are squires chosen?"

"Each town where a knight is stationed is required to take on the training of candidates for knighthood. Knights may choose a trainee over the age of thirteen to be a squire.

Twice a year, half of the knights and squires gather for a tournament."

"How are the trainees chosen?"

Robin gulped. "I've always wanted to be a knight like the stories. Before the tournament, there are races, tests and other things like that. The ten best go to the training grounds. Most times only one will be chosen. That day I could have already been a knight the way my heart raced. It sunk each time another kid rubbed my face in the dirt and the others laughed."

"That doesn't sound like a good day."

"I thought I was strong, but everyone else was stronger, faster. It took everything I had not to give up. I'd bragged about how I would be chosen, and if I failed, I wanted bruises to show for it."

"Right."

"I was ahead of everyone at the obstacle course. I had nothing to lose, so I took risks until the final challenge – a wall eight feet high. No matter how I jumped I couldn't reach the top. I finally dragged a log over and used it to climb the wall, but I was careless dropping on the other side and twisted my ankle. I had to crawl the last few paces to the finish line. Sir Garraik stood over me and asked if crawling was honourable for a knight. I told him it was better than giving up."

"I think I had convinced myself I'd failed, so when Sir Garraik called my name I fell over after jumping out of my chair. He didn't like my crawling, so I hopped over to him."

"'Convince me I didn't make a mistake' was all Sir Garraik said to me before he sent everyone home."

A knock on the door interrupted them, Robin jumped up to open it for Edward who pushed a cart into the room.

"I have been asked to report that your fellow trainees refused to allow the servants to bring your goods. They said they would carry it all themselves. I expect they will start showing up at any time."

"Thank you, Edward."

"I shall go and make sure they don't get lost looking for this room." He bowed and left.

Sarge watched as the girl pushed the cart over to him.

"It is kind of a tradition." Robin lifted the lids from the plates.

"My hands don't work as well as they once did. You'll have to cut up the food for me."

Robin talked as she cut up meat and cheese "Though Hal is the only one we had to move from one building to another. The others were left by their masters to complete the training, so we moved everything out of their room. Swept it out, then moved them back in." Robin pushed the cart so Sarge could use it as a table. "It sounds silly, but none of us thought about not doing it."

"Traditions are important." Sarge pointed to her chair. "Make yourself a plate and eat with me." She looked like she was going to argue but sat and filled a plate.

As they demolished their meals, a giant of a young man showed up with her chest on one shoulder. The others had stacks of books, armfuls of clothes. "Put the chest over by the nook." Sarge pointed. "The books can go on the desk for now, clothes on the bed."

The trainees filled the room with energy, and Sarge soaked it up. He couldn't remember the last time he'd been surrounded by youth. As work slipped into shenanigans, Sarge rapped the flow with his cane. "Line up."

The trainees snapped into their places, laughing as the big one firmly moved Robin to the front to form a sixth line. The spacious room burst at the seams.

"Introduce yourselves." Sarge nodded at them.

"Hal…" By the time each of them gave their name, where they were from, and who their master was if they were squires, the light from the window was dimming. The trainees sat on the floor around Sarge. The cart, completely picked clean, was pushed out into the hall.

"I am Master Sergeant Christopher Severson; you may call me master sergeant or just Sarge." Sarge scanned the room. "I will need you to answer questions for me, but not now. Time for you to leave."

"You should give Robin your colours to wear." Hal bowed and chivvied the crowd down the hall.

"We're going to need a bigger room for our bull sessions." Sarge looked around.

"Bull sessions?" Robin turned from where she was folding her clothes and laying them out on the trunk.

"Informal meetings like the one we just had where we talk about whatever we're interested in at the moment." He stood and walked slowly over to the window. "Looks like we aren't on the ground floor. I'd rather not need to have people carry me any time I want to go outside."

"Let me talk to someone." Robin tugged on the rope, when Edward knocked, Robin waved him in. "Edward, I would like to speak to the seneschal. As wonderful as this room is, we've discovered it won't suit the master sergeant's needs."

"If you would state your needs, I will send a message to Master Henri."

"I would like adjoining rooms. One for sleeping, the other for meeting with people. It should fit at least twenty comfortably. It should also give access to outside without the need of stairs." Robin said. "It restricts the master sergeant's movement if servants must carry him up and down stairs daily."

"One other thing," Sarge lifted a finger. "I would like colours for my squire to wear. Does anyone have this green and gold for their colours? Yellow would be satisfactory if gold is reserved."

"Colours with gold must be assigned by the king," Robin said. "But we should ask."

"If you don't mind waiting for him to have time for that discussion, we will do that."

"Certainly," Sarge said. "If you bring me paper, I will draw the badge I would like." Robin caught a glimpse of arcs and angles as he drew with quick strokes then handed the paper to Edward.

Edward bowed and left.

"I must go and bathe," Robin said. "I won't be very long. If you need anything call for Edward."

"I will sit here and think until you return." Sarge smiled at her. "Don't feel the need to rush."

***

The glow of being a squire had worn off and now she needed to keep this old man happy and out of trouble or she'd be sent home for sure. Robin walked over to the trainee baths, not sure where else to go. Was it only yesterday she'd sparred with Hal? It felt like a different life. She'd have to ask if it was like this for the other squires.

The bath was dim, and the water not as hot, but she didn't want to wait for the fires to heat it, so climbed into the tepid pool. A squire, and maybe a squire with gold colours, and maybe a squire with no future.

Sarge was old and fragile. She needed to do her utmost to help him. After listening to him in the War Room, Robin believed with all her being he was the hero they needed. But convincing some others might be difficult. Anyone who wanted to dismiss him would have to go through her. She wasn't going to mess this up. It was her last chance.

When Robin arrived at the room, she heard voices inside. After knocking to announce herself, she entered the room. Sarge sat chatting with a man in the king's livery.

"Master Henri came to get more details in person." Sarge smiled at Robin. "I'm afraid you'll have to stand."

"Welcome, Master Henri, you honour us by coming in person."

"When I assigned these rooms, I had imagined a different person. Now that the master sergeant has graced us by answering the call, it is clear these will not do at all. Unfortunately, all the suites on the main floor are either in the royal wing or already being used by others whom it would not be politic to move out." He lifted a hand. "I have a solution in mind, but it will require the king to agree. If that doesn't work, I will endeavour to find something suitable."

"We are grateful, Master Henri."

The seneschal bowed and left.

Robin helped Sarge change into a nightshirt, then dug a bell out of her trunk. "This is a keepsake from my grandma, but it will work well." She placed it on the side table within Sarge's reach. "If you need something, ring the bell. Loudly as I'm not always a light sleeper. If I must care for myself to serve you, you must also allow me to help as much as I can."

"You are right. I will remind you to rest, and you will remind me to ask for help."

Robin changed into her nightgown and climbed into bed. Sarge's breathing came through the tapestry. She hadn't shared a room since leaving home. There was something comforting about not being alone.

She began to list to herself all the tasks she had to accomplish the next day but fell asleep before she got to number three.

Movement in the night woke her, but when she peeked out of her nook, Sarge was pulling the blanket up. She had to remember he wasn't helpless but fell asleep again before she could consider what that meant.

CHAPTER 6

Robin woke early as usual and slipped out of her nook. She washed her hair and changed into her everyday trainee uniform. Sarge snored away in his bed. *Should I stay until he wakes?* She shook her head; he'd be angry at her. Instead, she scribbled a note for him and left it under the bell. Another idea came to her, and she rang for Edward.

"I'd like you to let people know if they hear a bell ringing in the room, it means the master sergeant is asking for help." Robin frowned. "Don't be obvious; he doesn't like being weak."

"I believe the woodwork in this hall is due for polishing. Later in the morning, I will check on him to see if he's ready for breakfast."

"Thank you, that's a load off my mind."

"If I may make a suggestion, the king's physician has expressed an interest in meeting the master sergeant."

"Perhaps after supper, he could drop by for a social visit. Sarge likes company."

"I will inform him." Edward smiled as if it was a secret between them. "Enjoy your training. If you get stronger, so will he."

Robin walked briskly until she got outside the palace, then sprinted to the training yard. The familiar weight of mail, armour, and backpack settled her nerves, and she began her morning run.

In the third circuit of the yard, someone joined her; one of the trainees was early. Robin grinned and pushed her pace a bit. The trainee kept up with her. *Haven't done the agility work in a while.* Side steps, crossovers, and short strides at a double pace made her muscles burn, but it felt good.

Crispin walked into the yard and his jaw dropped. Robin laughed, then switched to running backwards. Sir Garraik matched her, and she lost track of her feet. Completing a roll with the backpack was tricky, but she didn't think she looked like a complete klutz.

"Sir Garraik," Robin said as she kept up her run, "you honour me with your company."

"I wished to speak to you before training."

"Do you wish to go to the corner?"

"This is fine." He didn't appear the least bit out of breath. "You have been caught up in big events and will be meeting with important people, not all of whom will like your energy and forthrightness."

"That's right, you told me to learn tact, but I've been so busy helping Sarge get settled, I haven't had time to think on it. How do I learn? It isn't like swordplay where I can practice by crossing swords in the training yard."

"No, it is not." Sir Garraik picked up the pace, and Robin stayed with him. "You did well enough with young Lencely, but Lord Huddroc would not be a good enemy." He sped up again until they were flying around the yard, and the trainees gathered in the center to watch out of the way.

"Line up," he called and swerved to stand in his place. This time Robin remembered to form her own line. She breathed deeply until her heart slowed its racing. "Out of shape?" Sir Garraik raised a brow at her.

"Sir, I find I recover faster if I'm honest with my body, but I do have a way to go."

"Wise." Sir Garraik walked around her. "You come early to run in training armour and wear a pack. What is in it?"

"Sand." Robin lost the struggle to not drop her head.

He put his hand out, so she shrugged the pack off and handed it to him, ears burning. “I’d guess you’re trying to create at least the weight of a suit of plate.” He put the pack beside him. “Why?”

“I’m not strong enough, Sir.” Robin lifted her head to meet his eyes. “I’m the smallest, so I work harder to keep up.”

“Ah.” Sir Garraik stepped back. Robin itched to put her pack back on, but he’d made no sign of permission. “Not everything can be conquered by determination. Squire Robin, step forward and lead the warm-up.”

She gulped but took two strides forward before spinning to face the trainees.

“We’ll start with punches…”

At the end of the warm-up the others looked wrung out, even Crispin gasped for air. Robin breathed heavily but not as hard as usual. She didn’t think she’d worked hard enough.

“While the trainees recover, I’d like to cross swords with you.”

Robin nodded and bolted to fetch her buckler, sword, and helmet.

They walked out into the centre of the yard.

“When you are ready, squire.”

Robin lunged forward but misjudged her measure and only blocked Sir Garraik’s cut by a desperate swipe with her buckler. *Slow down, idiot.* She backed up a little. Defeating Sir Garraik wasn’t a possibility, but she’d show him she was going to try hard at it. She grinned and leapt to the attack.

They circled the yard while Sir Garraik took everything she threw at him without the least bit of difficulty.

"My turn." Sir Garraik switched from defence to attack. Robin relied on keeping on the outside of his measure, but though he was only a bit smaller than Hal, the knight was as fast as Crispin. She concentrated on pushing the cuts and thrusts aside, but it felt like trying to move a boulder with the point of her sword.

Sir Garraik didn't give her any clue when he lunged. Like Hal, his sword blew through her attempt to block. Robin staggered back but couldn't get her footing, and he gave her no time. She dropped her sword and snatched at her knife but couldn't get it into play before his sword touched her throat.

She dropped the wood blade and sighed. At least she hadn't made a complete fool of herself. Sir Garraik extended his hand and pulled her to her feet.

"Thank you for the match." He bowed.

"You honour me." Robin bowed lower, before recovering her knife and sword, and returned to her spot.

"You need more strength in the arms." Sir Garraik looked at the trainees. "What did you see?"

The trainees analyzed the match, pointing out where she'd been too eager or not eager enough. At the end, Crispin took a deep breath.

"She might have had you with that knife." He looked like he expected a blow in response.

"Why didn't she?" Sir Garraik crossed his arms.

"If she'd caught your sword, it might have given her the time she needed."

"Hal, she beat you by doing something unexpected when normally you would have clinched the match. It is the same here. The moment of victory can easily become the moment of our defeat. Squire Robin refuses to accept defeat. Without a sword, she'll use a knife. Without a knife, I'm guessing she would still try something. That is an invaluable asset in a fight to the death, but if your opponent is honourable, there is no shame in surrender. Don't force someone to kill you."

"Sir," Robin raised her hand. "How do you know?"

"You can't always, but you need to read your opponent as much as you read their swordplay."

Robin opened her mouth to ask how, then closed it. Another test.

Through the rest of training, she let the question rattle around in the back of her head. She already used the heaviest sword she could find but weighting it further didn't feel right. She'd tried wearing weight on her wrists, but the balance wasn't right.

Why did she need strength? To hold off his sword. At the end of the session, she was no closer to an answer.

When Lencely and his friends arrived, Robin set it aside to concentrate on teaching them. Sparring with them was harder than with the other trainees. She had to hold back just enough to make them push their limits. *Is this what Sir Garraik thinks about all the time?*

"How can you train all day and still have this much energy?" Lencely fell dramatically to the sand.

"That's because Robin follows her rules." Crispin grinned at her.

"Rules?" Lencely sat up and looked curious. Robin understood; she wasn't sure what Crispin was talking about either.

"One." Crispin held up a finger. "Never walk if you can run. Two, if training is too easy, make it harder. Three, everything is training."

"Those are good rules," Robin said. "Wish I'd thought of them."

After they finished and Robin was putting her gear away, Lencely walked back and filled the waterskins. She couldn't imagine him as the nasty brat she'd first met.

"What's in the pack?" Lencely leaned against the wall. "No one else has one."

"Sand." Robin willed her ears not to turn red. "I wear it when I'm running and working out to make me stronger."

He came over and hefted it. "I can't imagine wearing extra weight. The training is hard enough as it is."

"Rule number two," Robin said.

"Right, where do I get one?"

Robin pointed to a cupboard. "In there, you'll have to ask one of the groundskeepers for the sand. Don't overdo; build up the weight gradually."

"How long have you been doing this?" Lencely hefted the pack again, then handed it back to Robin.

"Since the first year I was here." Robin hung it up and adjusted it to sit straight. "That would be four years I guess."

"You are crazy."

***

After her bath, and the usual teasing from her friends, Robin dressed and headed up to her room, she had to correct her feet before they climbed the stairs to the barracks. She'd barely thought about Sarge all day. Guilt struck her. She hoped he hadn't been bored.

Standing outside the door was a page in the king's livery.

"I'm to take you to your new quarters," the boy piped. He chattered about helping with the move until they arrived at a huge pair of black oak doors. The knocker echoed loudly in the hall.

"I don't think I've been here." Robin looked around. "It's older than the rest of the palace."

The door opened, and Edward ushered them in.

"The master sergeant is in the bath." He held a finger to his lips. The boy nodded and sat on a chair near the door. "Danael has been assigned to the master sergeant as his runner."

"Good." Robin smiled. "He seems like a nice kid."

"He's pure rascal, through and through." Edward glanced back at the boy. "But he'll work hard not to lose his position."

"What is this?" Robin turned around to scan the room. Old tables and chairs filled the room, with enough seating for thirty people. A fire burned in the fireplace at the far end. The cupboard in the right corner looked incongruously new. On the left, a door stood open.

Edward led her through the door, and Robin had to stop and stare. This room was almost as big as the first, with its own roaring fire. Couches and chairs formed a sitting room to the left. A four-posted bed with a side table stood in the corner. She walked over to the desk, piled high with books, papers and maps.

"Where's Sarge?"

Edward nodded toward a door in the wall. "On the other side, bathing. Master sergeant will need to have staff bring hot water for him. This is all that remains of the old palace. The present king's great-grandfather built the new one, tearing most of the old one down in the process. This is what remains of the commanding knight's rooms."

"Wow." Robin ran her hand along the leather forming the seat of the chair in the corner. "Is this the chair from the other room?"

"The master sergeant expressed a liking for it."

She poked at the pile on the desk and almost started an avalanche. "We need bookcases, a map box, and some way to organize all this paper."

"The bookcases will arrive tomorrow. I will request a map box." Edward peered the pile. "Perhaps one of the secretaries will have suggestions about the rest."

A bell rang from the direction of the bath.

"If you'll excuse me." Edward went to help Sarge.

Robin went back to Danael who sat on the chair showing no evidence of boredom.

"Hello, I'm Squire Robin."

"Danael." The boy glanced at her.

"I have a job for you." Robin grinned wryly. "I'm new to this, so let me know if I'm doing something wrong."

"Sure thing." Danael stood up at attention.

"First, the palace physician was invited to drop in this evening, but that was before the move. Let him know about the change or get someone to wait to guide him here. Second, the other trainees may want to visit; please inform Squire Hal, or another in trainee grey of the change."

"I'll get one of the littles to wait at the other place, then run your errands."

"Good thinking."

Danael took off like an arrow from her bow. *Rule number one.*

Back in the bedroom, Sarge sat in his chair wrapped in a soft robe.

"How was training?"

"Eventful." Robin sat on the floor. "I learned that Sir Garraik is in better shape than I am. I think he approves of my training with extra weight but told me I need to strengthen my arms."

"What are you doing now with the weight?" Sarge stared up at the ceiling.

"I run in armour with a backpack of sand, wear it during the warmup and sparring too if I can."

"So you're working your legs and heart and lungs." Sarge tapped a finger on the arm of his chair. "Let's start with something you do anywhere. On your front, support yourself with your arms, your feet should be on the toes."

"Like this?" Robin took the position he'd described. He pushed her feet together with his cane and made her move her hands about until he was satisfied.

"Now lower yourself until your shoulders touch your thumbs. Keep your back straight, don't arch or sag. Okay, back up to the starting position. Keep going."

Robin raised and lowered herself, adjusting to Sarge's comments. It didn't feel too difficult, but by the time she'd counted to twenty, her arms were aching. She had to stop at forty-six as she couldn't return to the start position.

"Impressive, as I expected," Sarge said. "That's your starting point. Forty push-ups, that's what I call them, every morning and night. When they get too easy, we'll add to your count. Now onto your back. Bend your knees, feet flat on the floor, arms crossed over your chest. Good, now use your stomach muscles to sit up as far as you can, hold it for a count of three, then relax. We'll do forty of these too. Younger people call them crunches, supposed to be safer than full sit-ups."

Danael knocked and entered the room, giving Robin a strange look.

"Got lucky and bumped into the physician's apprentice. The trainees were all busy, but I asked the hall steward to pass on the message. Put a little at the door anyway; it's good practice for them." He bowed slightly and returned to his chair.

"Don't know how he can sit still for so long." Robin rolled to a sitting position.

"Kneel on the floor, sit back on your feet, keep the tops of your feet flat on the floor." Once again Sarge used his cane to adjust her position. "Now, see how long you can stay there."

Her legs complained immediately, but Robin quashed them and forced herself to stay in place until she thought she might never walk again.

"Not bad." Sarge waved around the room, "now walk it off."

When her legs began to return to normal, he waved her over.

"Kneel again."

Robin stifled a groan and did what she was told.

"This time pay attention to your breathing: in through the nose, out through the mouth; completely fill your lungs, then empty them."

With a bit of correction, Robin found the rhythm.

"Good, now, while you are breathing, run through the last match you fought."

Robin played out her fight against Sir Garraik, replaying parts in slow motion.

"That's fine, stand up."

Robin stood without thinking, then looked at her legs. "They don't hurt as much."

"You knelt for three times the length of your first try." Sarge tapped his head. "If you concentrate on the pain, even if to endure it, your muscles tense and it gets worse. When you concentrate on something else, along with the breathing, you relax into the posture and can hold it longer without thinking about it."

"Anything else?"

"Let's leave it at that for a week or so." Sarge smiled at her. "You don't get strong overnight."

"Yes, Sarge."

"Time to do our homework." Sarge jabbed his cane at the desk. "Find me the detailed map of Vilscape and the pass."

Robin sorted through them. Some had been marked, but others had no indication of what they were until she unrolled them.

"Why so many?" She asked as another roll wasn't the one she wanted.

"Maps of most of the important locations in the country," Sarge said. "Too tight a focus on one location is not good."

She found the one Sarge wanted and pulled over a small table to unroll it on. "I've asked for a mapbox to store them properly."

"Good." Sarge rapped his knuckle on the map. "If you were going to stop thirty-thousand soldiers, where would you set up?"

Robin ran her finger along the pass. "The map says this is the narrowest point, but there's no way of knowing that without going."

"Right, there is a way to draw maps to show that, but it takes a great deal of work and know-how. If you look closely, you'll see two x's, I'm told that is a defensive position. Between there and the town, what's the next best place?"

Robin located the spots and looked for the x's. "They have them all marked."

"I would hope so." Sarge chuckled. "That's their country. The problem is the defensive positions; none of them will stop that army. A battle in my world was the same, two thousand people held a pass against a much larger force for days. Eventually, the enemy found a back route and the defenders were slaughtered."

"Doesn't sound hopeful."

"A vastly superior force will eventually win, even if it is just by wearing the smaller army down. But the smaller force can slow the big one and buy time. The commander has to know when to cut and run, or you end up losing more than you can afford." Sarge shook his head. "It's dancing on the edge of a knife."

"So what can we do?" Robin studied the map of Vilscape itself. "How long would this wall last?"

"Good question." Sarge sighed. "It depends on how many soldiers you can sacrifice in the defence. Say we send all ten thousand of our soldiers up there. They won't all fit on the wall, but the large force would let us spell off the defenders, so exhaustion won't be an issue as quickly. But that's assuming the enemy doesn't find a way to flank the wall. Even all things being equal, thirty thousand will defeat ten."

"All things being equal?" Robin looked up at him. "How do we make things unequal?"

"You have the making of a strategist." Sarge patted her hand. "Strategy is about the aims of the attack. So putting multiple defensive positions is good strategy for us, as long as we don't let it cost us too dearly."

"Our goal is to stop the army." Robin ran her finger over the map as if it would give her the answer. "Our strategy needs to make things unequal in our favour. We can't change the numbers, so what can we change?"

"What does an army need?"

"My pardon, but supper is here."

"We'll have to set this aside for the moment, lass." Sarge tapped the table with his cane. Robin pushed it out of his way. She walked beside him to the room with the tables and chairs.

"Might as well look at different scenery when we can."

Robin sat Sarge and put a plate together for him, cutting up his food.

"Edward, call the lad in to eat."

"The runners have their own mess."

"That may be true, but one can learn a lot about someone at the dining table."

"As you wish." Edward whistled and Danael ran up. "The master sergeant has invited you to join him in a meal."

Danael's eyes widened so that Robin worried they'd fall out when they went wider at the site of the food. He bowed deeply. "Thank you, Master Sergeant." He scurried around to the other side of the table. Robin noted with approval he didn't take anything from a plate she hadn't served from, and he didn't take a lot.

They ate in silence. Danael looked like he thought he'd died and gone to heaven. He eyed the sweet Robin put in front of him. "If I each too much, it will slow me down." He stood and bowed to the master sergeant and a shallower one to Robin.

"Edward," Robin pointed to the sweet, "set this aside. Danael can eat it when his work is done."

Danael skipped back to his chair as Edward returned the plates to the cart.

"Be sure to eat, Edward," Sarge said.

"I'm used to eating at morning and night, Master Sergeant."

"At least make a sandwich for later. It could be a long evening."

"Sandwich?"

"Two slices of bread, meat and cheese and whatever else you want between them." Sarge demonstrated with meat from the last plate. "Easy, stand up food. This is yours if you need it."

Edward reluctantly put the plate with the sandwich aside.

"Visitors, Master Sergeant." Danael ushered in two men. Robin recognized one as the apprentice who treated the trainees' minor injuries.

"Master Sergeant." The other older man bowed slightly. "I am Master Louis, the king's head physician; my assistant Peter."

"Welcome, have you eaten?" Sarge looked up at the men.

"We have come straight from the king's hall."

"Then we will move to the sitting area in the other room. Robin, if you will?" She helped him up and stayed beside him as he led the way.

"I must say." Master Louis settled into a chair while Peter perched on one a little behind. Robin pulled a seat over to be closer to Sarge. "There are a few families in Kingstown who are dark like you, but they do not live any longer than most. I have never had the privilege of meeting one as extraordinary as you.

"Not extraordinary, just old." Sarge brushed off the comment.

"I heard rumours that you have seen a hundred winters."

"True enough, but in my world that isn't terribly unusual."

"This is a social call, so I will restrain my questions."

"Appreciated." Sarge nodded his head. "When I have a better handle on things, we can arrange a more formal visit."

"Since I don't know this world very well, could you tell me about the practice of medicine here?

As they talked, Robin had the feeling Sarge knew a lot more about medicine than he was letting on. From the occasional hard glances from Peter, she wasn't the only one.

"You have some medical experience?" Master Louis asked. "Your understanding is deep for one not trained."

"I had basic medical training in the army. Needed to be able to patch people together so they'd live to see the doctors. Growing old is its own education."

"More visitors," Danael announced from the door.

"I will take my leave." Master Louis stood and bowed to Sarge and nodded at Robin.

Robin watched him leave. "I'm curious about your basic training."

"Mostly stopping bleeding, keeping people breathing, immobilizing broken bones." Sarge thumped his cane. "You should have some of that already."

"Yes, Master Sergeant." She ducked her head, then turned to watch as the trainees entered.

"This is what I call living." Crispin came in craning his neck to scan every corner.

"Manners." Tamlyn swatted him. He rolled his eyes but sat down. Tamlyn sat beside him on the couch, the others took seating wherever they could, including the floor.

"Hope you don't mind the brats tagging along." Jalliet pointed at Lencely and his friends. Lencely opened his mouth but shut it without saying anything.

"Not at all." Sarge straightened in his chair. "Robin, summarize what we were talking about before supper."

"We were talking about how to make things uneven in our favour. We can't add more people to our army, nor can we remove numbers from theirs, not without putting our own people at risk."

"Thank you." Sarge patted her hand. "What does an army need to fight?"

"Weapons."

"Training."

"Discipline.

The trainees rattled off a list.

"That's a good start, but it is all about the fighting. What do they need that isn't connected directly to the fighting?"

Jalliet's stomach rumbled. "Sorry, I missed supper."

"Food," Crispin said at the same time.

"Yes, supper is food." Jalliet looked daggers at him.

"No, I mean an army needs to eat."

"How much would it take to feed thirty thousand people?"

"My father complained about eating dry bread and smoked meat on patrol," Hal said.

"How much?" Tamlyn asked.

"Bread the size of his fist." Hal held his up. "Maybe more the size of Norm's fist. He pointed to one of the other squires. "Meat more like Robin's fist."

"Did he carry it himself?" Robin asked.

"No," said Oswait, one of the other squires, the most junior next to Robin. "My grandfather talked about being a quartermaster. He drove a wagon and had people to help him with the food, spare clothing, weapons and stuff."

"Running an army is complicated," Lencely said. "My father is always talking about morale. I'm not sure what it is, but he thinks it's important."

"It is indeed." Sarge thumped his cane. "Morale is a soldier's emotional capacity to fight. The best-fed army won't fight well with poor morale, though being fed, clothed, and safe will boost morale."

"If we were going to go after their morale, we should attack those food wagons." Crispin leaned forward.

"Easier said than done." Oswait looked at Sarge. "Grandfather said they were well-guarded. He did say sometimes he wasn't sure who they really needed to be guarded against."

"Wouldn't even a wagon run out eventually?" Jalliet frowned. "You'd have to have wagons to replace the empty ones."

"Father says the people at the most danger from an invading army are the villages and farms, not the army." Lencely scratched his head. "It would make sense. If they got food from close by, it would be easier."

"You have just described supply lines and why some countries burned their fields and fouled the wells before they retreated."

"They burn their own food?" Tamlyn frowned, "but what would they eat?"

"If they're retreating, they'll be heading for a city." Hal scratched his head. "But it won't be just them getting hungry. Those farms feed the city too."

"Correct." Sarge thumped his cane again. The dialogue went until Hal stood and announced they needed to return to their barracks.

Without the bodies and chatter, the huge room felt empty.

"What did you make of the conversation?" Sarge twisted to look at Robin.

"The war begins long before the battle. Can you win a war without a battle?"

"There are no winners in war, only those who lose less badly." Sarge took a deep breath. "Yes, a war can be ended without a battle, but there needs to be enough reason for both sides to come to the table."

Robin wanted to ask more questions, but the sombre look on Sarge's face made her shove them aside for another day.

"Are you ready for bed?" She yawned.

"One more thing." Sarge leaned his head back. "Tell that boy it's time for him to go back to wherever he lives when not working, if he hasn't already. If he's still here, ask him to run a message to Sir Garraik asking for a meeting tomorrow. Time I started earning my keep."

"Mmmph." Danael peered up at Robin. "Oh, it's you."

"Sarge has said it's time for you to go back to your room."

"What if he needs me in the middle of the night?"

"You can't sit here all night and be any good in the morning." Robin thought about Sarge telling her to care for herself. "Sarge will be displeased if you don't eat and sleep properly."

"We're supposed to stay where we're assigned." He set his chin stubbornly.

Okay, I did ask. "How about this – Master Sergeant wants you to run a message to Sir Garraik asking for a meeting tomorrow. He didn't specify a time, so at Sir Garraik's convenience. When you get back here, you can sleep on the couch."

"I'm fine here."

"Why make the master sergeant come to you? If you need to be available, then the couch makes sense."

"I guess so." Danael stood and shook himself like a dog. "Sir Garraik, a meeting tomorrow at his convenience." He dashed off and Robin returned to Sarge.

"He's going to sleep on the couch, in case we need him," Robin explained to Sarge. "Makes sense as I haven't seen a pull to summon a servant."

"Give him a pillow and a blanket from my bed. There is more than enough." Sarge stood and leaned on his cane.

Robin helped him get ready for bed, then tucked him in.

"Goodnight." Robin checked to be sure the bell sat on the side table. She put out the candles except for one in each room for Danael. As she'd expected, a nook with a tiny bed waited behind a curtain next the room with the bath. It might be more suitable for Danael, but for once, Robin was glad she was small.

Danael returned carrying in the candle from the hall. He saw the pillow and blanket, blew out the candle, and thumped onto the couch. Robin went into the bath and washed her face. Back out in the room, she checked on the boy, tucked the blanket tighter around him, then changed into her nightclothes and crawled into her own bed.

CHAPTER 7

Robin put on her armour and backpack before she remembered she was supposed to do what Sarge called crunches and push-ups. She'd forgotten last night too.

Doing push-ups with the backpack weighting her back was impossible, but she vowed to wear the pack while doing the exercises someday. Even the armour made it harder, but she counted the forty push-ups and crunches off then picked up her pack and started her run. Today she ran as fast as she could until she had to stop, then walked, then ran again.

Instead of pushing herself to exhaustion. Robin knelt as well as she could in boots and armour and worked on the breathing. Instead of reviewing a fight, she ran through the conversation from yesterday. *How does he get us working our heads like that with only a few questions?* The sessions with Sarge were different from anything she'd experienced from the history tutors.

"You continue to surprise." Sir Garraik stood in front of her, an odd expression on his face.

"Sir." Robin moved to stand up.

"When we're gathered, perhaps you'll explain this."

"I think it might be more effective after the warmup."

"As you will."

When Robin told them it was from Sarge, no one complained, but she didn't like how she explained it. *Sarge uses fewer words.*

"Never give an unnecessary order," she told herself.

"What was that?" Sir Garraik looked over.

"That's enough for now." Robin stood up. "Will keep working with Sarge on it and pass it along to you."

"Squire Robin, you said something before we stopped." Sir Garraik glowered at her.

"My apologies, Sir. It is something Sarge said to me. 'Never give an unnecessary order.'"

"I see." Sir Garraik looked up at the sun. "Hal, lead the trainees in grappling. Robin, come with me."

"Sarge has asked to meet with me." Sir Garraik strode along at a pace that had Robin jogging to keep up. "Do you have any idea what he wants?"

"He said something about earning his keep."

"Ah."

Sir Garraik knocked on the door. When no one came, Robin opened it and waved Sir Garraik in. "This way sir."

Sarge sat in his chair, nibbling on a biscuit. An empty cup sat beside him.

"Welcome, Sir Garraik, you honour me." Sarge nodded. "If you don't mind, I will remain seated."

"That is fine, Master Sergeant." Sir Garraik sat on the chair Robin pulled over for him. She sat on the floor beside Sarge. Sir Garraik gazed at her for a moment, then leaned toward Sarge.

"Robin tells me you have decided to earn your keep."

She bit her tongue to keep from protesting. Sir Garraik brought her for a reason, and it wasn't to argue with him.

"That's right." Sarge patted her head.

At least he doesn't scratch me behind my ears. She almost laughed aloud at the image.

"A squire shouldn't repeat her master's words carelessly."

Sarge laughed and Sir Garraik's eyes widened slightly. "I trust Robin to not repeat my words carelessly."

"Explain why one should never give an unnecessary order." Sir Garraik spoke like he was executing a cut with a sword.

"Simple." Sarge almost patted Robin again but put his hand back on the arm of the chair. "If you get people used to being told each step, they will always expect you to explain each step. Do you order the troops to make camp, or do you order each step of the process?"

"I see." Sir Garraik frowned. "I wasn't sure why a squire would decide an order was unnecessary"

"Right." Sarge looked at Robin. "Which would you rather have, someone who obeyed your orders exactly or someone who obeyed your order based on the situation they are facing?"

"When we are training with sword or grappling, Sir Garraik keeps telling us to read our opponent, so I would want someone who would read their opponent."

"What if they disobey your order?" Sir Garraik rasped at her.

"It would depend on why." Robin spoke slowly to give herself time to think it through. "If they disobeyed because they didn't like the order or if they thought they knew better, that would be a problem. I would probably remove them from their position. But if they disobeyed because they understood my intentions but knew they wouldn't work in that situation, I'd want them around."

"I see." Sir Garraik rubbed his chin. "I'm not sure I agree. An order is an order. A soldier can't be expected to understand the larger needs of the battle. I don't want the trainees thinking they know more than their superiors."

"As you say." Sarge thumped his cane. "Now about why I asked you to meet with me. I believe I understand enough to make sensible suggestions. If you would request a meeting with the king and whoever else should be included, I will begin doing what I can."

"I will pass on your request immediately. Squire Robin, return to the training yard and tell Hal to move to the next part of training." Sir Garraik stood and bowed deeply, then strode out of the room.

Sarge waved at her. "Off you go."

"Yes, Sarge." Robin paused and turned back. "Where is Danael? I expected him to be here."

"I sent him to arrange better sleeping quarters for you. If he's going to sleep here, he can use the nook, and I'll have a corner curtained off for you."

"Thank you, Sarge." Robin headed back to the yard, then remembered rule number one, and broke into a sprint.

***

"Pardon, Squire Robin, your presence is required in the War Room." Danael bounced on his toes.

"Excuse me, Hal." Robin dusted the sand from her uniform. She'd have to wait until later to wash it off her skin.

"Race you," Robin said and bolted toward the palace. Danael's indignant shout came from behind her.

They arrived at the top of the stairs at the same time.

"Hold, Danael." Robin tried to focus on her breathing as Sarge taught her, and her heart slowed quickly. "Wait outside the room."

"Yes, Squire." Danael looked at her with what might have been respect.

At the door to the War Room, Robin gave her uniform one last brushing and tried to straighten it, before knocking and entering the room.

"Sire." Robin bowed as she saw the king in his seat. Sir Garraik sat around the corner to the king's right, a mage to the left. Lord Huddroc sat next across to him.

"Take a seat, Squire." The King pointed to where a chair was set beside the master sergeant.

Robin sat beside Sarge who smiled at her before turning his attention to the king. The map of Vilscape lay on the table with weights on each corner. Other rolls were standing in a box behind the king.

"My understanding of my role as Squire Robin's master that I am supposed to educate her, so please accept this as part of her education." Sarge leaned back in his chair. "Robin, please summarize our discussion from last evening with the trainees."

"May I stand?" Robin looked at the king. "I believe I can think better on my feet."

He nodded, so she stood and tried to organize her thoughts. Lord Huddroc harrumphed and shifted in his seat but didn't say anything. Robin related the discussion without the side trails and jumps in topic.

"Hmm," Lord Huddroc rubbed his thumb on the table in front of him. "So I take it you are suggesting attacks on their supply lines along with defence along the pass?"

"If I were to add anything, it would be to find a way to attack their morale." Robin crossed her fingers behind her back.

"Very astute." Lord Huddroc nodded and looked at her without glaring.

"Lord Huddroc, what would you suggest our first response be?" the king asked.

"We stand no chance against them until they enter the pass." Lord Huddroc went back to rubbing his thumb on the table. "In the pass, we can hold them at the defensive points, as Squire Robin pointed out. The problem is it will cost us dearly at each point. I have five hundred men and women in my garrison, few of them with any field experience. I fear we'd lose more than we'd gain."

"In my world, a general used dummies to make the enemies think they were much greater in numbers than they were. It meant the opposing general took a more conservative approach to the battle, allowing time for reinforcements to arrive." Sarge looked up at a corner of the room. "If the enemy found each barrier to be defended only by dummies, they might be unsure at the next barrier."

"I would think they would rush the barrier faster." The king tilted his head.

"Certainly, the commanders would desire the soldiers to do that, but soldiers are a superstitious lot if they had any doubt about the nature of the defence, for instance, that magic was involved."

"For a mage to intend to use magic to kill would mean losing their soul and soon, whatever will they had."

"I know nothing about magic here." Sarge leaned forward. "Obviously, you were part of the ritual the day I arrived, so you summon. What other forms of magic are there?"

Robin hid her giggle as the king rolled his eyes and leaned back. She soon discovered why as the mage droned on and on about the minute details of magic. Small things like purifying water or preserving food were simple, but the more one wanted to do, the more complicated and dangerous the ritual.

"Lord Mage," Robin asked, "how familiar would the average soldier be with the constraints on magic you describe?"

"I hear complaints about how useless mages are, but as soon as they want water cleaned…"

"I understand. They are fixed on results, not on process." Sarge leaned back. "The officers might know better, but the grunt on the front line will be ready to believe anything."

"An odd way of putting it, but yes." The mage nodded.

"An attack on the enemy's morale is different from an attack on their life?" Robin closed her eyes and chased an elusive idea through her thoughts.

"I know of no magic which can directly affect a person's mental state." The mage sounded impatient.

"In sword play, we will pretend an attack to get our opponent to move the way we wish." Sir Garraik said. "Could we use magic in the same way?"

"What are you thinking?" The mage looked interested despite himself.

"You told us one of the magics which are of moderate difficulty is moving inanimate objects."

"The heavier the object, the more draining it is, and the longer the drain lasts too."

"But you would be able to, say, have the dummies fall over dead as if they'd been moving up to that point?" Sir Garraik raised a brow.

"That would be simple enough, though I fail to see how that would help." The mage frowned

"We don't need the dummies to fight the enemy, just for the enemy to think they were." Sir Garraik almost smiled.

The mage sat back thoughtfully. "Yes, that could be done. You'd need a mage at each barrier. It might be more effective to vary the nature of the spell to create more uncertainty. But that won't stop thirty thousand soldiers."

"But it would slow them down. They'd eat more food than planned, and that would stress those supply lines Robin spoke of." The king grinned broadly at the mage.

"Don't we need to stop them?" The mage scratched at his head.

"Only until the winter closes the pass." Lord Huddroc clenched his fist. "They will only have two months at most to cross the pass and subdue Vilscape."

"That is true." Sarge sighed and rubbed his chest. "Only this attack is most likely one of the feints Sir Garraik spoke of."

"A feint, with thirty thousand?" Lord Huddroc pushed his thumb on the table as if to crush the invaders.

"Thirty thousand what?" Sarge leaned forward. "From what I've gathered from the bit of reading I've done, the empire is structured more strictly feudally than Caldera, with a lot of the people on the bottom being slaves in all but name."

"Slaves won't fight well," Lord Huddroc said.

"They don't need to if they are only to pull us out of position." Sir Garraik rapped the table. "A good sword wielder will use a feint to control what their opponent is planning to do. What if we ask ourselves what the empire would gain by us putting most of our forces in the north?"

"It would leave the west wide open." The king almost shouted. "We need to protect the west. A lot of our food is grown there."

"Which brings us to the reason for this war in the first place." Sarge put a hand on Robin's arm. He looked a bit pale.

"They need food." Robin stood but held onto Sarge's hand. "We need the west because we can grow more there than in the Caldera. If the empire isn't growing enough to eat…"

"Makes sense." Lord Huddroc's thumb speeded up. "The few traders who came through the pass before winter only wanted food, and they paid well for it."

"We can't defend the west and the north at the same time." Sir Garraik said. "We don't have the numbers."

"Your Majesty," Robin interrupted Sir Garraik. "Sarge isn't well. May I send for the physician?"

"Of course."

Robin ducked out of the room and sent Danael running, then ran back to Sarge's side.

"Hold on."

"Sorry, lass, just tired. Been overdoing it the last couple of days." Even Sarge's voice sounded grey.

"We could adjourn our meeting," the king said.

"No need; can rest here easier than getting back to my room. If Robin needs my help, I'll speak up."

"We will continue at least until Master Louis arrives." The king sat back in his chair. "So, Squire Robin, what's next?"

Robin's heart pounded and her mouth went dry. *What would Sarge say? He'd ask a question.*

"What's the minimum number of people we need to delay the attack until the winter?"

"The garrison won't hold long against those numbers, even if they are slaves." Lord Huddroc looked at the table as if it might hold the answer. She knew how he felt.

"Let's start with the worst case that they have two months to move their army and make their attack." Sir Garraik said.

"How long would it take to move that many soldiers?" Robin asked.

"On level ground, they could move four or five leagues a day." Sir Garraik rubbed his eyes, "At least that's what my mentor, Sir Mattew, said. The rest of the day they are starting or stopping."

"Their camp is on the plain, about twenty leagues to the pass, then another twenty from the beginning to the end of the pass. That's eight days just to march from there to Vilscape." Lord Huddroc started to look more hopeful. "There are five defensive points along the pass. If we can hold each one for three days, that's another fortnight. The pass itself will slow them down. The idea is to get to where the worst part starts, camp, then cross in one day if all goes well. Then camp at the other side, before continuing down to the plain and onto the imperial road. With that many, they won't be able to cross the pass itself in one day. They'd have to send smaller groups or lose a lot of soldiers. Say three weeks to a month to get into position." He leaned back. "We can't hold them for a month, not with five hundred."

"If each time they stop, it takes them candles to get started again, how many times can we force them to stop?" Robin pulled the map over and studied it. "Could we make fake defences just so they stop to deal with them? If they don't know if a barrier is defended or not, they'd have to treat each one like it was defended."

"Could work, but it would need more people to build them. We won't be able to work on the defences much before they start marching toward us." Lord Huddroc said.

"But we could get the materials ready." Sir Garraik pulled the map over to peer at it. "Even if it only buys us a few days, it would be worth it."

"What's the next fallback position after Vilscape?" Robin asked.

"There isn't one." Lord Huddroc grumped. "Once they're past us, the kingdom is wide open."

"We need another wall." Robin squeezed her head with her hands. "Sir Garraik, if I may?" She pulled the map over to her. Sarge reached over and peered at it, then tapped a more detailed map of Vilscape.

"There is a wall." Sarge gasped in air as if speaking was beyond his strength.

"Right." Robin pushed the map over to Lord Huddroc.

"You're thinking of the south wall. It's just there to keep the animals and bandits out. Wouldn't stand long against a real army."

"What if we make the whole town into a wall?" Robin leaned on her hands. "Empty it of all food and drink, then burn the rest when we have to retreat from the main wall? They'd be ready to take supplies from Vilscape, only to find it on fire and still blocking their way."

"If we're going to lose the place anyway, no need to hand it to the enemy." Lord Huddroc slumped, "Burning it is a final contingency to allow the people to escape."

"We don't have to wait for the weather to work on Vilscape." Sir Garraik clapped his hands. "We evacuate the townspeople, then turn the town into hell for the attackers. Could reinforce the gates and build traps."

"I'd need a thousand soldiers as well as my garrison. We could double up all the positions on the main wall and still be able to spell the soldiers off for at least half the day. Would need some luck, but it is possible." Lord Huddroc looked rejuvenated. "Need to get started right away. The pass could be open in six weeks."

"Sir Garraik, see that Lord Huddroc has what he needs."

"Engineers," Sarge whispered.

"Engineers?" Robin leaned down to him. "What are they?"

"Build."

"Build?" Robin looked up at the others. "I think he's saying we need people to build stuff."

Sarge nodded.

"Right, I will ask the Regulars for people with building experience," Sir Garraik agreed.

Master Louis entered the room and waved Robin out of the way, then took Sarge's wrist.

"Heart is beating as well as expected. I suspect he's just worn out. All of us need to remember the master sergeant has seen a hundred winters." He tapped Sarge's shoulder at the last comment. "My men will carry him back to his room, and I will leave someone with him until he starts to recover his strength."

"I'm in your hands, Doc," Sarge whispered.

"Squire Robin, if I may have some of your time?" Lord Huddroc put a hand on her arm. "Let Master Louis do his work."

"I will see you soon. Get some rest." Robin stepped back to let two men with a stretcher in beside Sarge. They efficiently lifted and laid him in place, then picked up the stretcher and followed Master Louis out the door. She didn't realize she was crying until Lord Huddroc gave her his kerchief.

CHAPTER 8

In Lord Huddroc's suite, Robin sipped at watered wine. Though Lencely drank the same wine as the men, she didn't trust herself.

"I misjudged you." Lord Huddroc sipped on his unwatered wine. "And your master. I came to the king prepared to demand the troops I needed to defend Vilscape. It would have stripped the kingdom bare and left us open to invasion."

Robin had no idea what to say, so she sipped at her wine again.

"The master sergeant asks one question, and it changes how we think about the world." Lencely put his cup down. "It is like when Sir Tehnfield teaches me a new technique. When it works, my understanding of swordplay changes, usually showing how little I know."

"I trained under Sir Matthew. My father sent me to take the test to get into the class. Thought I would learn more if I'd earned it. Took me three tries to pass, then I had to toss out what I assumed I knew about the sword." Lord Huddroc peered into his cup.

"Perhaps I was lucky not to know much about the sword." Robin mused. She sipped at her wine, then put it down. "I think Sarge combines knowledge with an understanding of the limits of trying to *give* people knowledge. He's big on letting me experience things by trial and error."

"I would love to take you back to Vilscape with me." Lord Huddroc lifted a hand. "I have no intention of trying to separate you from Sarge. Something is happening between you and the master sergeant I have not seen before. Perhaps it comes from standing on one of the points during the summoning."

"I have never been a squire, so I don't know." Robin looked down.

"It is like you have a connection, a special feel for what he's saying. It was hard to believe a squire was not only speaking at the war table but commanding respect from experienced knights. So, what I would like to do is go over the defence of Vilscape with you as if you were the master sergeant."

"I will do what I can," Robin settled herself. Lencely stood to leave. "Sit." Robin pointed at the chair.

Lord Huddroc raised an eyebrow but didn't say anything.

"Let's start at the beginning. I need to delay that army for two months."

"Are you familiar with strategy and tactics?" Robin asked.

"I'd like to think so."

"Let me start by stating what I understand from the meeting." Robin closed her eyes and imagined Sarge sitting beside her, his hand on hers. "The goal is to delay the army until they are caught by winter. Our overall strategy is to set up as many nuisances in their way as we can and do it in a way that will chip away at their morale. The tactics we are using are to create a series of defensive points, some we will fight and hold as long as we can without taking losses. Others will be undefended. At both, we will use dummies to make it look like we have more people than we do and to make it look as if we found a way to use magic against the army."

"What I'm worried about is what happens when we need to defend the wall."

"You know the area and what needs to be done. Sarge would tell you to trust yourself."

"What is the enemy's strategy?" Lencely leaned forward eyes bright.

"The council agrees with the master sergeant's opinion this is a feint to pull our army out of position." Lord Huddroc sat back. "Their strategy appears to be to bring overwhelming numbers and walk over us."

"The master sergeant told a story about a battle in his world where a few soldiers held out against a larger army. The battle ended when the invaders found a path through the mountains and were able to flank the defenders."

"There are paths, but you have to be mostly goat to cross them," Lencely spoke up, then reddened. "The Goat Club is dedicated to finding them."

"I will be asking for their help." Lord Huddroc smiled. "In my day we called ourselves Goatmen. There are other small passes farther to the southeast. If one connects to the empire, it will be trouble if anyone gets through. I'll double the sweeps and flush out any invaders."

"What do we do with anyone we capture?" Lencely asked.

"I wish I knew. If we hold prisoners, we'll have to feed and guard them. We can't honourably kill someone who has surrendered."

"Don't take prisoners." Robin had her fingers on her temples. "Send them back. Feed them a good meal and let them glimpse the encampment of the king's army outside the walls."

"They'll just be back to fight us again." Lord Huddroc frowned.

"We are concentrating too much on time." Robin smiled. "What else will cause them to fail?"

"We beat them back," Lencely said.

"They have to bring food across the pass for each person who is marching."

"We attack their supply lines." Lencely jumped up. "We can get above them before they get to the wall."

"Once the supplies are across the pass, they are as good as in the enemy's hands." Lord Huddroc rubbed his chin thoughtfully, "but a few troops on the far side of the pass could wreak havoc once the main army has passed. They'd have to make an early crossing to get in place."

"The winter crossing killed four out of five. How hard is an early crossing?"

"Normally it would be a coin toss."

"Vipan could do it," Lencely said.

"He could." Lord Huddroc looked at Robin. "My second son, he made it his mission to learn every foot of the pass. He's the one who suggested the defensive points and wanted a full-fledged fortified town on the far end. We also haven't had a civil conversation in years."

"You are going to give him what he's been demanding for years," Lencely said. "He'll take it and be happy."

"That will mean putting himself under my command. I fear I've burned that bridge."

"He doesn't hate you." Lencely looked at his toes. "Just what he sees as a problem no one else wants to admit."

"You've talked to him?"

"He's my brother."

"That he is. Can you contact him for me?"

"I will." Lencely nodded vigorously. "He's a commander with the Regulars. I can get a message to him to meet you on the road."

"Ask him to bring his troop. I'll get Sir Garraik to sort out the chain of command for him to act on his own."

"I'd better get moving if I'm going to catch a messenger at the gate. May I take the horse?"

"Don't kill either yourself or the horse." Lord Huddroc clapped his hands, and a man in livery entered the room.

"Lencely has an urgent mission and needs a horse. See to it, Camerson."

"Yes, my lord."

"Now, I'm almost afraid of what comes next." Lord Huddroc shook his head. "The villagers can set up the camp and make it look like it is full of soldiers. It will take everything I have to rebuild after, assuming there is an after."

"That brings up the town." Robin stared at the ceiling. "Burning it will be a start but could be trouble if they use the rubble against us. Maybe building traps to make it dangerous to move anything. Like the barriers, we'd need just enough to force them to check everything. How long would it burn for?"

"I have no idea; we've always focused on putting fires out."

"There is one more thing, going back to prisoners." Robin sighed, but Sarge whispered to her insistently in her head. "You need a plan for when they surrender."

"Surrender?"

"Think about it. We're going to block their supply lines, force them to push the time limit. Even if they left on the day two months is up, some are going to be trapped on our side. Do we let them starve and freeze?"

"I see, but how would we guard that many prisoners?"

"What do you usually do with prisoners?" Robin picked up her cup and took another sip. Tension crawled up her spine into her head.

"Most prisoners are bandits. If it's the first time we've caught them, they give parole not to go back to banditry. Try to send them to villages where they need labour. The plague created a huge labour shortage. Even without this invasion, we'd have been in trouble soon."

"What if you treat the prisoners the same way? Parole and set them to labour, though not as slaves. Pay them."

"We do that, they're going to want to stay…" Lord Huddroc laughed. "And that starts solving the labour shortage."

A knock interrupted them.

"My lord, Master Vipal has come to speak to you." Camerson stepped back and let a man in who looked like a younger version of Lord Huddroc. He wore the Regulars' brown uniform, only a rank and unit badge distinguishing it from the wool clothes that any woodsman might wear.

Lord Huddroc stood.

"I was in the area. I thought it would be quicker to come myself." Vipal spoke in a cold, clipped tone.

"I need to set something straight." Lord Huddroc took a long breath. "You were right. All those years, all those arguments, if I had listened…"

"Girl, I could use a glass of wine."

Lord Huddroc started to say something, but Robin jumped in. "Right away." The bottle sat open on the sideboard. She found a goblet inside and poured wine for Vipal.

He accepted the cup and took a long sip, then studied her again.

"Those aren't Vilscape colours, but it is a uniform. What division?"

"I am a trainee under Sir Garraik and the master sergeant's squire." She bowed to him, then to Lord Huddroc and let herself out of the room.

***

"You asked me to wake you in time to see Lord Huddroc off." Edward stood beside her holding a candle. "Apparently he is a believer in early starts."

"Thank you, Edward." He left the candle on the table beside her bed. She changed into her uniform quickly, then washed her face as she passed the basin. Danael had a foot sticking out from behind the curtain. Robin resisted the temptation to tickle it.

Edward waited for her in the hall. He led the way to the courtyard where Lord Huddroc and his retinue prepared to leave. Lencely stood to the side, a mutinous look on his face. He brightened as Robin stepped up beside him. Jalliet waved as she climbed into the coach. Oswait was mounted and concentrating on soothing his horse, which looked nervous with all the activity.

"Jalliet is going to Vilscape, she's Geoffroi's betrothed. Oswait is his squire. I knew Father was going to leave me here." Lencely didn't look at her. "I didn't know how much it would hurt."

"You angry with him?"

"No, I'm worried. He's leaving me here because if things go badly, I will be the next Lord Huddroc."

"I'm certain neither of you wants that to happen."

"Good morning, Squire Robin." Vipal came over to them. "I apologize for my rudeness last night."

"Think nothing of it." Robin smiled

"You are as gracious as my father described, and this one," Vipal ruffled Lencely's hair, "has talked about little else. I thank you for taking my brother under your wing.

Father is in the center of things, so I will pass on his message to you. Please continue to watch over him. Lencely has been asked to treat you as if you were squire to his master."

Lencely turned to Robin and bowed low. "I place myself in your care and pledge to obey you as I would my father."

"I will do my best to guide you. I'll see if Sarge will take you as a page."

"That's a good idea." The king strolled over to them. "Lencely."

Robin worried Lencely was going to fall over.

"Your majesty," Vipal bowed deeply. "I am ever your servant."

"Try to get your father to take care of himself, and if he can stop the invasion too, I'd appreciate it."

He strolled away to talk briefly with Lord Huddroc as he came over to them.

"Lencely..."

"I know, Father. It's all right. Robin is going to train me. You owe me a match."

"I look forward to it." Lord Huddroc put his hand on Lencely's head for a moment, then turned away.

"I must clear out my room. We are going to bunk with the pages." Lencely walked away.

"Too bad we didn't meet earlier; we could have had some great arguments." Vipal nodded at Robin.

"Next time we meet."

***

Sarge slept, his colour better.

"As he would say," Master Louis packed up his bag, "his body is worn out; he pushed himself too hard. The best thing is for him to be moderately active. Take short walks, get outside, but also give himself plenty of time to rest."

"I can set Lencely and his friends to encourage Sarge to move around and keep an eye on him. Lencely may become the master sergeant's page."

"An excellent plan." Master Louis smiled at her. "Here is a tea you can make. It is a bit of a restorative. No miracles, but it should ease some of his pain."

"Pain?" Robin looked at Sarge. "I thought he was just stiff."

"Imagine how you feel at the end of an extremely rigorous training session. That is probably close to what he experiences constantly. If he keeps exercising to a gentle routine, it will help with the stiffness and perhaps some of the pain."

Robin headed out for training, though she would arrive late after getting up so early. It was still better than moping about in the room with nothing to do but worry. She asked Danael to sit in the room with Sarge. The boy shrugged and headed to the bedroom.

The trainees were in the middle of warmup, so rather than disturbing them, she did her sit-ups and push-ups.

"Squire Robin." Sir Garraik waved her over.

"You were late."

"Yes, Sir Garraik." Robin kept her eyes forward. "I was needed to meet with the physician."

"You think that is an adequate excuse?"

"My first duty is to Sarge, then my training." Her heart pounded, whether in fear or anger, she couldn't say.

"None of the other squires are allowed to be late."

None of the others is squire to a fragile old man.

"You want to say something?" Sir Garraik snapped the words at her.

"No, sir." Robin lifted her chin. Sir Garraik would find a reason to punish her regardless.

"Very well, you will spar with each one here, from the youngest to the oldest. Get your gear and return on the double."

Robin sprinted to the equipment room, put on her training armour, picked up her sword and buckler, then jogged back to the centre of the training yard.

A rope made a circle in the sand. The trainees held their swords and grinned at Robin.

"A lethal strike or one of you steps out of the ring. If the match is less than ten exchanges you will repeat it." Sir Garraik crossed his arms. "Hal, judge on the other corner."

The first in line stepped into the ring and saluted her with his sword. Robin listened to her breathing, when she was calm and ready, she lifted her sword. "Ready."

Robin concentrated on keeping her movements the least she needed to fight her opponent. After ten exchanges she'd finish the match. It was hard on the young ones, to be defeated so casually, but she needed her energy for the squires. After the first five matches, Robin realized she was repeating the same forms. Each of the squires started with one of a few different attacks. Robin wondered what would happen if she changed the forms.

She'd learned this parry for that cut or thrust, attack when the opponent was in that position. Robin experimented, using unexpected parries, attacks at odd moments. Varying the rhythm was more work, but she was too focused on her experiments to care.

With the mail and practice armour, the usual attacks centred on weak points: under the arms, the head and neck. The trainees became uncertain, fumbling their parries. Robin had to pull her cut more than once to keep from ending the match in fewer than ten exchanges. After ten matches, her opponents tried different openings, but their follow-up was slow as they had to think about what to do next.

Crispin stepped into the ring and saluted her. Then he waited, sword at the ready. Robin got the feeling whoever moved first would lose, but if she waited too long, she'd stiffen up. What were Crispin's favourite opening attacks? If he started with a cut to the head, she'd use her sword to push it up, then lunge. He'd jump back and to the right to use his buckler. The possibilities ran through her head until she ran into a block. She had no idea how Crispin would react to that series. How to force him to start the series?

She stepped forward as if she were lunging but instead cut at his leg. He parried and she had him. The thrust and parries, cuts and feints happened as she'd imagined. No matter how fast his attack. Robin blocked it almost before he started.

The moment came, he leapt forward in a stop lunge so quick it would have nailed her if she hadn't already been moving. Crispin expected her to step left and sweep the thrust away with her sword. She turned enough for his thrust to miss her by barely a finger's breadth, then stepped into him, caught his sword arm with her buckler hand. His buckler came over to protect him, but she stopped it with the strong of her blade. The point hovered at his throat.

"Match," Hal called.

Crispin gave her an odd look but bowed and stepped out of the ring. The squires were next. As she expected, they were harder to predict as they didn't depend on the same sequences of moves, but they moved in the same rhythm. Robin changed her rhythm, taking a heartbeat before an overhand cut to his head. He easily moved his buckler into place to block, only Robin dropped into a low stance and reversed her cut to thrust from below. He staggered back, and she kept up a barrage of attacks.

"Match." Sir Garraik said. The squire's foot was outside the rope. He bowed, but his eyes looked confused.

Finally, Hal stepped into the ring. He stretched and grinned at her.

"I think your streak is going to end here."

Robin saluted him. Hal wouldn't be easy to defeat. His reach and strength would force her out of measure. All he needed to do was push her hard enough to get her out of the circle. It didn't help that her sword felt like lead in her hand.

Strangely, Hal stayed closer to the patterns of the younger trainees than the other squires, but he wasn't put off by shifts in rhythm. It was like he refused to fight the way she wanted, which would mean he knew she was predicting the pattern. He was going to change it himself.

Robin kept just out of his measure, but Hal was relentless.

She caught sight of the rope in the corner of her eyes. He'd driven her to the edge of the circle. He's going to charge, and he's waiting for me to try climbing him again. What's the last thing he expects?

Robin grinned. If it didn't work, she'd be chewing sand.

Now. Hal didn't telegraph his thrust, it almost caught her, but the closer the miss, the better for her plan. The follow-up to the hard thrust was his charge to sweep her over the rope. He held his buckler like a battering ram.

Robin tossed her sword to grip his sword arm with both hands. Then she lifted her feet, dropped to the ground, pulling his arm with her. It forced him to bend over, letting her plant her shoulder in his gut and heave him toward the rope. Hal put his full weight on her trying to grab her with his buckler hand. She ducked under and to the side of his arm. The big squire staggered off balance as he spun to face her. The sword lay in front of her. Her right hand snatched it up as her left found space on the hilt. She needed the extra hand to move the sword. It felt like lead in her hands, or maybe her arms were lead. The air hissed as she circled with the sword to push Hal's in the same direction he was already moving.

Even off balance and stumbling, his sword tangled in hers, Hal still stopped himself on the edge of the circle. Robin jumped at him, planting both feet on his thigh, then pushed away as flat to the ground as she could. Hal fell backwards. Robin's back slammed into the sand. The air puffed out of her, but she rolled to her knees, then stood shakily, her sword still at the ready.

"Match."

Robin stood and assessed her body. If this was how Sarge felt, no wonder he moved with so much care.

"Squire Robin." Sir Garraik's voice had an odd note in it. "Would you care to explain how you won seventeen matches in a row?"

"Sir," Robin's knees gave out and she thumped to the ground. "If you don't mind, I'll stay sitting for a bit."

"That seems like a good idea," Sir Garraik said.

Someone handed her a waterskin. She gulped some, poured more over her head, then finished the water.

"Squire Robin, are you going to make me wait for your answer?

"No, sorry, sir. You making each match lasting at least ten exchanges gave it to me." She tried to order her thoughts. "It is all about patterns and rhythm. If I could read the pattern, then I could push the fight to where I wanted it. Change the rhythm, and it changes how people respond to attacks, too slow or too fast. That gave me the opening I needed."

"I thought you were reading my mind," Crispin said. "You blocked me like you already knew what I was going to do."

"I did. I forced you into a pattern and controlled the fight from that moment."

"The cut at my leg." Crispin shook his head. "I lost as soon as I parried that."

"Sorry." Robin peered up at him.

"Sorry?" Crispin laughed. "You have to teach me how you did it."

"Every swordfighter has a style. The more experienced you get, the more you learn to stay fluid." Sir Garraik pointed at Robin. "What she did was to read the pattern, then be able to change it. I don't know more than three knights in the kingdom who can do that. Now three knights and a squire."

He knelt in front of her. "I realized during our match that you were shifting patterns. I wanted to see where you could go with it."

"Sir, are you one of the three?" Robin stared at him.

"I am. It took me ten years of being a knight to spot it, another few years to figure out how to make it work for me. If you can teach it, you will be the first. My master told me, and I didn't believe him"

"I will try my best." Robin tried to get up and failed.

"Trainees, I believe Squire Robin will need some assistance back to her quarters. Please make sure she gets there and rests." Sir Garraik tilted her chin up with a finger. "Rest well, two days from now, it's my turn."

CHAPTER 9

"Blast it, lass. I told you to take care of yourself." Robin woke to see Sarge sitting beside her bed.

"How long have you been sitting there?" She pushed herself up to face him.

"Too damn long." He thumped his cane on the floor in front of him. "That Lencely fellow was by and wanted to be my page. What do I need a page for?"

Robin slid off her bed to kneel before Sarge.

"Master Sergeant, I am sorry for worrying you and that I agreed to watch over Lencely without speaking to you." Robin kept her eyes down. She didn't want Sarge seeing the tears threatening to fall.

"Bah, you're my squire, not my slave." The master sergeant's voice ground like the day he first appeared.

"I am your squire, that means not making your life more complicated. I will talk to Lencely and make some other arrangement."

"No, you will not." Sarge raised his voice. "You made a promise. I'm not going to be the reason you break it."

Robin shrank down. Knights got angry at their squires; she'd heard stories from the other squires.

"Yes, Master Sergeant."

"So tell me about what put you into this shape." His voice had no give in it.

Robin told him about being late and the punishment.

"Is that a normal punishment?"

"It has happened a few times since I started training, but Sir Garraik said he wanted to push me to see if I could make it work." Now that she was talking about the day before, her stomach settled down.

"So, it wasn't just a punishment."

"I guess not."

"Would you have accepted the challenge if it hadn't been framed as a consequence for tardiness?" He didn't sound as much like a rockslide now.

"Probably." Robin still didn't quite dare to look up at him. "I want to get stronger, better."

"Why?" The edge was back. "It was foolish. You could have done permanent damage to yourself."

"I wouldn't have learned about the patterns any other way."

"Tell me about these patterns and why they are worth putting yourself in bed for a full day?"

"A day?" Robin looked up at him. "I was asleep a full day?"

"That's what I said." Sarge frowned. "Your friends dumped you here, and you lay like the dead all night and today."

"I was just a little bit tired."

"What kind of idiot takes on seventeen duels in a row, then says she was just a little tired? When Hal walked in with you like a rag doll in his arms, I about died. You're my squire. If anything happens to you, it's on me."

"I don't know what is happening to me." Robin jumped up and pounded the bed. "I was just the smallest trainee. Suddenly, I'm a shield maiden, a squire to a cantankerous old man from another world, and my trainer tells me he only knows three knights who can do what I did."

"What you did?" Sarge pointed to the floor. "Sit down and explain in words this cantankerous old man can understand."

"I spotted that the trainees fell into the same patterns, sequences of action. I could get ahead of them and know when the opening would come and how to take advantage of it. Crispin said it was like I was reading his mind. Maybe it was because I did your breathing to calm myself before I started."

"And just knowing these patterns meant you could defeat them?"

"I still had to be sharp. Knowing what was coming still meant I had to defend against it in a way to my advantage. Hal almost beat me anyway. His strength and reach were almost overwhelming. In the end, what gave me the victory was doing the last thing Hal expected."

"And what would that have been?"

"Grappling." Robin giggled. "I wish I could have seen his face when he realized what was happening.

"You went hand to hand with that giant?"

"He was going to push me out of the ring, so I had to use his strength against him." Robin described what she'd done."

"Leverage, planning, improvising." The master sergeant closed his eyes. "And a lot of luck. I'm going to have to have a look at your unarmed combat. Patterns and rhythm, huh? Interesting. They show up other places, in battles and diplomacy. Pay attention; try to spot them outside of the arena."

"Yes, Master Sergeant." Robin stood. "I'll get dressed."

"Like hell you will," Sarge growled at her. "Put a robe on and come out and eat dinner."

***

Sarge looked at Robin sleeping again after supper. *I'm a damn fool.* What did he know about kids? Yelling at her like that. He tucked the blanket a little tighter around her and resisted the temptation to brush her hair back.

Edward had cleared away the remnants of the food. Danael sat cross-legged on the couch. The kid only had two levels, full speed or stopped.

"Danael." Sarge sat in his chair.

"Yes, Master Sergeant."

"Find Sir Garraik and tell him Master Sergeant Christopher Severson wants to talk to him immediately. Don't let anything stop you. Kick his door in if you have to. Once you've given him the message, find Lencely and tell him I expect him here at breakfast tomorrow. I will have work for him."

"Find Sir Garraik, tell him you want to see him immediately. Find Lencely and tell him to show for breakfast."

"You've got it."

The kid took off like a shot. Sarge sat and rapped his cane on the floor. He'd met officers like Sir Garraik before who ruined good soldiers acting with the best of intentions but no thought.

Sometime later, Sir Garraik strode into the room and planted himself in front of Sarge.

"What you mean by summoning me like a recalcitrant squire?"

"Sit down, you're going to give me a stiff neck."

Sir Garraik reluctantly sat across from Sarge.

"I'm not used to pages kicking my door until I opened it."

"I told him to kick your door in if he had to. I guess he isn't big enough yet."

"This isn't a joking matter." Sir Garraik frowned.

"I'm not joking." Sarge pointed his cane at the knight. "If I was twenty years younger, I would have kicked in your door myself. You worked my squire to the point of exhaustion on a flying chance she might have some esoteric skill. I've seen people like you ruin good men by trying to rush them into something they aren't ready for. Robin needs to be working on the basics, building a foundation for later."

"She's better than that." Sir Garraik leaned forward. "I haven't seen such potential in all my years of training."

"So what?" Sarge thumped his cane. "Potential is another word for not ready. Are you prepared for the consequences if she climbs out of that bed and can't fight?"

"Nonsense, Robin–"

"I've seen it happen to stronger people than her!" Sarge shouted at him. "She doesn't know who she is. In days, she's gone from one of twenty trainees to someone who exchanges 'good morning' with the king, speaks at council and is listened to. Now you tell her there are only three other knights you know who can pull off her trick. If her nerves break, you're going to lose her and if you're lucky, you'll be left with a mediocre, undersized trainee."

"I..." Sir Garraik stopped and took a deep breath. "Robin is your squire. I have overstepped my authority. I just..."

"You just wanted to be the guy who trained Robin Fastheart." Sarge slashed at the knight with his words.

"Yes. No." Sir Garraik stood and paced around. "I don't know. I wasn't thinking about that."

"No, you weren't thinking," Sarge snarled at him. "Now I am going to tell you what you're going to do. First, this match you have tomorrow, it will be in the afternoon. You're going to win. She has to know that no matter how special you told her she is, it doesn't make her invincible. Second, you will tell her the match is a graduation ceremony, that you have nothing left to teach her. Last, you will assign her to a regular unit. To become a commander, she needs to know how the boots on the ground do things."

"I will not single Robin out. No matter how it is sweetened, she will see it as her fault." Sir Garraik turned and pointed at him. "So this isn't a graduation, and she hasn't learned everything I can teach her. I won't injure her to win the match, but I'm not going to go easy on her. All the squires will be assigned to regular units as class one soldiers for two months. It will be three months before the pass opens. That gives us time to help them integrate what they've learned. I will speak to the knights and explain things. The next stage of training would normally be with the knight in the field."

"That is acceptable." Sarge nodded. "One last thing, I would like to have the squires for the full day before they leave. There is essential training they must have before they go."

"In return," Sir Garraik held up a hand, "you will continue your sessions with the trainees. I don't care what you call them. One day in four, they will meet with you. And one day in four you will meet with the knights. Bring your cane. You're going to need it."

"Very well." Sarge reached out a hand, and Sir Garraik clasped it before bowing and making his exit.

"Hope I wasn't too hard on the kid." Sarge leaned his head on the cane.

***

Sarge lowered himself into the chair Lencely had carried from the room. Gord and Rud, two of his buddies, had taken turns with Lencely carrying the thing so Sarge could sit and rest on the way. They were typical boys, distractable, nattering about the strangest things, but they stayed with him and his snail's pace without complaint.

He was the last to arrive at the training yard. The king and the rest of the council sat on what looked like folding chairs against the facing wall.

"Hmmph, it's becoming a circus."

"The king sends his apologies." A servant came over to Sarge. "I am Wilson, His Majesty's personal servant. The council insisted on coming, even though his Majesty forbids any refreshment other than water." Wilson smiled slightly. "In truth, his Majesty wanted hard bread, but we couldn't find any. He asks if you have need of anything, you are to ring this." The man handed a bell to Sarge.

"My pages, Lencely, Gord, and Rud." Sarge waved his hand at the boys and gave the bell to Lencely to hold.

"I am pleased you are so well-served." Wilson bowed to Sarge and returned to the king's side.

"It is going to get warm," Sarge told the boys. "Make sure you get enough to drink."

Lencely ducked into the equipment room and came back with two waterskins. He hung them on the back of Sarge's chair.

Sir Garraik finished talking to the trainees and had them form up beside the council. He and Robin walked out into the centre of the yard where a rope ring was laid out. They saluted the king, then turned to salute Sarge.

Sir Garraik wasn't as big as Hal, but Robin still looked like a child beside him.

Sarge expected some signal to start, but Robin darted in with a quick thrust. Sir Garraik parried it easily. Lencely gave Sarge a blow by blow of the match, getting more excited with each exchange.

After a few minutes, Sir Garraik took control of the attack and chased Robin around the ring. The knight moved every bit as agilely as Robin but with a minimum of energy.

Sarge grew exhausted just by watching, but Robin looked to be speeding up. Then as Lencely rattled on about cuts and parries and more, Sarge rubbed his eyes. Both were moving to defend almost before the attack. *Must be the patterns she talked about.*

The watchers on the other side pointed and muttered to each other. The swords blurred and even Lencely stumbled to silence. Sir Garraik and Robin fought on. Robin jumped forward as the knight's sword brushed her hair. A loud crack echoed in the yard, and Robin tossed away the broken stub of her sword. She pulled a knife from behind her back.

"Hold." The king stood and strolled into the circle. "Squire Robin, I admire your tenacity, but you have both ably demonstrated your skill. This is not a tournament where a winner must be declared. I would not put either of you at risk."

Robin looked like she might argue, then she bowed to the king and to Sir Garraik. They walked toward Sarge.

"Help me up, boys." They had him standing as the three stopped in front of them

"Master Sergeant, you have my permission to stay seated if you are unable to stand. There is respect due to age as much as to royalty."

Robin stepped forward to stand beside the boys, facing the king and Sir Garraik.

"Your Majesty," Robin bowed low, "I am honoured that you came to watch."

"I'm now very glad I didn't rush into a match with you. I'm not sure it would be good to have the king thrashed by a squire. Toward the end, I admit, I was unable to follow the action. It seemed best to call a halt." The king pulled a cloth from his pouch. "I had decided on the colours, but it didn't seem adequate to simply send them to you."

Sarge bowed the best he could with the boys' support. The king put into Sarge's hand an embroidered badge bearing a shield with the master sergeant's insignia based on Sarge's drawing.

"You may wear this on shirt, cloak, or tunic. These colours are given you and those who serve you to wear, and for your heirs in perpetuity."

"Pardon, your Majesty, but I'm long past producing heirs."

"There is more than one way to choose an heir. I wished to leave you the option to do with as you will." He handed a badge to Robin. "Should really be your master granting you his colours, but I wanted to thank you personally for your service." He bowed and kissed her hand, turning her face red.

"You, you are too kind." Robin stammered.

"Now to business." The king straightened. "Sir Garraik is sending the squires out to get experience with the Regulars. I heartily approve. In your case, I meddled somewhat. As far as the squad you will work with knows, you are a squire learning how they do things, but the commanding officer knows I will be very upset if anything untoward happens."

"I appreciate your concern." Robin had recovered her composure. "When do I leave?"

"The day after tomorrow. The Regulars will provide you with all the gear you need and a uniform. Take your mail and a small bag for personal items, but it was suggested to me that you not bring anything you aren't prepared to leave behind. Wear your badge if you wish."

Robin ran her finger across the badge in her hand, then handed it to Sarge.

"I have little I need, and while nothing would make me happier than wearing the master sergeant's colours, if I am to learn as much as I can from this, I need to be one of them."

***

"You boys be sure to take care of the master sergeant." Robin fought back tears. "I'm counting on you."

Lencely straightened and saluted her. "Of course, we will."

"Lass, be safe and come back to us." Sarge leaned on his cane and put his hand on her shoulder. "I had Edward put this together. Doesn't do any good to have knowledge if you don't have the equipment to use it. There are bandages, needle and thread, and whatever else I thought might be useful. Master Louis gave you some packets of herbs with instructions. Each of you has a kit. Use it as you need."

Robin slung the bag over her shoulder, saluted the master sergeant, and left while her feet would still carry her. The other squires waited for her outside and together they walked to the gate. A woman in the brown uniform of the regular sauntered over to Robin.

"Wasn't kidding when they said you was small. Hope you c'n keep up." The woman didn't introduce herself but spun and walked briskly out the gate as Robin jogged along beside her.

Part 2

CHAPTER 10

Sarge sat in his chair wondering if he'd made a mistake. The suite didn't feel right with Robin gone. Lencely, Gord and Rud had taken over Robin's corner.

"We've finished putting Squire Robin's stuff into her trunk," Lencely reported. "Gord sewed your badge on like you wanted. Three of your shirts have them now."

"Good work. Ask Danael to come here, then you can relax for a bit."

"Right away, Master Sergeant." Lencely jogged out to the door of the suite where Danael insisted on sitting, waiting to answer the door or run a message.

Gord and Rud sat on chairs and pulled out worn cards to continue some endless game they were playing.

"Master Sergeant?" Danael stood in front of him.

"Yes, Danael," Sarge straightened in his chair. *Focus, idiot.* "Please ask Sir Garraik when the next council meeting will be held. Wait for the reply."

Danael dashed away.

"Gord."

"Aye, Master Sergeant."

"Run to the kitchen, I would like to have suitable food and beverage for the knights for this evening. Let them use their judgement."

Gord raced away.

"Rud."

"Master Sergeant."

"Take the bell out into the hall and ring a few times. Wait for Edward. If he doesn't show, find a servant and ask them to pass a message to him."

Now alone in the room, Sarge scanned the place. I will do my part, Robin. You do yours and come home safe.

***

Robin followed the woman into a rough-looking inn. Four men sat at a table in the corner a plate of crumbs showing they'd eaten their breakfast.

"This is the one." The woman pushed one of the men along the bench. "Don't know whose idea it was, but we're stuck wit' her."

"What'cha waitin' for. Park yer butt." One of the men slid over and patted the seat beside him, leering at her.

"My name is Robin Fastheart." She scanned the unimpressed faces. "I would like you to forget that I am a squire. From this moment I am a new recruit in your squad. Please treat me as such, no special treatment."

"Ain't that nice." The woman didn't quite sneer. "Where's your kit?"

"I was ordered to bring my mail and this," she slapped the satchel at her side. "For the rest, I am to be equipped as any other Regular."

"Let's see t'mail." The man who patted the bench had moved back.

Robin pulled her tunic off.

The woman stood and walked around her, drew her knife and poked Robin with it a few times.

"Tis better than any we have."

"If it will fit any of you, you are welcome to it."

The men laughed and made space for her. She put her tunic on and sat down.

"Innkeep!" The woman called. "Another plate."

A girl brought over a plate of bread, cheese, and a bit of meat. Robin helped herself to the bread and cheese. The man beside her piled meat on top. "Don't skimp, you'll need the energy, and ye never know when yer next meal will be."

"Thank you." Robin tucked into the food. The woman ate twice as much in the same time.

A man in an apron came over.

"You off then?"

"Aye, was supposed to have two weeks furlough. Orders changed." The woman stood and stretched. "Here's your chit for our stay." She dropped a piece of wood on the table and a few coins with it. "Y'know we 'preciate you looking after us special like."

Robin jumped up along with the men.

"Since ye've got no kit, ye c'n carry the grub." The woman handed her a bag. Robin thought longingly of her pack in the equipment room, then used the draw string to fasten it to the strap of the field kit, as Sarge had called it.

They left in single file, Robin staying behind the woman. People had started to come out on the street. A few shops opened and she eyed the goods as they passed. It had been months since she'd last left the palace compound.

"Gris!" A man came out of an alley. "You owe me ten silvers."

"Not a chance." The woman crossed her arms. Robin stepped back out of the way.

"You scared of 'im?" one of the men behind her put a hand on her back.

"Don't want to get in her way." Robin didn't turn around.

"A big guy like that, you think she'll be able to deal wit' him?"

"Please, she could take him apart in her sleep," Robin snorted. "Sure, he's big, but he's standing flat footed."

"I will make a deal with ye," Gris said to the man, "just 'cause I like ye. You get to me through this new recruit, and I'll pay the ten silvers. You lose, ye never bother me again, or I'll put my knife between your ribs."

The man licked his lips and drew a large knife.

"Hold this, please." Robin handed the satchel and food sack to one of the men. Walking out in front of Gris, Robin breathed deeply. She remembered Hal saying that he could lose on any given day. Her stomach tensed, and she balanced on the balls of her feet.

"Kid, you want a knife?" Gris asked from behind her.

"Nah, don't want to kill him by mistake." Robin tried to match the woman's way of talking.

"Your funeral. What flowers do you want on your grave?"

"Always b'n partial to daisies." Robin didn't take her eyes off the man, who finally appeared to be getting ready to fight.

He leered at Robin and whipped his knife through complicated motions.

"C'mon, sweetie, come here and I'll give ye my blade." He waggled his hips at her.

Robin rolled her eyes and watched until the pattern became clear. She launched herself at him when the only cut he could try would hit her mail. As the blade scraped against the armour, Robin grabbed his ears and jumped as she pulled his head down. Her knee crunched into his nose, and she rode him down to the cobbles.

His head hit with a hollow thud and his eyes went blank. Robin rolled him on his side, then picked up the knife. She cut his belt and took the scabbard.

"Cheap steel, but it's better than what I have. And he did say he'd give it to me." She took the satchel from the man who stared at her open-mouthed and fastened the scabbard to the strap.

"Let's go." Gris walked forward. Robin fell in behind her.

Gris led them to a building with Regulars coming and going. She signalled something to the guard with one hand and walked inside.

"Get the standard kit for her, Amby." Gris pointed at one of the men. "No games, we're out two months, and I don't want ye whining when she beats the crap out of you for shorting 'er."

"Aye, Gris."

Gris stalked along the hall, knocked on a door and let herself in. "Robin, with me."

Inside a man sat behind a desk. He looked up. "Gris, I thought you would be gone already."

"Needed t' gear up the new one." Gris poked her thumb at Robin.

"Her?" The man's brows went up.

"If ye bother looking, halfway from t' Dryad and here, Jock boy'll be lying on the cobbles. He's alive, but he's lost 'is good looks."

"Thought I told you to stop fighting in the streets." The man frowned.

"Jock pulled a knife on 'er."

"She took down Jock?" He looked skeptical.

"Ayup." Gris grinned at him. "I'm thinking you assigned 'er to me somethin' like a punishment. I'm stopping by to thank ye."

"Right, you've wasted enough of my time." The man returned to the paperwork on his desk.

Back out in the hall, they picked up the men and returned to where Amby stood beside a pack.

Robin opened and went through the contents, familiarizing herself with them and how Amby had packed them.

"My thanks." She nodded at Amby .

"Now we have to find you a uniform and a sword to swing." Gris took off again. Robin hoisted the pack into place and followed.

The armoury didn't look much different than the equipment room, other than the scale.

"Who's the kid?" The speaker clunked over to them, his one wooden leg giving him an odd stride.

"New recruit," Gris said. "Needs weapons, helmet, the lot."

"Right, don't try to pull a fast one on me, Gris."

While they argued, Robin walked over and began going through the swords. Barrels held bent and chipped blades; sharpened swords hung on racks. All had been well used. One blade drew her eye, it looked to be the length of the hand-and-a-half she'd snapped on Sir Garraik's breast plate. She lifted it down. The balance was perfect. Robin worked through a set of figures, the air humming from the blade's passage.

"What do you think you're doing?"

"Figured to save time." Hoisted the blade, then took a closer look. It looked ancient. The leather wrap on the hilt black from time. "I like this one."

"You like that one, huh." The man thumped up to her. "Do you even know what you're holding?"

"Looks to be a hand-and-a-half. Style's a bit old, but the steel is solid. She sings nicely"

"Close your mouth, Ferd, ye'll choke on a fly." Gris came up and slapped him on the back. "That happens to be the sword Ferd here carried in the field."

"Twas my father's, a knight give it to 'im." Ferd stalked around Robin. "Least you know how to hold it."

"If you would prefer me to choose a different one..."

"Here's the scabbard."

Robin sheathed the blade and pulled it a few times.

"Nice."

"Of course, she is." Ferd leaned forward to whisper. "Her name is Kestrel."

"Thank you." Robin fastened the harness on and again drew the sword. Adjusted the harness and repeated the process until she was happy.

"I'll need a buckler, and if you have a bow, I'd appreciate it."

"Go git a helmet." He pointed to a corner.

Robin found a simple helmet with a nasal guard, and Ferd returned with a buckler and a trio of bows. She strung and unstrung each one before choosing one.

"Doesn't have as much power, but it'll be easy to carry." A quiver holding twenty arrows added to the pile.

Robin returned to her pack and rearranged it to fit the food bag in. She strapped the bow and quiver to the pack, making sure she could reach them easily. The best way to carry the helmet was on her head.

After finding a uniform that, miraculously, almost fit, she was ready to go.

"What's yer name, girl?"

"Robin Fastheart, new recruit."

"If yer a greenhorn, I'm a dancer."

"I'm sure your performances are breathtaking." Robin let her lips curl a little. Ferd roared with laughter.

"You bring 'er back in one piece, Gris."

"Our job's dangerous, more than most." Gris patted him on the shoulder. "But you know me."

"Yep, trouble follers ye like a dog after a bone."

***

Outside they walked through the city. The roads sloped down toward the river. Robin fought temptation and lost.

"Gris, is it all right if we take a small detour."

"Ye got to go kiss yer ma goodbye?"

"Yep." Robin gave up on the hope.

"Lead on, long as it don't take us too long. Missed the mornin' boat already."

The closer they got to her home, the more Robin felt like a snail under the pack and all the gear.

"Robin, that you under all that stuff?" Tom ran out of a shop.

"Aye, tis me for sure. Where's me ma?"

"At the studio. Wait, I'll get you some bread to go." Tom darted into the shop and returned with a long loaf.

"Eat while it's fresh," Robin said. "Tom's da makes the best bread in the city."

Gris tore up the loaf and divvied it up. They ate while they walked.

"Yer boyfriend?" Amby asked.

"Friend." Robin breathed in the taste of the bread.

They rounded a corner, and the studio beckoned her. Her mother ran out.

"Robin, is that really you?" She took off Robin's helmet. "You're getting stronger."

"No taller though." Robin grinned at her.

"What's this?" Her mother looked at Gris and the men.

"Next part of my training."

"Wasn't Sir Garraik training you?"

"Yup, fought him to a draw, so he decided I need some real-life experience. My commander, Gris, and the guys." Robin waved at them.

"I got a message saying you were made squire. Who's the knight?"

"The oldest, most cantankerous man I've ever met. I expect this was his idea. His name's Master Sergeant Christopher Severson."

"Not a knight?"

"Tis complicated, Ma, and I don't have time to explain proper. Go up to the palace and ask t'see the master sergeant."

"Perhaps I'll do that." Her ma hugged her tight, backpack and all. "Your dad will be proud; he's driving wagons all the way up to Vilscape.

"Give 'im a hug for me when he gets back."

"What happened to all that proper squire talk?"

"Can't be sticking out, ma."

"Well, fine, but don't be calling the king 'yer maj'sty' again."

"Can't make no promises." Robin laughed along with her mother.

"Did ye really call him 'yer maj'sty'?" Amby asked sounding equal part horrified and fascinated.

"Yup, twas the old king. Good thing he had a sense of humour."

"What's the new king like?" One of the other men asked.

"He'll be a strong king," Robin said.

***

The river stunk. Robin had forgotten about that. She always did.

They rode a riverboat west and gradually the smell retreated, or maybe her nose grew numb.

"Time you meet the rest of the crew." Gris leaned back on the bench. "Ye know Amby, then there's Pul and Norin. Them's all squad members; I'm squad leader."

"I'm honoured to join you." Robin nodded to each one of them.

"We'll see if ye still think so two months from now."

CHAPTER 11

The entire council was present. Edward and some others had rearranged the tables and chairs in the hall of Sarge's suite to accommodate everyone. Besides the king and Sir Garraik, the mage, the archbishop, the chancellor and a representative from the Masters' Council, at Sir Garraik's suggestion, they'd also invited the local commander of the Regulars.

"Welcome, Your Majesty, and thank you for putting up with an old man." Sarge sat at the foot of the table, Lencely at his side. The other boys hovered in corners waiting to be called upon.

"I hear you are walking daily, but three flights of stairs is asking too much." The king grinned. "Besides, I've always liked this part of the palace. I'm glad to see it in use again. Now to business."

He brought the council up to date on the response to the threat. "Lord Huddroc spent an evening picking Squire Robin's thoughts on the defence of Vilscape. I'd like Lencely to report on the conversation."

Lencely stood and stammered out something.

"Stop, take a breath. Talk to me and let the council listen in." Sarge put a hand on the boy's shoulder.

"It was like one of your bull sessions." Lencely kept his eyes fixed on Sarge as he recounted the discussion.

"Very good, lad." Sarge nodded at him, and the boy almost glowed with the praise.

"Would you add your opinion, Master Sergeant?" Sir Garraik leaned forward.

"If these are indeed conscripted peasants, then attacking their command structure will be devastating. If this Goat Club can guide archers to safe niches to shoot from, that should be their orders."

"Concur," the regular commander whom Sir Garraik had introduced as Marshal Potter spoke. "In the Regulars, we concentrate on a fluid command structure. While it does have some drawbacks, it means picking away at our leadership isn't as devastating."

"Lord Huddroc should also have a plan to deal with a mutiny in the enemy forces. They will be hungry, poorly equipped, and not happy about being there in the first place. They could get to a point where they turn on their own command structure. It might be tempting to jump in to support the mutiny, but it could be very dangerous. The enemy will still be your enemy."

"What if we put some of our own people on the inside?" The mage was a different one, a younger woman.

"Would be a death sentence if they were caught." Potter rubbed his jaw. "But if we can turn a few of the prisoners we send back, it could work."

"Lord Huddroc is starting the work with his garrison and the villagers. They will work on making the town into a trap and building a camp to look large enough for ten thousand soldiers." Sir Garraik looked over at Potter. "We should start talking about the logistics of moving the extra thousand soldiers to Vilscape over the next month."

"Why not call up the Regulars from the villages in the area? Sounds like most of the action will happen after planting. Can't say for certain, but that should give you between five and eight hundred. The northern group has been monitoring for banditry and raiding through the small passes. Mostly they have nothing to do."

"My father talked about putting a hundred men on patrol," Lencely spoke up, then turned red.

"Smart man, we can take a lot of that duty. I can send orders to Marshal Wentron."

"I thought the Regulars made up most of the garrison at Vilscape?" The king leaned back.

"They do, Your Majesty, but only a few are local. That's work for them that want to be Regulars regular like." Potter cracked the tiniest of smiles. "If you pardon me saying, Your Majesty, the real logistical nightmare will be moving soldiers west and meshing with Sir Kenly's command."

"I would like you to work with Sir Garraik on a plan." The king tapped the table. "We are playing with the enemy by having a larger camp than we need. Can we do a similar thing in the West?"

"That we could, Your Majesty." The guild representative, Master Fuvian, waved a hand. "Happens the West put in an order for updated equipment. Normally part of the Regular's pay is their gear and weapons, but we could buy back what we can to distribute to others. Could call them the Irregulars."

"The royal treasury is in good shape," the chancellor said as he folded his fingers in front of him. "We could spare enough to pay people on top of the Regulars for a month, maybe two."

"It would be a good investment. The Regulars spend their pay any place they go. That means work for the guilds and, of course, taxes for the treasury." Master Fuvian beamed at the table. "The Master's Council is willing to loan the crown a substantial amount of money. War is bad for business, at least for most of us."

"At what interest?" The Chancellor peered at Master Fuvian.

"We are more interested in gaining some concessions from the crown than in interest on the loan."

"Bring a list of those concessions to the chancellor as soon as possible." The king tapped his fingers on the table. "Marshal Potter, Sir Garraik, if you need to travel west to meet with Sir Kenly, perhaps going soon would be best."

"Your Majesty." Sarge leaned forward. "All the discussion has been about how to fight the empire, and we need to be prepared for that, but we also need to discuss how not to fight the war."

"Not fight?" Sir Garraik's wasn't the only brow furrowed around the table.

"The only way to win a war is to not fight it." Sarge leaned back and rubbed his temples. "In a war, there are only those who lose and those who lose more."

"We should plead for peace?" Marshal Potter made a face.

"Why are they invading in the first place?" Sarge scanned the table.

"They are the empire. Every new emperor has to try their luck with annexing the west." Sir Garraik shrugged. "Not quite a hundred years back, we sent aid to the West, which was an independent kingdom then. The war almost destroyed their country. Caldera put a lot of gold into helping them rebuild. The last heir to their throne married the eldest prince. Their oldest son became Duke of the West. Except under rare circumstances, such as war, they function as an independent region with their own laws."

"The west would have a member at this council, but Sire Ghemphi took ill and returned home just before you arrived. The duke has appointed a replacement who should arrive in the next few days."

"Thank you, that makes things clearer. Pardon me for asking, but could the west want to join the empire?" Sarge forced his hand not to clench.

"They have been invaded many times over the past hundred years and have always led the fight against the empire. The present duke was a young knight during the last major incursion. There is always a certain amount of raiding." Marshal Potter leaned forward to get better eye contact with Sarge. "I can understand you, as a stranger, needing to ask."

"Thank you for clarifying." Sarge relaxed a little. "A delegation to the empire would need to come from both provinces."

"What would we say to the emperor. 'Please don't invade us?'" The mage didn't quite roll her eyes.

"Let's go back to why the empire is invading. In a hundred years, they've thrown small forces at the west, but now they have thirty thousand just to make us send our forces north." Sarge frowned. "That suggests they want the war to cause as little destruction as possible. What do they get if they own the west?"

"As part of the reconstruction, Caldera gave them our farming practices." The chancellor stared up at the ceiling." As a result, the west grows enough surplus to sell to us and to the empire."

"Wars are fought over resources. The excuse may be imperial pride, but resources lie at the bottom, if you dig hard enough. How much do you know about the present situation in the empire?"

"Not much. The plague went through there before it hit us." The king rubbed his eyes. "The envoy to the empire died, we have been too busy rebuilding to send a new one."

"Something to consider, then, is that the empire needs the growing capacity of the west badly enough to try to invade and take it over. What can you bring to the table that would be more valuable than control of the west?"

***

For a few seconds, Robin watched the boat move away from them, then turned and followed the others along the trail up the bank.

"There are roads along both sides of the river, but why walk when we c'n ride?" Amby hiked along beside her, pulling at the straps of his pack. "It always takes a while to settle into carrying the load again."

"Slow down, Gris, you're killing us," Norin whined.

"Fine then, I'll let the new kid set the pace." Gris waved Robin forward. "You've got point, kid. Just walk forward until I tell you otherwise."

Robin nodded then let herself fall into a rhythm. Keeping up with the long legs of the rest of the world, she'd learned a stride that wasn't quite a jog. She could keep it up all day.

"There'll be a side trail on your right. Take it," Gris ordered her. Robin couldn't have said how long they'd been walking. She'd spent the time reviewing her most recent matches and imagining alternatives.

The split came up and she turned. This trail was rougher with roots running across it. She concentrated on her footing until they reached a clearing with a creek burbling past one edge.

"This'll do," Gris said, so Robin stopped and looked around. "We camp here t' first night back. Though it's light enough we c'd make another league or two."

"Please, please no." Norin dropped his pack and lay flat on the ground. "Tomorrow, you set the pace, Gris."

The others entered the clearing and copied Norin.

"Expected the pack to throw ye off more." Gris lowered hers and stretched.

"I've been working with a pack since I became a trainee." Robin bounced on her toes. "This is only double, maybe not quite triple, the weight."

"You trained with a pack?" Amby pushed himself up on one elbow.

"Since I was twelve winters." Robin put her pack down. "Running, warmups, even sparring sometimes."

"You ran in a pack?" Pul put his arm over his eyes. "I never thought knights were quite human."

"The others didn't; just me. I wanted to be stronger."

"How could you survive running?"

"Don't think I could run in this." Robin nudged it with a toe. "Isn't balanced right and it's too loose. My one at home has a waist strap so it doesn't bounce. I could probably rig something up to show you later."

"Later." Gris sat and reclined against her pack. "Pul, the pots, get them out for Robin. Water first, then get firewood, enough to last the night if need be."

"Sure thing, Gris." Robin took the largest pot from Pul and filled it with water. She tasted it, much better than the water from the barrel in the training yard. After that, she dug out the rope from her pack and headed off into the woods.

"Robin, if you get turned around, whistle and we'll whistle back. The forest is easy to get turned around in."

There wasn't much wood to be found close to the clearing, so she kept meandering along, picking up what she found and made a bundle. When the bundle was large enough for her to think about returning to the clearing, she heard voices.

Robin crept toward the sound. When she could hear well enough to realize she didn't understand them, she lay the bundle down and walked as quietly as she could toward them. Three men sat around a fire, one reached over to stir something in the pot. She couldn't see any weapons but wasn't going to take any chances and backed away until she could pick up her bundle.

In the city, she'd be able to find her way easily, but the forest looked nothing like that. She'd start by getting more distance between her and the men.

"Hey, kid, you get lost?" Gris stepped out from behind a tree making Robin squeak.

"I'll need to learn my way about the forest."

"Time enough for that." Gris jerked her head behind her. "Let's get back 'fore they fall asleep."

"Gris, there are three men, not far from here, that direction. I didn't see any weapons, but I didn't understand them."

"Stay here, I'll take a look." Gris vanished into the trees. She reappeared a few minutes later with a bag in her hand and a wide grin. "Foresters. Speak the old language of the west. Most people do 'round here."

Gris led the way back to camp, pointing out landmarks and getting Robin to look back frequently to see what the back trail looked like.

The men had cleared out a circle of blackened rocks, and Gris told Robin to drop her bundle there.

"Score, gents. Robin spotted some foresters. They said she was respectfully quiet for a new recruit, sent some mushrooms for us to enjoy."

***

They travelled mostly north along tiny tracks. Robin used rope to make a waist strap for her pack. It wasn't perfect, but it steadied the load. She grew used to sleeping under the stars when the weather was dry and found she loved the sound of rain on the tiny tent when it wasn't.

To pass the time, Gris and the men taught Robin bits of Westron or, as they called it, Fhayd. She fetched water and wood, using the opportunities to practice her woodcraft. She patched up small cuts with the kit Sarge sent with her. Occasionally, they'd stop at a tiny village. At one, Robin splinted a young boy's arm and made him a sling. At another, Gris bought a dress for Robin and had her put it in her pack.

"Never know when it will come in handy."

Gris had Robin hunt with her bow.

"Don't carry them myself; not much use in the forest."

Robin struggled to get close enough to deer for a shot. They ate a lot of squirrels and birds Gris called grouse. She wouldn't shoot unless she was certain of a kill.

"We're hunting bandits," Gris said in a rare moment of openness. "A big guy named Andre in particular. He raids both sides of the border and leaves a trail of bodies. You see him, you make like a mouse, hear?"

"Yes." Robin stirred the rabbit stew in the pot.

One day, Robin spotted a deer alone in a clearing. She held her hand up for silence and strung her bow. Leaving her pack and sword harness on the ground, she made her way around the clearing so the breeze would be in her face. The deer munched on the tall flowers in the sun. Its head went up, but it stared at the opposite side of the opening. It wandered closer to Robin. She had an arrow on the string and another stuck in the ground beside her

When she pulled the bow, the slight creak made the animal pause and stare at her. Facing her straight on, it froze. She didn't have a shot, but Robin refused to give up. Gritting her teeth, she pulled the bow to a full draw, using her back muscles. *The push-ups must be helping.* She huffed at the deer, and it spun to flee. Her arrow struck and vanished into the animal. It made two bounds then collapsed.

Robin left her bow with the quiver and walked slowly toward the unmoving deer. Her da had talked about hunting on the road. She drew her knife but froze as the deer coughed. She couldn't see any blood. *Did I miss? But it fell.*

"Not bad shooting, boy." A big man stepped out of the forest flanked by two men on each side. They had swords drawn. "If ye weren't wearing that brown, I might have let you join me."

"You'd be Andre then." Robin held the knife in front of her, wishing she'd brought the bow. None of the men carried one. If they'd been hunting the deer… *One more in the forest, probably with an arrow nocked and ready.*

The man licked his lips. *He's enjoying this.* The deer coughed again. Robin kicked it and it jumped up and bounded toward Andre. Robin ducked behind the deer as an arrow scratched its back. Now she knew where the archer was. While the archer was nocking another arrow, she moved to put Andre between her and the danger in the forest. The deer staggered and fell in front of one of the men. He jumped on it with his knife.

"Leave it." Andre bellowed. In the second he was distracted, Robin leapt to the attack.

Andre swung his sword. The cut was slower than she expected. She ducked inside his reach. His left hand moved at lightning speed and caught her around the neck. He squeezed her air off and sneered. "I b'n killing before y'r pappy was born. Do y'wan' it with the sword or the fist?" He laughed and the others cheered. His mail only came halfway down his forearm.

I'm not dead yet. Robin flipped the knife in her hand and then slashed up, cutting into his left wrist. Blood spurted in her face as he roared and dropped her. She hit and rolled, snatching the buckler from her waist. His sword thudded into her shoulder and something crunched inside. She spun away, her left arm screaming in pain.

Sir Garraik would have called the match, and they'd send for Master Louis. This was no match. Robin charged under his sword arm. *If his mail is too short.* She ran her knife along the inside of his thigh. The blade ground on mail. She ran behind him as he swung the sword backhand. With her left side hurting, she couldn't climb him or defend with the buckler.

She tried his leg again, stabbing into his knee. It jammed into flesh and he fell backward almost landing on her. Robin jumped toward him, knife aimed at his neck. He blocked unbelievably fast, putting his blade between them. Though it made her shriek in agony, she made her left hand pin his sword with her buckler. With her right she slashed his other wrist.

As she rolled into the flowers, an arrow skittered across her back.

"Boss," a man in rough leather ran up to Andre, swinging back and forth as he searched for Robin. A shout came from behind him, and the man spun to look toward the archer.

Robin jumped on his back, stabbing his throat, then jumping off. From the corner of her eye, she saw the archer, arrow on his string charging toward her. Desperately, she dove into the flowers again, blessing her small size.

"Gotcha!" the archer shouted, and Robin dove to the side. He laughed and aimed at her, then an arrow bounced off his armour. He lifted his bow and loosened his draw to look around for the other archer. She ran at him, as he brought his bow back to aim at her and grinned evilly. Her buckler in her right hand smashed into the bow, knocking the arrow askew. The momentum of her charge carried her into him, and he staggered back. She kicked his knee, then landed on him, her dagger at his throat.

"Ye should leave some fun for us." Gris waded through the flowers to stand over Robin. The archer had his hands open and flung to each side. "What part of being a mouse did ye forget?"

Robin stood, backing away from the archer. None of the other bandits were left standing.

"Thanks," she said. "I knew I had to buy time for you to get into position."

"Buy time? I thought ye were going to take 'em all down yerself. We saw yer nail the buck, then Andre swaggers out and I'm swearing, 'cause I let you go wit'out help." Gris shuddered "Could have died when the deer jumped up."

"Then ye' were like a fae." Norin came over and pointed his sword at the archer. "Never seen anyone move like that."

"It's amazing how being about to die will do that." Robin swayed, then sat on the ground abruptly.

"Tis normal after battle." Gris patted her on the head. "Breathe it out. Now, what are we going to do with this'n?"

"Don't kill me, I c'n help you. Take ye t'the gold."

"Gold?" Gris didn't sound like she believed him.

"Empire people hired Andre to move back and do 'is raiding on this side."

"Which one of ye is the empire's spy?" Gris leaned over the trembling man. "T'wouldn't be you now?"

"Dubson we called 'im. The fae cut 'is throat."

"Amby, Pul, check 'im out, right to the skin; may as well t'others too."

"Norin, tie this scum up. Tries anything, skewer 'im."

Robin watched them work, holding her left arm; it didn't hang right.

They buried the bandits, then Amby cleaned the deer. He slung it over one shoulder and carried it to where the packs were sitting.

"What's up with ye' arm?" Gris peered at Robin.

"Andre's sword caught m'shoulder, did somthin' to it."

"Village not far from 'ere. Has a sawbones. We'll git to it tonight."'

***

They made it into the village just as the sun set. Gris led the way to a house and banged on the door.

An older man answered, saw Gris, and stepped back. They followed him into the house. Gris had the bow and Robin's satchel. Their prisoner carrying Robin's pack. Norin sat him in the corner, then sat facing him, and took out a stone to run along his blade.

"Who's injured?" Their host paid no attention to Norin or the prisoner. "You never come by unless someone's hurt."

"Ye know why." Gris frowned at him but pointed at Robin. "She's got somethin' wrong with 'er shoulder."

"Let me see, child." The man moved the arm and Robin hissed. "You will have to take the mail off."

Getting the armour over her head had Robin almost weeping from pain.

"Tch, you should have better padding." He poked at where blood stained her shirt. "Rings cut into the skin. You mind taking the shirt off?"

Robin pulled her knife and cut her shirt from the neck to her elbow.

"That will work too." He inspected the purple and black bruise on her shoulder, then gripped her arm and twisted. Robin screamed. The pain receded, but unconsciousness was already claiming her.

CHAPTER 12

Sarge sighed; they'd been arguing in circles for days.

"I still think we need to stop them before the empire will even consider negotiating." Sir Garraik picked up his cup but played with it instead of drinking.

"The question is whether we can." Marshal Potter looked over the papers in his hands again. "Say the majority of the army coming at Vilscape is conscripts, they'd still need a core of people who knew what they were doing and were loyal. Without some other hold on the soldiers, I wouldn't want to have less than one in twenty experienced, trustworthy people."

"So fifteen hundred?" The Chancellor stared up at the ceiling. "That's near the same as we are sending to Vilscape. How many can we expect in the west?"

"Pardon, sirs." Wilson stepped into the room and bowed. "The Duke of Fhayden is here to join you."

A man in travel clothes stepped around Wilson. Though older than Lord Huddroc, he still moved easily.

"Your Majesty, I apologize for showing up on such short notice, but given the content of your last communication, I thought it prudent to come in person."

"You are more than welcome, brother." The king jumped up and went to clasp hands with the duke. "Come join us."

Gord pulled a chair over to the table for the duke, and Rud brought him a cup of water. They bowed and returned to their corners.

The duke sat and nodded to the boys.

"I prefer to be addressed as Lord Allin; I'm not big on ceremony." He winked at the king, then turned to Sarge. "You must be the master sergeant. We will get to know each other more later, but let me express my gratitude that you are here."

"The longer I am here, the more thankful I am to be among you."

"I heard some of your discussion as I came in." Lord Allin leaned forward. "Part of the reason for my tardiness was that I waited for reports from my agents in the empire. As dire as things may feel, I wasn't ready to risk my people by not following the schedule."

"I gather you have something akin to answers to some of our questions." Sir Garraik drank his water, and Rud came to refill it.

"Not hard answers, but perhaps better than guesses." Lord Allin nodded to him. "The truth is the empire is in deep trouble. They've had crop failures the last two years and have eaten through much of their reserves. The emperor has legions stationed in the northern provinces to quell unrest. My people estimate they could put fifteen or twenty thousand in the field."

"Is there a way to increase their internal troubles?" Marshal Potter rubbed his chin thoughtfully.

"It is something that I have considered but hesitated to take such action without conferring with His Majesty."

"Civil wars make bad neighbours," Sarge said. "Either you'll get pulled into the conflict, or it will spill over into your country."

"That, indeed, is part of our thinking." Lord Allin smiled grimly. "It is difficult enough now not to get sucked into empire politics."

"We're back to stopping them at the border." Sir Garraik leaned back in his chair. "And that with less than ten thousand soldiers."

"We have made a step forward." The king stood and leaned on the table. "We know why they are taking this desperate gamble. This war is life and death for them as much as it is for us."

"Well stated." The mage tapped her lip. "Lord Allin, do you have any knowledge of why the crops have failed?"

"Not in detail, no. Their farming is very different from ours. Nobles own large tracts of land which are worked by peasants. The peasants are allowed to live on the land and eat from the excess of the harvest."

"If we ignore their plight and defeat them, the empire will only get more desperate. It doesn't sit right with me." The king sat down slowly. "But is there anything else we can do?"

"Sire." Sarge rapped his cane on the table. "The good duke has brought us the information we need to move forward. In my world, we talk about using the carrot and the stick."

"We have a similar saying here." Marshal Potter smiled.

"My suggestion is we plan to defeat the empire in the field." Lord Allin leaned forward and slowly scanned the table. "The knights and the marshals are the people to plan the strategy and make it work. We also must plan a delegation to the empire to offer an alternative to war. An offer of peace won't work if we don't have the strength to back it up, but we cannot end the conflict with military strength alone. I will, with the king's permission, undertake the delegation to the empire. I have a very competent heir, which makes me the logical person of rank to go."

"Let us adjourn and return tomorrow with the beginning of plans for both the carrot and the stick." The king stood and nodded to the gathered council. The rest stood and made their exit.

“Rud, ask Danael to run and find Edward, ask for refreshments. I’m sure Lord Allin is hungry after his trip.” Sarge pushed himself to his feet. “Lord Allin, if you would join me in my chamber, there are more comfortable seats for my old bones.”

“It would be my pleasure.” Lord Allin bowed to me. “I must admit to a great deal of curiosity since I heard of your arrival.”

Once Sarge was installed in his favourite chair and Lord Allin was comfortable in a chair across from him, Lencely retreated to the corner.

“Lencely, sit down and join us, Gord and Rud as well.” Sarge raised a brow at Lord Allin. “These are my pages; I would be in great trouble without their help.”

“You have them very well trained.”

Sarge laughed. “I know nothing about training pages. They have worked together to become invaluable supports. Lencely is their leader and my teacher.”

Lencely turned beet red and stared at his shoes, but Sarge caught a wide grin on his face.

“I had hoped to meet your squire as well, but I’m told the squires are with Regular units. I plan on sending the suggestion back to Sir Kenly.”

“I’ve long thought it impossible to effectively command an army if you are unaware of how the people on the front think and what their capacity is.”

“I like to think I know my people but have to admit I’ve never considered going on a sweep with them.”

“What I would like to talk to you about, Lord Allin, is how battles are fought. Coming from another world, I am not familiar with this world’s tactics.”

"We don't have a standing army, but the empire does. Their equivalent to our knights fight from horseback in full armour. We have been fortunate not to see them in the last twenty years. They are, by all accounts, immensely proud and unwilling to take part in what they see as common raiding. We will not be so fortunate this time as the intent is to take over our country. There is honour and land to be gained."

"Heavy cavalry, do we have any forces on horseback?"

"A few units do, but truthfully horses are expensive, and without a paid force to do the training, they are the exception. Since our knights are moving from being a privileged class to trained commanders of the army, they don't fight as a unit, though all of them can ride and use a lance, at least in tournaments."

"How many knights?"

"The noble sons all become knights but are not expected to serve in the same way as the others. There are ten noble families, so they would be able to field maybe fifty. There are another fifty to eighty active knights from Sir Garraik and Sir Kenly who command a legion each, to those who command smaller units. The marshals are what hold our army together. There is one marshal for each Thousand, and each has a knight. The knights come up with strategy, and the marshals work on making the strategy work. We have tournaments every year with two Thousands facing off against each other. So one year in five, we test the practicality of the system."

Edward arrived with the food and the discussion ranged far and wide, with the pages forgetting their nerves and jumping in.

"This has been most stimulating." Lord Allin stood and bowed to Sarge. "With your permission, I will bring my squires and pages next time."

"You are certainly welcome to do that, but we have regular informal sessions. There is ale for the knights and water for the trainees and pages. Lencely will explain the system if you will allow him to walk you to your rooms."

Sarge relaxed in his chair when the duke had left with Lencely escorting him.

"Gord, have you ever heard of people fighting with pikes?"

"Master Sergeant?"

"Long sticks with blades on the end."

"You mean spears?" Rud glanced at Gord.

"No, longer, much longer." Sarge closed his eyes. "Numbers, training, technology. Can't do much about the first two in the time we have, but maybe the third."

***

Robin lifted her buckler and winced. Harald had told her to exercise the shoulder gently, and it didn't hurt so much as complain.

"Quit yer wool-gathering." Gris smacked Robin's helmet.

"Sorry, working my shoulder."

"Work your shoulder while you stay sharp."

"Aye."

Robin hung her buckler on her hip and paid more attention to her surroundings. Norin walked behind Oscor. The bandit had been warned if he ran away, he would be left dead for the scavengers. The Regulars made him nervous. Robin terrified him. She didn't like being the stuff of someone's nightmares.

The forest had been thinning out in the week since they'd left the village doctor. Robin wished she could pull her bow but wasn't up to it.

"We oughta camp fer t'night." Oscor apparently couldn't talk without whining. Or maybe that was the result of almost dying at the hand of a fae. He wouldn't be convinced she was as human as him. "Don't wanna arrive at night."

"Yeah, night's a good time for an ambush," Pul said.

"Not that; tis haunted." Oscor turned to glare at Pul, then paled when Robin caught his eye.

"Movement ahead to the right," Robin spoke quietly without pointing.

"Fine, we'll camp. I know a spot near." Gris didn't speak any louder than before as she turned into the thicker brush. Soon they arrived at a beautiful spot by a waterfall. A shadow hinted at a cave in the sheltering cliff.

"Looks like a good spot for a trap," Pul muttered.

Gris led them down to the side of the pool.

"Put your packs against the cliff for now." Gris waved a hand. "Robin, you're in charge. We're going to catch a few winks." She ducked behind the waterfall and disappeared, followed by Pul, Amby, and Norin.

Robin dug the pot out of Pul's pack and filled it at the pool.

"Never drank waterfall before." Robin put the lid on the pot and set it by the rock. Splashed water on her head and put her helmet on her pack, then took a stone from her pack and drew her sword, inspected the edge and set to work on it.

"Sit," Robin ordered Oscor when he shuffled toward the cave behind the waterfall. "Move again and I'll cut your feet off." She didn't look up from her work.

Oscor fidgeted and moved his hand toward a rock.

"Want your hands cut off too?"

He froze in place, then shook violently.

"Don't wanna die; don't wanna go to hell." He murmured the words as if he feared her cutting his tongue out.

Robin ignored him.

A stick cracked at the top of the path down to the pool. Oscor screamed and bolted. Robin slashed the first arrow from the air and grabbed her buckler. The bandit got between the archer and Robin in his panic. The second shot pierced his neck and he fell back onto the path. She backed behind a bulge in the cliff and continued using her sword's reflection to watch for movement above.

An archer stepped out on the cliff over the opposite shore, but before he could aim, an arrow bounced off his helmet. The man swore as he jumped, landing too close to the edge. The ground under him gave way, and he fell to the rocks below. The other archer ducked back into the trees.

Someone shouted orders above; it didn't sound like Fhayd.

Two men with blackened armour sidled down the slope, swords and bucklers at the ready. They didn't look nervous. The way they moved warned her they were used to working together. Robin stretched back, lifted her helmet to her with her sword and planted it on her head.

They were almost to the narrowest part of the path. If they pinned her against the cliff, she'd be dead. Fighting two experienced soldiers, she was probably dead anyway, but she wasn't going to go cowering in fear.

When Robin ran out to face them just below the narrow part of the descent, the men laughed and said something to each other which only made them laugh louder. She lifted her sword and buckler and grinned in return. One of them moved ahead and walked toward her.

At the point when she expected him to lunge and use his body to push her over, Robin stepped forward and slashed a cut at his neck, at the same time she scattered a handful of stones on the path under his feet.

The soldier moved his buckler to bat her cut aside, stepping forward to attack. His lead foot landed on the stones and slipped. Robin reversed her cut and thrust at his neck hoping to put him more off balance. He'd waved his hands in a reflex action to regain his balance. Her sword slipped past to catch his open mouth. The man grabbed her sword as he fell off the path. Robin let it go rather than be pulled off balance. The other soldier charged, but instead of running across the narrow bit, he jumped with his sword held in front of him, buckler hand reaching for her.

She could try to scuttle back, but Oscor's body was there to trip her. The man's bulk would push past any block she tried. Instead, she dodged toward the edge of the drop. His sword tore her shirt and scraped on her mail. As he landed, the soldier swept his sword to push her off the path. Instead of trying to avoid it, Robin grabbed his arm and leaned back, pulling him with her. The soldier's momentum carried him past her. Dropping the sword, he tried to grip her arm, but she yanked herself toward him, striking his chest with both feet. As he plummeted to the pool, Robin caught the edge of the rock and drew herself back onto the path. Picking up the soldier's sword, she saluted whoever was at the top of the path and waited for the next attack.

"Good grief, girl. Don't you have any sense at all?" Gris sheathed her sword and walked toward Robin. "You should have retreated into the cave when it started."

"Careful, there's loose stone on the path." Robin held up a hand while she swept the path clear with her foot.

"There were six of them. Got two with your bow, must be blessed or something, I was never more than a mediocre archer. Amby ambushed them from behind, then Norin and Pul hit them when they turned to attack Amby…" Gris stopped and pointed. "Are those bodies in the water?"

"Two." Robin leaned against the cliff face. "That's why the loose stones."

"Right."

"And why I didn't retreat. They'd have pinned me down."

"So you took on two empire soldiers on your own." Gris shook her head. "You're good, but not that good. You have the fae's own luck."

"Every fight could be the one where I die." Robin led the way down to the camp. "So there is no reason to hold anything back."

"Pul's right; knights aren't quite human. Weren't you afraid?"

"Of course I'm afraid, how could I fight properly if I wasn't?" Robin dropped her helmet on her pack, then sat and leaned against it. "Half the reason those two died was they knew they'd won the fight."

"I think I get it. You always know you can die, so you never underestimate your enemy." Gris sat beside her. "It makes sense in a twisted way."

"Thanks, I think."

"I'm going to ask you to do something. You can refuse, it isn't an order." Gris sighed. "We have two prisoners. They are empire people probably scouting us out and creating problems like Andre. I need to get information from them. We play them. You make a fuss about torturing them; I forbid it. While we're arguing how to question them, they won't be thinking we can understand what they say to each other."

"Even to argue for torture…" Robin hung her head. "If anyone hears of it, I will never make knight."

"I will get one of the others." Gris levered herself up.

"No, I will do it, but I'll do it my way." Robin sighed then stood up beside Gris. "From here on, call me Fay. Let the others know."

"Fair enough." Gris headed up the path. "We'll be bringing the prisoners down in half a candle."

Robin stripped off her uniform, mail, and gambeson, then waded along the shore of the pool until she had to swim. It took several dives to find her sword. The others would have to retrieve the bodies or not. Back on shore, she put her mail back on over the dress, then her sword harness. Lastly, she used some of Oscor's blood to draw patterns on her face and arms. When the others marched the prisoners down to the camp, Robin was sitting on a rock working on the soldier's sword.

As they passed her, she jumped up and slashed at the prisoners.

"Fay, hold!" Gris shouted.

Robin's sword stopped just touching the neck of the older of the pair. She stared into the man's eyes for ten beats of her heart, then turned and went back to her sharpening.

"Sorry, Fay's parents were killed by bandits. We found her after she hunted them down and killed the lot. One hid from her so we were bringing him to our commander for questioning. Looks like he didn't make it. Good thing we have you." Gris sat them against the cliff. "Amby, keep Fay from killing them. Pul, Norin, you collect what you can from the bodies in the pool. I'll deal with the one over there."

Amby sat between Robin and the prisoners. She growled at him but ignored them after that. When she'd finished the sword, she started on the knife, then inspected her sword before oiling each of them and returning the knife and sword to their scabbards.

Hope I'm not making a mistake. Too late now. It's just one more fight.

CHAPTER 13

Sarge drew formations with chalk on the tables. The knights looked doubtful, but Marshal Potter studied them carefully, making copies and sketches of what Sarge described.

"It will be Regulars at the front; we can do this. Making the pikes is not a problem." He looked around the table. "The most important thing here is that you show the Regulars you believe they can make this work."

"No knight will express the slightest concern about the Regulars' ability with the new weapons." Sir Garraik's voice made it clear he was issuing an order to the others present.

"Since it isn't feasible to bring pikes to Fhayden and train our people, I will leave it in your hands and work on recruiting archers. You've given me some interesting ideas on how to use them. Once my son is up to date, I will continue to the empire and try to open negotiations." Lord Allin sat back. "As much as I have enjoyed my visit, the days are passing. Fighting might start in as little as a month."

"Once this is done, I will do my best to return the visit." The king leaned on his elbows and massaged his neck.

"King Federick, I believe your father would be very proud of how you are managing this crisis."

"I thank you." The king sat straighter. "One last string for your bow. Some of my agents have been discussing possible marriage, mostly with the independent cities to the south. But nothing is decided yet."

***

The squires and trainees poured over the diagrams and asked endless questions. Sarge let the discussion rove where it would. Rud dug out maps of the border between Fhayden and the empire, and they argued about what would be the best ground to fight on.

"The forest isn't good ground for a set battle." Tad, one of lord's squires, tapped the map. "There is too much opportunity to split them up, and they lose their advantage."

"They'd be foolish to try to march down the centre." Hal peered at the map. "There are several fallback positions."

"That is why we are trying to convince them all our forces are at Vilscape. Let them take the easiest path, then ambush them." Lencely leaned over the map.

"Why not just form up and block them?" Tad looked over at the much younger boy.

"Morale." Lencely grinned. "They will be thinking they have an easy march to Fhayden, then they'll all be back for supper. When we come out of nowhere it will be a knock to their confidence."

"This will be the empire's best. They won't be pushovers." Tad bent back to the map. "But then we've beat them every other time they've tried. We could hold the river fort. It isn't much more than a garrison, but it's close to impenetrable."

"If they're smart, they'd just bottle us up in the fort, then keep going." Another squire put a biscuit on the map. "Say this is their main force. Each time they come on a fortified position, they need to either reduce it or leave people to hold the position to protect their supply line. By the time they get to Fhayden, their army will be a lot smaller, even without battle, but not small enough."

Sarge let them ramble. Gord, Rud and another group were talking about the best way to use the pikes. Another bunch talked about getting ahead of the invasion and setting up, using tricks to make it look like they had an overwhelming number advantage.

Though the ideas were wilder, the discussion matched what the knights talked about.

None of them knew the war had already started. Before he left, Lord Allin, Sir Garraik, Marshal Potter, and Sarge had met with the king through the night. There would be spies in Fhayden. It was essential they report back what the empire wanted to hear. Control the information and control where and when the battle happened. The western legion was being called up and ordered to muster at Fhayden.

Forests weren't good for battle, not the way this war would go, but they were great for hiding troop movements.

Robin would be back in a few weeks. Sarge looked forward to hearing all that she'd been up to.

***

"Order me to heal the prisoner," Robin asked Gris when they were out foraging to feed the extra people.

"Can you?" Gris picked mushrooms and dropped them in her bag.

"Don't know, but he'll die for sure if I don't try." Robin dug up a tuber. "Hard to get information from a dead man."

"All right then, but how are you going to that without revealing the act?"

"Very reluctantly." Robin grinned.

Back at camp, Gris called her over.

"Fay, get yer butt over here." Gris pointed at the younger prisoner; his arm was discoloured around a cut on his forearm. "Heal him."

"No, enemy." Robin shook her head violently.

Gris pointed to herself. "Who am I?"

"Commander." Robin bared her teeth at Gris.

"Heal 'im, or ye're on yer own again." Gris put her hand on her sword. Robin spun and ran into the woods.

"She run wild for who knows how long. Times I think she's more animal than human." Gris's voice followed Robin.

She found the satchel where Gris said she'd leave it. The bandages looked too civilized. She filled a cup with water from her skin, then added the herb Master Louis had labelled to stop wounds from going bad. He had moss which was supposed to help stop bleeding. Once the water had turned an ugly green-brown, Robin pushed the bandages in to soak up the colour. Her mother had once taken her to a mender who'd used moss on a scrape on Robin's arm. She gathered some and wrapped it in the discoloured bandage. Slowly, Robin picked up the curved needle and thread. The man's wound gaped open. If she closed it, would it heal better?

A finger dipped in the sludge at the bottom of the cup painted green patterns over the remnants of the red.

Better get it done before I lose my nerve. Robin packed up the satchel and left it for Gris to retrieve. With the cup of sludge, bandages and moss, she returned to camp.

The prisoners were tied to separate trees. Close enough to talk, too far to touch. The sick one had his good arm tied. Robin dragged him so he couldn't move his good arm, then sat on his shoulder and gripped the wounded forearm to inspect it. Since she was more animal than human, she sniffed at the arm and almost gagged at the reek of rotten meat.

Closing the wound wouldn't do any good. The man was as good as dead. *Robin refuses to accept defeat. Sir Garraik said that.* She slashed away the remains of the sleeve and before she could second-guess herself sliced at the wound.

With the first cut, the man screamed; with the second he went limp. The older prisoner screamed curses at her.

Gris stalked over and Robin growled at her, blinking tears from her eyes. Gris put her hands up and backed away.

Somehow the blood was harder to deal with when it wasn't a fight. Robin swallowed and prodded at the arm, sniffed again, then cut more. She repeated that until no odour of rot hit her nose. The herbs were supposed to be taken as tea, but the man wouldn't be drinking anything. She smeared it in the wound, then pulled out the needle and thread to sew up the arm. His arm looked horrible when she'd finished. If he lived, he'd never wield a sword again. She packed moss along the still-bleeding cut, then wrapped it with the bandage. Sarge had warned about making a bandage too tight. She bound it tight enough to hold everything in place and watched for the fingers to discolour. When they stayed pink, she drew a sign on his forehead with the mix of blood and sludge on her fingers.

The older prisoner had stopped his noise, and the others were talking, but they sounded far away. Robin wanted to get up, run away, but her body refused. The ground hit her hard, then hands lifted her and carried her away.

***

When she woke up, Robin was certain she'd blown her wild-girl act, but if anything, the prisoners were even more scared of her.

Two days later, the prisoner could sit up, eating and drinking. Gris forced him to drink the herbal tea Robin made for him. His colour had returned to normal.

I sat on him and cut his flesh. Is that any different than torture? Robin watched him from the corner of her eyes.

"Let's walk." Gris strolled past her. Robin followed her into the forest.

"I don't think I'd have the guts to do what you did." Gris picked a leaf and played with it. "You saved his life, but from their conversation, they think you are fae, not a wild child. That's shaken them badly. The older one is a century leader. There are always empire soldiers causing trouble of some kind, but usually young bucks out to make a name for themselves. He keeps talking about escaping to report. This is more than just a nuisance raid."

"I'm going to tell you something, but you have to keep it absolutely secret." Robin took a long breath. "The empire is planning an invasion of Fhayden. They've assembled a huge force to attack Vilscape. The master sergeant thinks it's a feint, meant to make us move most of our troops north."

Gris shook her head and crumpled the leaf in her hand. "Please tell me someone has a plan."

"We do, but it involves letting the empire think we've taken the bait. Master sergeant, the king, and the council are working on it."

"The master sergeant and the king?" Gris glared at Robin. "You're no ordinary squire. Aside from the way you fight, no squire I've met knows national secrets, even if their master does. You said 'we' like you're part of the council. Just who are you?"

"To be honest, I hardly know." Robin leaned against a tree. "The king asked me to be part of a summoning. That's how the master sergeant got here."

"Got here from where?"

"Some other world. He's seen a hundred winters, and most of that either fighting battles or teaching people about them. He has a way of making me see the world differently."

"Summoning is high-powered magic; are you a mage?"

"No, we needed a knight, a mage, a priest, a peasant, and a shield maiden."

"A shield maiden." Gris put her hand over her eyes. "Ye know anything about shield maidens?"

"Only that they can't have, you know."

"That's the least of it." Gris paced in the tiny clearing. "They were fearsome warriors, even knights didn't want to face 'em. Some had magic, different from the mages. The king of Fhayden a long time back didn't like 'em and started knighting women. The shield maidens died off without the support of the crown."

"But I'm not a shield maiden. I just stood on the point of the star because the king asked me."

"The king asked you to act the part of a shield maiden, but the magic wouldn't have worked if ye'd been playin' at it. Or possibly the magic made ye one because ye were nearly there anyway since the king appointed you." Gris pointed at Robin. "Ye notice any change after?"

"I won seventeen straight matches in one day." Robin slid to the ground. "I fought Sir Garraik to a tie."

"Ye defeated Andre, as close to a monster as a man can get, then two more men while I gave orders to my squad. Then ye killed two elite empire soldiers. The ones we fought were children next to that pair. Damn, I was done wit' all this." Gris wheeled around and dropped beside Robin. "When I said t' maidens had died, that ain't strictly true. My family handed down traditions, mother to daughter. I wanted nothin' to do wit' it, so I run away and become a Regular."

"What do we do?" Robin put her head on her knees.

"Damned if I know." Gris put a hand on Robin's shoulder. "But ye can't ignore it. I'll teach you what I c'n, but t'ain't much. Spent more time avoiding lessons than learning."

"I'd appreciate that," Robin whispered.

"So here tis. Intention is everythin'. Ye decide to kill, people die; to heal, they live."

"The prisoners think I'm fae, you're telling me I'm a shield maiden, Sarge is teaching me to think like him."

"Tradition says the fae started t'shield maidens." Gris sighed. "Those patterns you drew, they's supposed t'be fae words. No one knows what they mean. Listen, girl, ye keep your mind on what yer doin'. First off, ye stop playing at being fae. God only knows what will happen if ye keep it up. We dump the prisoners on someone else. Then we gotta sit and talk about this invasion ye mentioned."

***

Late that night, Robin slipped up to where the prisoners slept. She cut the rope then jumped up into the tree over the older prisoner.

Dropping a branch on him worked to wake him up.

"Thou art free. Take thy freedom and a message to thy Emperor. 'Consider carefully.'"

The man asked a question in his empire language, then in Fhayd, then Calderan.

"Who are you?"

Robin kept her lips sealed. Gris had only been able to coach her on the one phrase in the prisoners' language.

He didn't ask a second time but woke his companion and they crept into the shadows of the forest.

When she was sure they were gone, Robin jumped from the tree and returned to her blankets to sleep.

***

"What happened to the prisoners?" Amby didn't sound upset.

"Robin let 'em go last night on my order." Gris leaned against a tree. "Followed their track far enough to know they ain't stopped running."

"It's a relief to be back to Robin." She scrubbed at her face, hoping the green came off completely.

"I'm guessing there are no beds or baths in our future." Amby shrugged.

"We stop at t'fort, Cassidy'll keep us there for days to entertain 'im."

"And we have better things to do than entertain that slob." Pul stirred the fire to get it burning again.

"Damn right." Gris grinned at them. "By my count, we've three weeks before our Robin flies home. We's taking two of them to hunt spies. Be they bandits or the empire's elite, none return home."

"We're hitting the shadows," Norin sighed. "And here I thought we'd have a nice normal tour this time."

"Ain't been nothin' 'bout this tour could be called normal." Gris rolled her eyes. "Ye get geared up and I'll explain to our Robin."

"Ye' ain't t'only one wit' secrets." Amby dumped out his pack, turned it inside out, and pulled clothes from a hidden pocket.

"We's not a regular squad, though we work with 'em. We's hunters, girl. When folks threaten Fhayden, we make 'em go away."

Robin emptied her pack and searched the bottom. The clothes she found were soft and light in mottled green and brown.

"Keep us hard to see and hard to hear." Norin pulled his on.

Robin shed her mail and the dress, putting her uniform jacket over the light gambeson before putting the mail back on, then covering it with the mottled clothes. She lifted the buckler, then dropped it onto the pile. "I was told not to bring anything I wasn't prepared to leave behind." She copied the others who sorted through the pile, setting most of it aside. When they were done, their loads had been cut in half.

Robin didn't look back at the pile in the clearing. The only things she kept from Kingstown were her weapons and the satchel. The last rested in her pack, not at her waist. She'd snugged the pack close with a rope at her waist. By the time they'd walked a league, she'd forgotten it was there.

Gris had them in a new marching order. Sarge would have approved. The only command was for Robin to hold the centre. They'd spread out with Amby behind her somewhere, Gris up ahead, and Norin and Pul to the sides.

***

The enemy soldiers had camped in an easy spot to defend, backs against an enormous fallen tree. Their fire barely a glow in the twilight. Two sentries watched the approach through the sparse forest. One huddled on the top of the trunk to watch their back.

The one on the tree was Robin's job. If they were like the elite, their mail would cover their head and throat. With a helmet, it would be a near-impossible shot. At least he didn't have a visor.

For three days Gris and the others had given Robin the most intense training she'd ever experienced.

The sentry was good, they kept their eyes moving, but not startling at the sound of small animals. Robin nocked her arrow and drew her bow. It would be a coin toss which way they'd fall, *if* she did the impossible and made a kill shot.

A shout came from the darkness. The sentry tensed but didn't turn around. The soldiers in the camp weren't panicking but making enough noise for her to guess there were five more.

"Sorry," Robin said. The sentry snapped his head around to look in her direction, an arrow already nocked on his bowstring. Her arrow struck the lower rim of the helmet. She dropped her bow and ran forward as he fell back into the camp, landing on the fire.

Terror won the toss over stealth. She drew her sword and knife and dropped into the midst of the momentary confusion. Her opponents would still be night blind from the fire.

When Gris entered the camp, she relaxed her grip on her sword.

"Damn girl, what did ye think ye're doing?"

Robin used a scrap from one of their cloaks to wipe her face. "Who would expect an enemy in the middle of their guarded camp?" Her voice caught.

"'Tis wrong but necessary. Won't likely help."

"You're right." Robin drew a shuddering breath. "But I don't ever want it to be easy."

While Amby, Gris, Pul searched the bodies, Robin dug out her satchel and ordered Norin to sit.

"It's going to hurt." Robin cleaned out the cut on his calf. She crushed the herbs and let the dust fall into the cut. Norin gritted his teeth as she stitched up the cut, then wrapped it with moss and bandages. "Don't fuss with it."

He caught her hand. "Remember this is also what you do."

"Thanks."

***

"We head south tomorrow." Gris sat beside Robin. Since the green clothing didn't absorb blood, they were more brown than green. "Don't relax because you're on the way home."

"Sir Garraik said that the moment of victory is also the most dangerous."

"Sounds like he might be an okay guy, for a knight."

Robin sat her watch, the fire banked down to where it didn't even glow. She walked in random paths around the camp watching for movement, listening for a change in the sounds of the night. Wearing her helmet limited her view, meaning she had to constantly turn her head to scan the dark. When a twig snapped, Robin didn't look but dove forward into a roll. The arrow buzzed over her head.

"Attack!" Robin shouted and drew her sword and knife. She moved as if she were drunk. If the archer couldn't predict where she was going, they couldn't shoot her. Shadows streaked toward the camp from all directions. Noise from the tents reassured her the squad was awake. So she ran to the attack.

Fighting in the dark when the enemy was ready for her was very different from being the one doing the ambushing. Cuts and thrusts came at her from nowhere. Robin defended as she slowed her breathing. *See the pattern.* A blade scraped along her helmet. If the enemy's blade was here, then they were…she lunged, her sword point connecting with mail. Her opponent coughed. She'd hit his throat where mail protected it.

Instead of backing away, Robin hammered at the target with her knife and the crossguard of her sword until their sword dropped and they fell choking to the ground. She turned to the next attack.

I will kill them all. The fight fell into a rhythm, the patterns helping her to fight as if it were day, not the black of night. A kick to the enemy's knee sent them off balance. She flipped her sword and smashed the crossguard like an axe into their helmet.

Blows glanced off her mail, leaving bruises behind, she wouldn't feel them until later.

Then there were no more attacks.

"Squad?" Robin called into the dark.

"Amby."

"Pul."

Silence.

One of the others stirred the fire into flame, and Robin took stock. Eight bodies in blackened armour, two in the mail of Regulars. One of them coughed, and Robin ran over to find Gris bleeding from a hole in her gut. Her own heart fluttered in pain.

"Lie still, I'll get the kit." Robin fell to her knees beside Gris.

"One o' 'em got me wit' a spike." Gris tried to sit up and moaned, then coughed more blood. "Not even you's going to heal me of this." She fumbled at her neck and yanked off a blood-covered amulet. "Wear this, ye have more right to it."

As if removing the amulet drained Gris of the last of her strength, she dropped her head back. "S'way i' shou' be. Dying t'bloody death I deserve." She gripped Robin's hand. "Grieve if ye must, but don't avenge me."

Robin stayed by Gris' side until her hand went slack and her breathing stopped.

"Norin's gone too." Amby put a hand on her shoulder. "Sometimes, we're the ones hunted. Every time we go out, we know this. Doesn't make it any easier to bury the dead."

At dawn, Robin found a bit of cord and fastened the amulet around her neck, then helped to bury her comrades. Both Amby and Pul had wounds she needed to treat.

"Gris told me intent was important." Robin knelt by the mound of dirt. "I swore to kill them all. What if I'd sworn to protect you?"

"You can't protect everyone." Amby laid a flower on the grave. "They were her favourite."

Robin followed Pul and Amby south, having left nothing but her tears on the graves.

CHAPTER 14

Vipal looked back at his troop. They hadn't lost one to the pass, though more than one bone was broken.

"Remember our orders." Vipal gathered them close. "We do not engage with the enemy until they've passed. A squad out two leagues in front and a league to each side. Keep your swords loose, just in case. We march in broken step. I'll be with the vanguard."

They wound their way down toward the plain. There was no gorge on this side, but the road took advantage of every favourable slope.

After two days of marching, a scout came back to report. "Commander, the enemy is on the move. The vanguard will be here within two days."

"Enemy scouts?"

"A couple had unfortunate accidents. Nothing to show we are here."

"Good, recall the scouts. Staying out of sight is more important than knowing the enemy's movements. We already know where they are going."

"Yes, Commander. We expected that order, so they'll be rejoining us soon. "

"Messenger. Alert the column, but we are not going to battle-ready. Be clear. No change in pace."

"Yes, Commander."

Just before they lost the light, Vipal led his troop up a side valley, setting scouts to cover traces as they could.

"We're holing up here." Vipal cursed. The enemy was early. The weather on the plain must be good. "If you pray, pray that the pass has one more storm before the summer. No fires, we camp cold."

***

Hob didn't know if being in the front and facing danger first was better than being in the back and breathing dust. Wasn't like he had a choice.

Marching up the long winding slope made his legs ache. Only the promise of silver for his family kept him moving. He didn't expect to make it home. The silver was paying for his blood.

The air grew colder. Hob shivered, not from the cold, but the idea that the mountain hated them.

The overseer ordered them to halt and set up camp. The sun touched the tips of the mountains to the west before the tents were set up. The mess wagon came by and they ate.

For three more days, they tromped uphill. Each day got colder and the air less friendly. A few in their column fell, unable to breathe. The overseers ordered them to keep going, then left them to die.

On the fourth day, they reached a place where snow covered the road and stopped early.

"Double rations today, we march at dawn. You will be the first to gain glory for the Anca Empire."

Hob didn't believe the overseer, but his family had the silver, so he would march.

Marching in snow was a new kind of torture. His feet pained him, then went numb. His hands numbed too, like he was slowly dying.

"Don't stop. If you fall, you die." The overseer ranted at them until he lost his footing and fell screaming into the void.

They didn't stop, only death waited here. The mountain hated them. People in front of him fell to the road, some followed the overseer. He didn't think it could get worse. Then the snow and the wind started

They marched, and Hob wasn't sure if they hadn't somehow slipped into hell. Yet even in hell, the empire expected its people to do its will.

Night came to accompany the wind and snow. The only reason Hob kept moving was because he'd forgotten how to stop. He was sure he imagined the path going downhill. The wind faded, the snow grew lighter, then stopped. Walls rose on either side of them. When the last of the snow on the road vanished, Hob dropped, expecting to die. Others stopped and huddled around him; their shared warmth kept them alive.

In the morning, Hob woke and cursed. Feeling returned to his feet and hands. They'd gone from dead stumps to burning coals. Out of the five hands of Hundreds who had started through the pass, fewer than three hands of Hundreds were left. The overseers ordered them to wait, but Hob couldn't have moved even they'd wanted.

***

Men unloaded the wagon and used the beams to reinforce the rock fortifications. The mage's job was to prepare for the moment they gave up the position. He took out his chalk and began drawing the sigils. With this chalk, no matter how many feet crossed it, there would be no smudging. A small magic he was very grateful for.

They stopped when they couldn't see. The mage ate his food, warmed on the brazier at the back of the wagon.

Two more days they pushed themselves from dawn to dusk at the bottom of the crack in the mountain. The wagon left and another one arrived, this one filled with uniforms stuffed with straw. The soldiers set up the dummies, leaving some of them in lewd positions. Everyone dealt with stress their own way.

Now they waited. A wagon would bring them food in a week. If they were still here. If they were still alive.

***

"You need anything?" Lencely parked himself beside Sarge.

"Not at the moment." Sarge smiled. Lencely had taken to heart Robin's request to watch over him. Gord and Rud ran off to explore every nook and cranny of the ship. Lencely had to make one last check before he joined them.

"They are good boys." Edward tucked the blanket a bit tighter around Sarge. Every boat and barge in the kingdom ferried soldiers west. Sir Kenly's forces had already secured a perimeter around the dock where most of them would disembark. The boats would continue to Fhayden, where they would pick up the mustered Regulars and knights of the west. Their trip would be shorter, just to this dock.

When they tied up to the dock, the boys surrounded him like an honour guard as the soldiers marched off the boat, each one of them carrying a ten-foot pike. Sarge was impressed; they kept good order. When they were done, they turned and saluted Sarge as a unit.

A man in light armour and a cloak strode up the gangplank, then over to Sarge.

"Master Sergeant, I am Sir Kenly. I hope to be able to share a quiet cup of wine with you someday, but we have a war between now and then. I had to be sure to greet you myself." He saluted Sarge, then turned to the boys. "I know you already care for your master with all you have in you, so I won't tell you to watch over him. Instead, I will thank you." He saluted the boys, then left the boat. Minutes later they'd cast off and continued downriver.

"That really was Sir Kenly, commander of the western legion?" Gord asked as they leaned on the rail.

"So he said." Rud stared at the shore.

"He saluted us." Lencely put a hand on the other boys' shoulders. "Never forget this."

"Not like we would." Gord elbowed Lencely, and they became boys fooling around again.

"How many badges do I have?" Sarge looked up at Edward.

"Five, Master Sergeant."

"Make sure each of my boys has one sewn on their livery. They deserve more than a ribbon around the arm."

"I will take care of it."

***

A coach waited for them at the pier outside Fhayden. Sarge recognized the duke's colours. They rode past hundreds of tents with people swarming about them, putting them up or taking them down. These were the western Regulars. The gate into the city stood open and crowds walked in and out with no interference from the guard in the duke's livery.

The coach took them to a mansion surrounded by gardens beginning to green. A younger version of the duke walked to the coach to greet them.

"I am Sir James, Duke Allin's eldest son. It is my pleasure to welcome you to Fhayden. I would introduce you to the council, but there is someone here looking to meet you. The council can wait."

Sir James led them to a room off the main hall, matching Sarge's pace without effort. He opened the door.

"Some reunions require no audience." He smiled at Sarge, then stepped out and closed the door behind him.

A young woman waited by a window. She wore the brown uniform of a regular with the alertness Sarge had seen many times in soldiers returned from battle.

His boys sat him in a chair, then stood behind him. The soldier turned and Sarge recognized Robin, but her eyes were shadowed.

"Sarge..." Robin took a step, then hurtled toward him, kneeling in front of him, sobbing.

He pulled her to him and ran his hand over her ragged hair. Lencely snapped his fingers and the pages moved from behind Sarge to each stand by a door into the room.

"Master Sergeant, I did terrible things." Robin hiccupped.

"War is about doing terrible things." Sarge put a finger under her chin and lifted it so he could see her eyes. "A true warrior does what is necessary, then stops. There is no shame in tears, for as long as we feel pain, we remain human."

"Did you ever feel like this?" Robin's eyes had the haunted look he remembered in his mirror.

"More times than I care to remember." Sarge held her gaze. "For countries, war is a chess game. This many soldiers here, and we have this probability of victory, with this number of casualties. But for the soldier in the field, the casualties are people they know, friends or ones they didn't like. The enemy isn't numbers, but people with faces like theirs and the same red blood."

"I won't be able to talk about Regulars without thinking of Gris." Robin clutched his hand. "And each person who dies by my sword has their own family, their own Gris."

"The best commanders never forget the people at the front live and breathe, but sometimes they still must make awful decisions." Sarge patted her head. "Sit down and tell me about it. Telling the story can be as painful as cleaning out a wound but helps keep the soul from festering."

Robin sat in a chair and pulled it close to Sarge.

"Lencely, Gord, Rud come and sit with us." Robin waved to them. "You should hear this too."

***

Telling her story drained a weight on her chest Robin hadn't realized was there. The boys sat wide-eyed. She hoped they heard the pain as well as the victory, but they were young. They didn't need to learn her lessons until they were older.

Sarge watched her with neither condemnation nor pity. As she talked, Robin wondered what events put the lines on his face. How many were from memories of joy and how many from painful lessons? She'd tried to imagine what her face might look like at a hundred winters. The idea was ridiculous; she couldn't even imagine herself at twenty.

"What's all this about shield maidens?" Sarge frowned. "Nobody mentioned anything to me."

"It was one of the points of the star of summoning. The king asked me since I was the closest thing they could find to a shield maiden. I agreed, why not? It was the king asking. After the summoning, I never thought about it again, not until Gris asked about it."

"She thought the magic made you into a shield maiden so it could work?"

"Something like that, I guess"

"And you don't know anything about shield maidens?"

"Only what Gris told me. I'd hoped to ask her more questions, but…"

"Life happens, lass, she gave you good advice at the end."

"It's funny, both of you having the same name for me." Robin wiped her eyes.

"Maybe we shared the same laziness." Sarge smiled.

"I think you would have liked her."

"From your account, I think so."

"We need to research shield maidens." Lencely sat up straight. "I can help with that."

"We'll stay with the master sergeant so you can work on it, Robin," Gord said while Rud nodded vigorously.

"That's a place to start." Sarge nodded. "I expect to be spending time with Sir James. Gord and Rud can accompany me for most of that, but I expect they will want to meet my squire too."

"We'll start now." Robin stood up and signalled to Lencely. "My gear, what there is of it, is already in your suite. Any of the servants will take you there. It's on the ground floor, no stairs. I'm told they used to be the Dowager Duchess' rooms."

Robin saluted and left, shadowed by Lencely.

"I've been here for two days. The library is a sanctuary. Nobody starts conversations there."

They jogged up four flights of stairs, and Robin walked straight across the hall through double doors.

"It says something about whoever built this palace, that the library is grander than the throne room," she whispered to Lencely.

"Hello," the librarian, Marian, greeted them. "Sir James has given you free run of the library. Who is this?"

"Lencely is the master sergeant's senior page. He is aiding me in research the master sergeant has requested."

"Ah, pleased to meet you, Lencely." Marian nodded, then handed him a token. "Keep this on you whenever you come to the library."

Lencely accepted it with a bow.

"We are researching shield maidens," Robin told Marian, who frowned as if the topic wasn't polite.

"The master sergeant is interested since Squire Robin stood on the point of the star for the Shield Maiden."

Lencely put his hand over his heart. "You can imagine that he's interested in all aspects of what brought him here."

"Very well." Marian led them to the back of the library and unlocked a heavy oak door with an iron key that hung on a chain around her neck. "You will need me to let you in and out. Pull on the bellrope when you are done." She lit oil lamps that hung from the ceiling.

"You get the idea she isn't happy we're here?" Lencely said after the door closed and the lock thumped.

"From what Gris said, shield maidens weren't popular at the end. The king didn't actively ban them, but he offered an alternative with more status and less sacrifice." She pulled out the amulet. "Look for any books with a symbol that looks like this or mentions shield maidens in the title."

"Aye, Robin."

They worked around the room in opposite directions. For the small side of the room, there were a lot of books. Shelves went from ceiling to floor on all four walls, the only break being the door. In the centre of the room, shelves formed an open square that didn't reach the ceiling to let light from the lamp shine.

Lencely was flipping open books and thumbing through them.

"Don't take too much time on each book."

"Got it, but these are all stories, so I'm looking at the title of the stories."

"Good thinking."

The books on Robin's wall were histories from before Fhayden joined Caldera, but few of them went much more than fifty winters before that. She started skipping any book with a cover that didn't exhibit cracks on the spine. They didn't seem to be arranged in any order other than being histories; a biography of Duke Allin sat beside a summary of the war with the Anca Empire.

Pay attention to patterns everywhere.

Robin gazed into space and let the titles and topics flow through her mind. It wasn't alphabetical order either by author, title, or subject. All of the books here were locked away, probably because they contradicted the official history or weren't complimentary of the subject. They were preserved perhaps for no more reason than they were books and valuable.

Maybe they were arranged in order of how much they were disliked.

Robin moved to the other end of the wall and pulled off a book at random. It was a treatise on magic. Not the flowery but unspecific explanation any mage would give you, but a detailed discussion of why it worked the way it did. Mages wouldn't be happy to see this book outside of their college. Another one told how the independent cities were founded by pirates and brigands fleeing the precursor to the Anca Empire.

Robin adjusted her thinking. These books weren't just unpopular opinions; they were books that could kindle a political bonfire. They weren't just being hidden but protected. Who would be upset about the history of shield maidens? Knights. She widened her search to include books about knights and their development.

A book with the innocuous title of *A History of Knighthood* sent shudders down her back.

'The movement of power from Fae to Human' read the subtitle. Robin sat where there was light a looked through it. According to the author, the fae had ruled the Caldera and the western province of Faedom. Even then the northern border had been a point of contention, but the forces of the fae were indomitable and no human long survived an attempt to raid the fae.

Some humans lived on the borders, not quite fae territory, not quite human. The independent cities were older than the human kingdoms of Caldera and Fhayden. Their founders, running from pursuers from the human kingdoms, begged the fae to allow them to live in Faedom. The fae refused but conceded them territory far to the south on the far side of a river the fae named 'Shield' in their own language. Things went well for a while, then the humans wanted more territory. The fae refused again, but this time a heated debate rose whether the humans should be exiled or exterminated or made into allies against the growing menace of the north.

The compromise was the shield maidens. They were created to be a shield between the land of the fae and outside threats. More time passed as trade between the cities and the fae increased, and a population of half-human, half-fae grew. They were given the land between the Shield and the Earthsblood rivers. As the fae population shrank and the mixed grew, the fae withdrew into the forests, then into what was now Caldera. In Faedom, now called Fhayden, humans ruled and the fae became legends, the magical creatures of stories and myth who lived in mountains and trees.

A fae messenger came from Caldera, begging for aid, but died before she could explain what the menace was. A force travelled from Fhayden to Caldera but found the land deserted. Humans settled it and true history became myth.

The shield maidens weren't called such because they carried shields, but because they *were* the shield. They answered only to the needs of the land. Robin couldn't find anything about how they were commanded or even if they had commanders. The fae governed themselves in a manner incomprehensible by the humans of the day.

All that was the prologue to the rest of the history, but reading the first chapter, Robin found it echoed what Gris had said. The human kings didn't like people who weren't under their authority but were too afraid of the maidens to attack them directly, thus extending knighthood and its political privileges to women. The shield maidens faded into obscurity and legend. The knights became the protectors of the kings and the land was forgotten.

"What have they done to me?" Robin dropped the book on the floor and put her head on her knees.

"Robin, you okay?" Lencely came and sat beside her. "The stories are confusing."

"Tell me about them." Robin didn't lift her head.

"One is about a king who wants to build a road through the forest. A shield maiden stands in his way and the king gives up. His son tries, and the same thing happens, then *his* son tries, and there is no shield maiden, so he builds the road. It's weird, all they did was outwait the shield maiden."

"Shield maidens weren't immortal. She died defending the forest." Robin rubbed her eyes.

"There's another one where a knight is on a quest to slay a dragon that is devasting the country. He meets a shield maiden, and she goes along with him. When they meet the dragon, she asks him to wait while she talks to the dragon. He doesn't want to, but she convinces him. When she goes to speak to the beast, it snatches her up and flies away. Neither of them is ever seen again. The knight travels home, telling people how the shield maiden traded her life for safety from the dragon."

"Maybe she convinced the dragon to move by offering to go with it."

"One last story, this is even stranger." Lencely shifted on the floor. "A hundred knights are travelling to battle. They get to a river. To cross the river they build a bridge, but before they can cross, a shield maiden shows up and destroys it. They build another one, and she breaks that one. After they've built the seventh bridge, the knights form up to protect it from the maiden. There is a terrible battle, and she kills ninety-nine of the knights. Then before she dies, destroys the bridge. The survivor, the youngest of the hundred rides back to tell the king. The king names the river the Blood and forbade anyone to build a bridge across it lest it anger a shield maiden."

"The fae name for the river was Earthsblood. The humans shortened it to Blood and told stories about a terrible battle to explain it. You know, there is still no bridge along the entire length of the Blood."

"How do you know these things?" Lencely asked.

"I will explain later, but shield maidens protected the land, not people. Not that they wouldn't help people if it would help the land. The fae built no cities and had no roads, but humans needed both, so in time what the shield maidens protected changed."

"So, if you're a shield maiden, what are you supposed to protect?"

"To quote Gris, 'Damned if I know,' but I think it will come to me when it needs to."

"I'm hungry." Lencely rubbed his stomach.

"Go pull the rope." Robin went over to the history and place it back on the shelf, then followed Lencely out as Marian opened the door.

"Did you find what you needed?" Marian asked.

"I understand why a shield maiden was needed for the summoning. It is enough."

Marian nodded and locked the door behind them.

CHAPTER 15

Vipal cursed as he watched the confusion of the empire camp at the foot of the pass. Every day they sent five thousand soldiers into the pass along with wagons and the ever-present overseers who strode about with their crops, all too ready to mete out punishment.

None of them from peasant soldier to overseer to the general in his fancy coach were ready to deal with the pass. It would be a miracle if they had one in two survive, probably fewer for the horses and wagons.

Today only wagons loaded with beams and rope were left. The materials for siege engines. Twenty of them, plus the general's coach. Each wagon had four peasants working on it. One overseer railed at them.

A guard of fifty soldiers stood in formation around the coach. These were no peasant soldiers. Vipal wondered what they thought of guarding a general who sent his entire army off while he waited in comfort. For a moment he considered escorting the general across the pass, just to ensure his incompetent leadership continued, but they were going to stop those wagons.

The only question was who was leaving first. The overseer whipped the peasants by the lead wagon, and they pushed to help the horses get started.

"Let's go."

His men loaded a bolt on the ballista they'd made while waiting the last five days. One lit the rag on the bottle which replaced the iron head. He dove back out of the way and the other man fired the ballista.

The enemy wasn't expecting an attack. They'd barely made an attempt at sentries, and they mostly kept their own people in close. The coach was only fifty paces away.

The bolt roared like a dragon as it streaked on a flat arc to strike the coach. Vipal expected it to burn to distract the guards. It exploded into a fireball that consumed the closest guards and littered the rest with flaming chunks of wood and gobs of oil.

Vipal's troop charged and had the rest of the empire soldiers surrounded before they could respond. The officer, from the singed gold on his helmet, snapped an order at his soldiers. One drew a sword and charged, dying with several arrows sticking out of his body. The others dropped their weapons and prostrated themselves.

"Move the men, search them one at a time, no roughness unless they attack you, then they die."

The officer said something to his soldiers.

"You speak Calderan?" Vipal crooked his finger to call the man over. When they got closer Vipal realized she was a woman, but no less dangerous.

"I do, our former leader expected us to be able to understand the enemy's cries of surrender."

"Wise."

"Until he was executed for speaking too vigorously against this farce."

"I will ask you to give your oath not to attack us, then you may go where you will."

"Every path leads to death." She saluted. "I am Centuria Maysan. We were sent to die. If we return, we will be executed. I have no wish to cross the pass to die either. I will give you my oath to serve you. My soldiers will choose for themselves."

"When all have been checked, we will accept your oaths. Even those who do not swear to us, we will give what healing we can. If they do not wish to give their oath, they may continue on their way." Vipal pointed up the pass.

"Commander, the peasants are begging for mercy."

"Centuria Maysan, if you will translate for me."

They walked over to the wagons where the peasants prostrated themselves in front of him.

"They get the same deal as you. Explain it."

When the Centuria finished the peasants looked wide-eyed at Vipal, then burst into a babble of sound.

"I see they approve." Vipal nodded. "You are free. We keep no slaves. Work hard," he said in Ancan.

"So you too wish to understand your enemies, my lord." Centuria Maysan's lips curled up.

"Centuria, you will be in command of all the Ancans, soldier or peasant. This is a new start, make no distinction in treatment."

"As you command, my lord."

Within the candle, Vipal's troop escorted the Ancans and wagons down the mountain to where they were camped, leaving the still burning coach and what was left of the overseer behind.

"It seems a pity to waste this good lumber." Vipal waved one of his men over. "Jack, organize the Ancans, get them to use the lumber to build a hall. Centuria Maysan will translate your orders."

***

Hob limped through the slash in the rock. At midday the sun might shine for part of a candle; otherwise, they marched in gloom. The line of soldiers stretched ahead and behind as far as he could see, which didn't mean much in this place. A murmur travelled back through the line, and they bunched up as the front row stopped and the rest kept pushing.

"Stop, stop marching!" Hob shouted. An overseer glared at him, then took up the shout himself. His punishment for speaking without permission was to be sent to the front of the line to find out what had happened and report.

Soldiers cursed him as he wormed forward. At one point they passed him over their heads. The ones at the front of the line dropped him to the ground. He climbed to his feet and looked ahead. A barrier of rock and wood blocked their way at a point where the walls closed in so that a wagon would barely fit through.

Hob closed his eyes. The overseers would say to attack, but he knew even less about how to attack than he knew how to use the spear waiting in a wagon for him.

"Someone go back and tell the overseers we need instructions, spears, and shields."

The soldiers glared at him sullenly.

"If I must go," Hob walked toward the press in the canyon, "I will have to report how you have stopped without permission."

A wiry older man huffed and jogged toward the back of the line. Hob stared at the wall. It didn't look hard to take apart, but he glimpsed movement at the other side of the thing. Whoever was there wouldn't let them walk up and destroy their wall.

He sat on the stony ground and watched the wall.

"You the one who sent for command and spears?" The voice behind him didn't sound angry, but Hob spun and stayed on his knees anyway.

"Yes, master."

"Stand up."

Hob stood and looked up at a woman who stood a head taller than him. Her armour was steel mail in place of the thin gambeson he wore.

"I like you. My aide fell off a cliff. You'll replace him." She handed him a ribbon. "Tie this on your arm."

Clacking and murmuring announced the arrival of spears.

"So, what do you think? Should we just run at them?"

Hob snorted.

"They are watching? Why come out to fight us if we throw ourselves against their wall?"

She chuckled. "We can't sit and outwait them. We have a limited amount of food; we must attack."

"Yes, Master."

"Don't 'yes master' me. Think."

"Yes, Mas… We have spears. Do we have the shields?"

"God only knows, they aren't close."

"What about a wagon?" Hob screwed up his face. This thinking thing was difficult.

"What about a wagon?"

"Put men behind pushing. It will stop arrows. We hid under wagons when thieves would come to the fields."

"Good, I like it." The woman slapped his shoulder "The wagon should be here soon. Get the people together for your plan."

"Me?" Hob squeaked.

"What did I make you my aide for?"

"As you wish, Master."

Hob walked back to the crowd of soldiers peering suspiciously at the wall.

"A wagon is coming. I need four hands of men to push it into the wall so we can attack with our spears."

"Who made you general?" A big man loomed over Hob, his fists clenched.

Hob pointed to the ribbon on his arm. "We have our first volunteer. As a reward, he gets to choose if he pushes or rides."

"I ride, like an overseer." The man pounded his chest. Others stepped up to claim what they thought was a favourable position.

Ten soldiers climbed into the wagon.

"Lie down until we get close." Hob pointed to the men who were pushing with him. "Don't stop pushing until I say." Hob thought of something. It wasn't part of the plan, but he didn't want to ask, she'd only tell him to think again. That hurt as much as the overseer's crop. "Put extra spears in the wagon. When I say, throw them at the people on the wall."

Once the spears were on, Hob shouted and they pushed the wagon toward the wall, one hand on the wagon, one carrying their spear.

Arrows flew at them one of the pushers grunted and fell, but the wagon didn't slow.

"Spears, now!" Hob shouted. The ones in the wagon threw a few curses as arrows flew by. "Hold on! Stop pushing!"

The wagon smashed into the wall. The ones in the wagon did too. He hadn't thought of that.

"Attack!"

"What?" one of the men yelled.

"Stick them with your spear, idiot."

Hob got out of the way before he was stabbed by one of his own people. A man on the wall aimed an arrow at him. Hob threw his spear, then grabbed another one off the ground. The bow clattered to the stone beside him. He threw his second spear and picked up the bow and the arrow. He'd done his share of illegal hunting. He aimed at where the man had been. Something blocked the gap and Hob released the arrow, it disappeared through whatever blocked the gap.

The arrows had stopped, so Hob climbed the wall to look over. Bodies lay scattered about. Two hands of them, but no blood. He jumped down to investigate. They were bundles of straw in clothes. Hob took a set and put them on, they were nicer than what he had. He tied the ribbon to the sleeve of the brown clothes. Other men dropped down beside him.

"Take clothes from the dummies, and check for food."

Except for the now naked dummies, there was nothing but strange marks on the rock.

"We go back." Hob climbed over the wall, followed by twelve soldiers each wearing some brown. He had the only full set. After picking up the bow, he collected arrows. "Pick up the arrows on the way back."

Once back at the mob of peasants, Hob pointed to the wreck of wagon and wall.

"Get rid of that mess."

"You're a natural." The woman officer clapped him on the shoulder again. "What's your name?"

"Hob."

"Well, Hob." The woman flashed him a ferocious grin. "Don't be falling off any cliffs."

***

Robin couldn't stop herself from rolling her eyes

"Squire, you have a problem with what I'm saying?" Lord Paalip glared at her red-faced.

"No, my lord, as long as we ignore that it is a direct contradiction of the orders left by Sir Kenly, would mean recalling soldiers already on their way to fight, and is putting the safety of your goods over the lives of the soldiers, there is nothing wrong with what you are saying."

Robin met his gaze without flinching. The lord stood with his mouth open.

"Arrest her!" He pointed at her. None of the guards moved.

"Lord Paalip." Sir James leaned back. "My father left very specific instructions about who would command this campaign. Your name is not on that list. In fact, the only one in Fhayden who is on that list is the master sergeant here, and I should point out that Robin is his squire."

"I demand satisfaction." Lord Paalip jumped as if he was going to draw his sword at that very moment. The guards shifted. "You will meet my champion in the ring tomorrow at midday."

"No." Robin sat back and crossed her arms. "I will not harm another human over your folly or cowardice. I will me you in the ring or no one."

Lord Paalip looked on the verge of explosion, but none of the faces in the room showed any more give than Robin's. For days they'd wasted time blathering on about things already done and decided. The camp was gone along with all the Regulars. Most of the knights had gone with them. The remainder were to plan a final defence of the city.

"Lord Paalip," Sir James drawled, "considering your fame at the tournaments, you should have no difficulty defending your own honour, or you could withdraw your challenge."

"I am a noble of the realm." The lord sputtered.

"I am the Duke of Fhayden's heir and by his word acting in his stead. Squire Robin wears colours granted by the King himself, and she has already distinguished herself in fighting for this country. Either pick up your own sword or sit down."

Lord Paalip turned and stalked out of the room.

"Watch your back." The elderly knight sitting beside her murmured.

"Now about the defence of the city." Sir James rapped on the table.

"Defence of the city is foolishness," Sarge spoke up for the first time in days. Robin had thought him asleep. "If the empire's forces get to this city, we have already lost. Further defence will only cost lives."

"But we must put on some defence for honour's sake." Another lord leaned over the table.

"Will you be on the wall?" Sarge ground out the words. "Will you stand when the gate breaks and shed your blood on the cobbles? If not, it isn't your honour you are concerned with."

"How do we know you aren't an agent of the empire?" The lord pointed at him.

"You don't." Sarge stared calmly at the man.

"Asking a question is neither insult nor treason." Robin stood beside Sarge. "But choose your next words very carefully."

"Master Sergeant, what would you see as an honourable defence of the city?" The lord frowned.

"Using the wealth of the few to save the lives of the many by bribing the enemy not to sack the city."

The lord sat back and gazed up at the ceiling.

"My lord the duke has always had the good of the people in mind. I will endeavour to follow his example. If it comes to it, you have access to everything I own to use as you will."

Robin bowed to him. "You set a fine example for the city. I thank you."

The lord blushed and looked down.

"We are adjourned." Sir James stood. "Tomorrow we will plan how to best convince the enemy to spare our people."

Robin walked with Sarge back toward their suite.

"Sir Garraik told me to learn tact. I'm not doing very well."

"Tact is overrated," Sarge laughed. "Paalip heard exactly what he needed to hear."

"I'm glad you think so." Robin opened the door to let Sarge into the room first. A shadow shifted in the corner of her eye, and she threw herself to cover him. Something slammed into her back and she stumbled forward, her arms and legs not working properly. She twisted to not land on Sarge. Something scraped the floor sending agony through her.

Lencely, Gord and Rud ran toward her.

"Protect the master sergeant." Robin pointed to him. The boys hoisted him to carry him away, but a man in a black mask walked through a door on the far wall and pointed a sword at them. Footsteps behind her warned her another was coming, but she couldn't move. Black floated in her vision.

I will protect them. Robin set her teeth and tried to stand. The door closed behind her and the bar dropped.

"You're already dead, foolish girl." Pain shot through her as whatever stuck in her back was yanked out. "But you can watch these others go before you." The attacker reset his crossbow and put the already-bloody bolt in place. "Any more heroes?"

Gord pushed Rud and the master sergeant aside and charged the crossbowman. The crossbow snapped, and the bolt buried itself in his chest. Gord tried to step forward but collapsed. Somehow Lencely had Sarge's cane and was trying to hold off the swordsman.

Intention is key. Gris had said. *I will not let them die.* Her chest burned, and she shrieked as her entire body burned. The crossbowman was turning Gord over with a toe, laughing as if it was a great joke.

Robin moved before she knew she could. Her knife slashed through the crossbowman's throat as she passed him. The other man ran his sword through Lencely's leg. The boy wailed as he fell back still trying to hold up the now broken cane. The attacker lunged to finish him off.

Robin gripped the sword stopping the thrust as if it had hit a stone wall. Her knife plunged into the man's heart. He died before the sneer could fall from his face.

She ignored him and dropped beside Lencely. "Rud, my kit." She put pressure on Lencely's wound trying to stem the flow of blood. He was pale and limp. The satchel dropped beside her, and she pulled what she needed without looking, packing moss into the cut. Wrapping a bandage around his leg and pulling it snug. Her fingers drew signs on his leg, his forehead.

He wasn't breathing. She tilted his head back and blew air into his chest. *You will not die today.* The burning agony ran through her again, but this time Lencely screamed. She put him down suddenly exhausted. Halfway to Gord's side, her body failed her, and the world retreated.

***

The tears flowing from her eyes told her was alive. Robin sat up and scrubbed at them, then looked around. She'd been lying on Sarge's bed. Lencely occupied hers, still pale, but breathing.

"Sarge!" Rud yelled. "Robin's awake." He reddened. "Sorry, Squire Robin."

"Robin is fine; you've earned the right."

"But I didn't do anything."

"You stayed at the master sergeant's side. You did enough." She put a hand on his cheek, and a part of her noted the green patterns running down her arm to her fingertips. No time to worry about it.

"Now you need to keep by his side and Lencely's. Bring them north when you can."

She snatched her pack, stuffed what she needed it then dressed. When Sarge entered the room, holding a new cane, she was buckling her sword belt on, checking the knife at her back.

"Revenge won't help." Sarge stood in the doorway as if to stop her. "Gord won't be helped by more killing."

"I know," Robin's voice caught. "Make sure they treat him as a hero. The land is calling. A book, *The History of Knighthood* will explain."

"Heroics won't change the course of the war." Sarge's face looked like stone.

"I can't..." Robin drew in a long breath. "I can't *not* go, Sarge. It's not like I understand it either.

Sarge stepped to the side. "Be careful." He handed her the satchel.

"You too. Follow when you can." Robin ran through the halls, then out the door, the scenery blurring as she passed. Disaster brewed ahead of her, and she ran to meet it, wishing whatever called her had given her the time to mourn Gord as he deserved.

***

Sarge sat in his chair like it was a throne. Sir James knelt in front of him. The days since Robin left were torture. Only Lencely's rapid recovery and Rud's company helped him stay sane.

"We've laid Gord safely until we can send him home to his family."

"Good, be sure you tell them what happened. Him being a hero won't make the pain less, but it will give some meaning to his death."

"My deepest apologies, we haven't been able to locate Lord Paalip. His household is in chaos and my people have been unable to sort it out. For now, they are all being detained. All his property is forfeited to the crown."

"Paalip is the least of your worries." Sarge wanted to kick the man. "You had empire assassins with free run of your palace, and an agent sitting in your council reporting on everything you discussed. We must assume the empire knows our plans down to the smallest detail."

"I've sent runners after Sir Kenly, but…"

"I know, I've sent my own to deal with it. Trust her."

"How is she alive? The poison on that bolt should have killed her immediately."

"What do you know about shield maidens?" Sarge leaned on his cane.

"Shield maidens? You mean like in the fairy tales?"

"Listen well, son, we've got some talking to do, and I don't have much time to spare."

"Master Sergeant, the wagon is ready, Lencely says he's ready to go."

"Give me a few minutes, Rud. Check the room one last time to be sure you have everything. We won't be coming back soon."

"Aye, Master Sergeant."

"There is a book in a locked room in the library. Find it, read it." Sarge described the volume to Sir James, then pushed himself to his feet as Rud came back from his check. "Robin is no mere squire, but then, she never was."

Rud took Sarge's arm, and they headed out to the wagon, leaving the duke's heir staring at their backs.

CHAPTER 16

Hob watched as the soldiers attacked the wall. This was the third one. The first had been abandoned after their first attack, the second wasn't defended at all, but this one was giving them trouble.

The shields had finally found their way to the front of the column. Men and women with shields and spears crept toward the wall through a storm of arrows.

"Call them back," his master ordered. "That's not going to work. Can't put an overwhelming rush together four people at a time."

"Retreat!" Hob yelled. The command went up the line until all were scuttling back instead of forward.

"Now what?" she asked.

"Fire?" Hob scratched his head. "They can't defend a wall that's on fire."

"We can't attack it either."

"Won't it be weaker? The wood they used to brace it will be burnt."

"Have it your way." His master waved a hand. "I'll leave it up to you."

"Yes, master." Hob bowed then ran over to the overseer. "I need a barrel of oil."

"What for?" The overseer stared down at him. "You may be wearing fancy clothes, but you're still a peasant." She slashed at Hob with her crop.

Hob went back to his master.

"Master, I have failed."

"Why is your face bleeding?"

"The overseer whipped me for overstepping my station."

"Oh, for heaven's sake, must I do everything myself?" She stalked over to the overseer. "Did you hit my aide?"

"Master, he..." her words died as the officer pulled her sword from the overseer's chest.

"Listen up." She waved her bloody sword, then crooked a finger to call Hob over. "This is my aide. You obey him because he's part of me, like my right arm."

The crowd murmured and another overseer ran over to her and fell to his knees.

"Command me, master."

She wiped her sword clean on the overseer's cloak. "My aide will tell you my orders. Do not mistake, you are no more than a peasant to me. That will be your blood if you fail me."

The overseer crawled to Hob.

"What do you require, master?"

"Oil, at least two barrels, a big hammer or axe, and rags."

***

The border was clear, no enemy as far as they could see down the road.

"Put a white flag on each wagon. I don't want any visible weapons."

They rolled into the empire picking up an escort from the fort on the far side.

"Why should I let you through?" The fort commander demanded.

"Why not? Which would be worse, the emperor hearing you acted in his place or receiving an envoy from a neighbouring country?"

The wagons rolled slowly deeper into the empire. The escort refused to talk to Lord Allin, but they did send a message ahead to let the local lord know he was coming.

On the second day, twenty soldiers in uniform surrounded them. One stepped forward yelling at them.

"No one move." Lord Allin put his empty hands to his side and spoke in careful Ancan. "We are an envoy from King Federick of Caldera, we bring the emperor gifts from the bounty of our fields."

"Food!" one of their escorting soldiers shouted, the driver pushed him off the wagon. Three other soldiers ran swords through the driver. In seconds every Fhayden but Lord Allin was dead.

The leader pointed a sword at Lord Allin.

"The emperor curses any who break truce."

"The emperor isn't here." The leader sneered.

"I've watched soldiers die from the curse." The soldier who had started the fight coughed then stared with wide eyes at the blood on his hand. He collapsed in a heap, another fell, then another.

"You poisoned the food. You planned to kill the emperor." The man's sword scratched Lord Allin's throat.

"Bring what the fool was eating, and I will eat it in front of you."

Another soldier coughed.

"Only those with blooded swords are dying." Lord Allin met the commander's gaze. He should have asked for a more active defence from the mages, but that would doom his task before it started.

"Take the wagons to the barn. I will bring the spy to the master."

***

Lord Allin winced as the guards threw him down in front of the noble.

"We caught a spy."

The noble sauntered over and nudged Lord Allin with a toe. "You are a Fhayden spy?"

"I am from Fhayden, but no spy. Your commander is hiding that he has robbed –"

The commander's boot knocked the rest of the air from Lord Allin's lungs.

"Desist." The noble glared at the guard. "Or I will question why you don't wish me to hear his words. Why should I be concerned that you were robbed?"

"They didn't rob me." Lord Allin worked his way to his knees, then bowed the best he could. "They stole from the emperor." He coughed and spat blood on the floor, carefully away from the noble's shoes. "What did your guards do with the four wagons of food I brought as a gift for the emperor?"

"My lord," the guard put his hand on his sword. Others put themselves between him and the noble.

"It saddens me that one of my commanders was so foolish." The lord flipped a hand, and several guards grabbed the commander and forced him to his knees.

"He cursed my men, half of them died on the road."

"And you brought him here to me? Hang him from his feet in the dog pit," the lord told the guards. "Then find those wagons. Take this man and treat him like a guest. Guard him carefully."

***

After a bath and new clothes, Lord Allin felt human again. His stomach burned. Eight of his people dead, because some guards got greedy. *Stupid, bloody, idiot.* He cursed himself. If he'd hired guards...

"My lord, the master is ready to see you." The servant knelt in the doorway.

"Lead me to him." Lord Allin banked the fire of his rage, he needed this noble to get to the emperor.

The noble sat on a low bench but stood and bowed to Lord Allin.

"The guards have been punished. Do you require to see their bodies?"

"I trust you as a noble of the Anca Empire to do what is right." Lord Allin bowed in return.

They sat and the noble motioned for wine.

"I am Marques Povost."

"The Lord Duke of Fhayden." Lord Allin hid his smile as the marques paled, then recovered quickly.

"It is such a dangerous time for you to be travelling with so few retainers."

"I worried that bringing a troop with me might be misinterpreted."

"Alas, you are right. What is this world if humans can't trust each other?"

"Much like it is now, Marques. Humans are not a trustworthy species."

"Not like the fae?" The marques leaned forward. "I heard a report that two soldiers passed through stating they had a message for the emperor from the fae."

"The fae?" Lord Allin sipped at his wine. "I have not heard them mentioned outside of fairy tales. What were Ancan soldiers doing to gain the fae's attention?"

"You understand, the foolish youth try to make a name by crossing into Fhayden and returning alive with proof of their escapade."

"A learned man such as you would know the treaty between Fhayden and the Anca Empire, signed by my grandfather and the emperor himself declares anyone crossing the border without an escort has sentenced themselves to death."

"And where is your escort, my Lord Duke?"

"Who do you think told your guards what my wagons carried?"

The marques spilled his wine. The servant rushed over to mop it up.

"Never mind that, fetch the captain of the guard."

When the solid-looking woman entered and knelt, the marques ordered her to find the man who'd commanded the duke's escort.

"How would I prove this man's identity?" She levelled a cold gaze at Lord Allin.

"He will have three gold rings in his pouch, one with a ruby set in it. He swallowed my signet ring."

***

Lord Allin studied his signet ring carefully but could see no evidence of mistreatment. He slid it on his finger. He'd gifted the gold rings to the marques as a token of his forgiveness.

The wagons were all but empty when the guard found them. The gold Lord Allin had hidden for emergencies was gone too.

"Lord Duke?" A young woman entered the room and knelt. "I am Jequilane, the marques's daughter. He asks that you to allow me to travel with you as a guide and surety against further mishap. Until we have safely arrived in the emperor's presence, I am your slave."

"Very well." Lord Allin stood. "I accept. You will conduct yourself in all things as the noble daughter of the marques."

"Thank you, my lord." She stood, head still lowered. "If you will follow me."

Outside a coach waited. Twelve guards surrounded it, commanded by the captain of the guard.

"My lord duke." The marques bowed low. "My own bodyguard will protect you." He pulled a letter from his vest. "I have written in my own hand a record of what occurred. I am sending with you these servants. They are yours to use as you will."

Lord Allin walked around them and shook his head. "They will not do. I must have a woman of an age to serve Lady Jequilane as chaperone, and one to be her maid. I will not allow her dignity to be challenged. If we are to meet with the emperor, she must remain Lady Jequilane."

"My lord, you are generous beyond my dreams."

"Father, Nan is despairing. She would gladly accompany me if asked. One of my maids, she has long straight black hair. She is quiet, but I believe that will be a blessing while travelling." Jequilane's eyes sparkled.

After another, plainer, coach had been added, Lord Allin boarded the front coach.

"Lady Jequilane, if you and your maid or chaperone would join me. I would appreciate the company on the journey."

As they started, Lord Allin subtly examined his companions. Jequilane looked out the window, while the maid stared at her with adoring eyes. The older woman, Nan Jequilane had called her, glared at Lord Allin.

"Madam, may I ask what is amiss?"

"Oh, she's just mad because I wouldn't let her bring a knife from the kitchen," Jequilane said without turning.

"Ah." Lord Allin pulled out his boot knife and sheath to hand it to the woman. "I trust you with my own blade, to protect your Lady's person."

"My lord." Nan reached to take the knife, hand shaking. "Servants may not own blades."

"It is my knife; I am asking you to carry it for me."

She hid the knife somewhere in her clothes, then looked out the window, the slightest of smiles on her face.

***

Robin rode the horse they had given her at the gate of the city. She was sore already, but from what she'd learned on the riding excursions Sir Garraik had led, patience would rule the day.

A mad gallop would have satisfied the urgency stirring in her gut, but Paalip had the better part of day's lead on her.

Farms stretched away from the road as far as she could see. Men, women and children walked the fields planting. Robin watched curiously. As a city dweller, she'd seen very few farms.

The day passed, then the next, the forest started to close in. She'd been so numb riding south that she'd seen nothing but the walls of the wagon. Now she passed foresters with immense logs on axles and huge wheels. She waved to them; they nodded back.

The trees grew close enough to the road to shade her. To warm up, she dismounted and ran beside her mare with reins in her hand. The horse kept eying her as if trying to figure out this human who ran instead of sitting in the saddle.

Men in brown uniforms stepped out of the forest.

"Pardon, Lady, but you may go no farther. It isn't safe."

"Have business to the north. Who can grant me permission to ride on?"

"Sir Kenly, but—"

"Tell me how to find him."

"I will guide you." One of the men walked into the trees, Robin rode after him.

The light had dimmed by the time they reached a camp spread out under the trees. Her guide left her with a sentry and headed back to the road.

"I will make sure your horse is cared for. The boy will take you straight to Sir Kenly."

She would not have been able to tell the knight's tent from those around, not even one guard watched. The boy walked in announcing a visitor for Sir Kenly.

"Hello, sorry for the poor hospitality." The knight wore only his light gambeson and a tunic.

"I am the master sergeant's squire, Robin. I have business to the north."

"It wouldn't be business with a certain lord who passed through yesterday?"

"Perhaps. I haven't been told."

"What are the names of the master sergeant's three pages?"

"Two now, Gord died protecting the master sergeant from assassins. Lencely is recovering from being closer to death than anyone should get. Rud continues to care for the master sergeant. They will come, not today or tomorrow, but when they get here, give them a guard and bring them north."

Sir Kenly found a scrap of paper and wrote on it before adding a seal with wax from the candle and his ring.

"Won't you stay the night? The forest is dangerous at night."

"I cannot. We will meet again, but my business is urgent."

"Then is there anything I can give you to help?"

"A bow, quiver, arrows, a helmet, and I will be fine."

The boy ran off to fetch the items, and Sir Kenly walked her back to the sentries. The boy arrived almost at the same time. Puffing, he carried bow and quiver on his back, a helmet in each hand and one on his head.

"Lady, I didn't know what size you would require, so I brought three."

Robin tried on all three and kept the one off his head. "Old fashioned, but it will do." It didn't have a nasal guard, instead a brim covered the eyes. As a bonus, mail hanging from the back circled around to fasten over her throat. She took her satchel from the horse stuffed, a few rations from the sentries in it, then bowed to them.

"I thank you, the land thanks you, Sir Kenly, and Sir Three Helms." She grinned at the boy. "I will leave the horse in your care. Treat her kindly, she has worked hard."

All night, Robin ran north. By all rights, she should have been exhausted, but the farther she ran the more refreshed she felt. The black night lightened to grey as she left the forest behind to see an army forming up at the fortress. Spears banged against shields as the soldiers worked themselves up.

"Messenger from Sir Kenly." Robin showed the first person she met. "Urgent." They passed her along until she arrived at the front line. A man in a brown uniform, so burdened with braid and embroidery it was a wonder he could move, stood on a platform, mouth open, as she interrupted his speech.

"You the commander?" She held up Sir Kenly's seal then stuffed it in her satchel.

"You will address me as Marshal."

"My pardon, your uniform looks nothing like Marshal Potter's."

Marshal frowned and waved her out of his way. "Whatever you are here for can wait."

"No." Robin projected her voice as her mother had taught her long ago to be heard all through the performance hall. "If you enter the Anca Empire, Fhayden will be doomed."

Rustling behind her said the troops heard her.

"Nonsense, superstition." Marshal puffed up and nodded to a man who could have given Andre an even match at grappling.

"Sorry, Lady, but'cher gotta move."

"No." Robin walked past the box and the pomp to set herself in the middle of the road. "You may not cross out of Fhayden. Sir Kenly has given no such order, nor has Sir James, heir of the Lord Duke Allin, nor has his Majesty King Federick."

"I was given orders to form up and attack!" Marshal was red and shouting.

The big man put his hand on her shoulder.

"Sorry."

Robin caught his arm and swung up like it was the branch of a tree. Her heel connected with the side of his head. She caught him as he dropped, drawing a sigil on his temple.

"I'm sorry too."

"You may not leave Fhayden."

"By whose authority?" The marshal pointed at her. "Archers, kill her."

No one moved.

"You asked by whose authority I stop you." Robin drew her sword and knife. "By my own authority. I am Robin Fastheart, Shield Maiden of the Realm, made so by the King's own hand." She pointed the sword at the army. "If you would invade the empire, you must kill me to do it."

Part Three

CHAPTER 17

Hob craned his neck to see the top of the wall blocking them from entering the city. He'd told the front line to wait in the space just before the crack widened. It was one hundred and seven paces from there to the wall. Each one he'd taken expecting an arrow to strike him.

The wall curved slightly so there would be more defenders than attackers at any one point. He walked the length of the wall, thirteen paces from one polished cliff wall to the other. A gate with heavy doors sat in the centre. Four, maybe five times his height, people looked out at him pointing. They were real, not dummies filled with straw.

The straw men weren't hard to destroy, even if their early attacks failed, the straw soldiers fell within three days. A group of his best warriors served his master while wearing some part of the brown clothes the dummies were dressed in.

A rope snaked down the wall at the other end and a man slid to the ground, then the rope was pulled back up. He didn't have a sword out, and he held his hands away from his side as he walked toward Hob.

The man said something Hob didn't understand, then he spoke again.

"You are from the empire."

"Yes." Hob pointed at the wall. "We've been sent to tear down your wall."

"The watch worried you might be one of ours from the uniform."

"Took them from the straw men." Hob slapped the wall. "This is a better wall than the others."

"Thank you." The man tilted his head. "Did you come to parley?"

"Parley?" Hob creased his forehead.

"It means for enemies to talk before a battle."

"Why would we?"

"Perhaps to learn if battle is necessary. We don't want to kill more than we must."

Hob's head ached, then he recalled the soldiers falling at the side of the path, people freezing in the snow, men with arrows through their hearts.

"We will parley."

The man whistled a series of notes. Another rope dropped and a woman slid down.

"She will stay at the bottom of the wall until you return."

"That is fair."

Another whistle and the people above lowered a rope. The man showed Hob how to hold it and fend off the wall with his feet. At the top of the wall men and women in brown stared at him. They held spears, bows, and other things Hob couldn't name. None spoke to him or made any threatening move. Maybe they were straw men.

"Come, I will take you to Lord Huddroc." The man waved for Hob to follow him. The people moved aside. The man must be this lord's aide. The wall was interesting from the top. It was wide enough for wagons to roll. A smaller wall not quite a man's height ran along both sides. Probably to keep the straw men from falling off. He walked to the inner side and looked over. A town lay quiet below. A few people in brown moving purposefully, but no market, no women, no children. On the far side of the town stood yet another wall. *Do they have to wall in the straw men?*

They went down spiral steps set within a tower beside the gate. They came out into a space wider than the one on the other side of the wall, but not as long. Everything he could see, even the roofs of the buildings were made of stone. The gates on the inside of the wall had heavy bars the size of trees holding them closed.

Across the open space, a building had guards standing by the door. The man led him over and through the doors. An older man sat at a table covered with paper. He looked up and made a sign with his hand.

"This is Lord Huddroc." His guide pulled a chair out at a table with no paper on it. "I will bring a meal. Are you hungry?"

Hob rubbed his stomach. He was a peasant who didn't know what it felt like not to be hungry.

"Yes."

The lord came to sit across from Hob.

"I am Lord Huddroc; this is my city."

"I am Hob." It didn't feel right to say just his name. "I am the master's aide."

"Welcome, Hob." Lord Huddroc smiled. He didn't look like an enemy, but soldiers stood close by with spears and swords. "I hope we can talk sensibly."

"Yes."

"Let me ask why you are attacking my city?"

"The emperor said to." Hob shrugged. "No one asks why."

"The emperor says to go there and start a war, and no one questions it?"

"Of course not." Hob rubbed his eyes; his head was aching again. "Does your emperor allow you to question him?"

"We have a king, not an emperor, but yes, he expects us to think for ourselves. In the end, we do what he says." Lord Huddroc shrugged and waved his hands. "He has ordered us to stop you."

"Why talk?"

"Why not? It doesn't hurt."

The man who guided him returned with a tray.

"My apologies for such a simple meal." He laid out plates of meat, cheese, fruit, vegetables. Bread that wasn't hard or at the point of moulding still steamed slightly, the smell making his mouth water.

Even the master didn't eat like this. She grumbled about rations. The peasants' gruel got thinner each day.

"Help yourself." Lord Huddroc picked up a slice of meat and bit into it as if it weren't worth silvers for each bite.

Hob tried the meat, and the taste made him sweat. How could it be so much better than the occasional animal they hunted? He had the same question about the cheese and the rest. This was food from the part of the harvest the nobles kept. If he told his brown men and women, they would fight just for the chance to eat from this tray.

They ate in silence, drank water that tasted clean without the taste of oak barrels or old leather.

"Listen." Lord Huddroc pushed the tray aside. "I understand you are under orders and won't hold it against you. If you wish to talk again, wave a white flag and come alone to the wall. Don't attack under the white flag. The gods will curse you."

"I will not attack under the white flag." Hob stood and bowed. "I must return to my master."

The guide packed the remains of the tray into a cloth bag and handed it to Hob. "A gift for your master, for allowing you to parley with us."

"I thank you for her." Hob bowed again. They left the building and returned to the wall where his guide tied the bag to his waist, then lowered him to the ground. The woman bowed and climbed up her own rope without needing help.

"Let the master know I would report to her in private," Hob ordered one of his Browns. She jogged off to return shortly with the master behind her.

"Where have you been?" The master frowned at him. Hob resisted the urge to throw himself at her feet.

"Parleying?"

"Really?" Her face relaxed. "Let's hear it." She led him out of earshot of the army.

"First, they sent this to you, as a gift, they said, for letting me parley." He handed her the bag and her eyes widened.

"Is this safe?"

"Their lord and I ate from the same tray as that food is from."

"Good enough." She tied the bag to her waist. "Now what did you talk about?"

Hob repeated the conversation as well as he could.

"Any ideas from seeing the wall?"

"All the people except Lord Huddroc were dressed in brown. They are straw men; they will fall in a few days." Hob said. "The gates are wood. The soldiers are straw. We attack with fire."

***

Once Lord Allin proved he had no intentions of stealing Jequilane's honour, Nan became a good travel companion. She told scandalous stories about the nobility which simultaneously had Jequilane giggling uncontrollably and eyes widened in fear.

Wonder what kind of stories they tell about me? Lord Allin had dedicated himself to improving the lives of the people who were the foundation of their realm, the farmers, craftspeople and more. The nobility hadn't liked it, some still didn't, but as their lives got better, those people were happy to pay taxes to the nobility. Some of the nobility took Lord Allin's reforms to bring them to their own people.

But Lord Allin wasn't flamboyant. He did his work in small increments. Any craftsperson had more variety in his life than he did. When his wife and daughter died in the plague, he'd retreated even further into his work, leaving James to pick up the ceremonial parts of the job. Too bad James had never found time to marry. Maybe when this was mess was done.

Lord Allin glanced over at Jequilane and her maid giggling over something. Perhaps…

***

They rolled into Ancapolis having encountered no more issues, but Lord Allin looked out at the city with beggars sitting in front of gold-plated gates and worried that the easy part had been getting here.

Soldiers escorted them through the city. The captain had ordered her guards to seal their swords in their scabbards.

"You will wait here for the emperor to call for you." The building had to be double the size of his palace and many times grander. They were assigned to rooms that were bigger than his at home. The captain set her guard on rotation, some to watch during the day, others at night. She allowed them to go out into the city in pairs.

"If you get into trouble, I'll let you rot. If you want to get drunk, buy wine and bring it back here."

"Jequilane, would you like to see some of the city?" Lord Allin looked out the window of their room at the exquisite gardens, and the tall wall with knives set in the top. "We would have to bring some of the Captain's guards of course."

Two days of all the comforts he could desire had bored him to the point of distraction. He'd turned down the offers of women or boys from the woman who ran the place. A slave, though she wore gold jewellery.

"If the Captain thinks it safe."

When he asked the manager of the palace, she assigned them two of her own guards and a guide.

"Take only two of yours. If you look too important, it could be dangerous." She smiled broadly. "This not a nice city."

The guide took them to see grand and beautiful buildings. They shopped at markets with fences and guards to keep the poor out. It was as if they'd only widened the walls of the palace, but Jequilane and her maid, who still refused to give her name to Lord Allin, looked to be enjoying themselves.

On the third day of excursions a soft-looking young man in a plain robe, but who wore a ruby the size of a hen's egg on a chain around his neck, accosted them. He looked no older than James.

"I haven't seen you before." He walked around Lord Allin like he was examining a horse he might buy. A glance at the guide showed her trembling. Not a man to insult then.

"I am visiting from Fhayden, waiting upon the emperor's pleasure."

"Really?" The man looked interested, then he saw Jequilane and her maid, and Lord Allin was dismissed from his attention.

"Ladies." He bowed to them. "Would you come with me? I can show you pleasures you've never imagined."

Lord Allin stepped in before Jequilane could respond. "She is mine, my lord."

"Well then?" The man raised his eyebrows.

"I will buy some wine, and we will speak on this." He led the young man to a secluded table and sat across the table. Jequilane and the maid took either side.

"Captain, ask the keeper to bring a bottle of their best wine." She nodded and strode into the crowd. "I very much apologize for any rudeness." Lord Allin lowered his head. "I am new to your city and do not know the rules."

"You travel to a place where you don't know the law?" The young man frowned.

"There are laws, my lord, and then there are the unwritten rules which may be even more dangerous to break."

The young man brightened. "A man of philosophy, how delightful." He leaned forward and took Jequilane's hand to caress. "What philosophy should keep me from this beautiful flower?"

"Even if she were but a flower, would you pick a blossom before your emperor?" Lord Allin glanced at Jequilane. She stared entranced at the man. The maid scowled jealously at the pair. Lord Allin nudged her foot and shook his head. She smoothed her face.

"It could be dangerous to step ahead of the emperor, but what is life without risk?"

The captain returned with the keeper and had him present the bottle. The keeper opened it, poured some into a cup tied to his waist and tasted the wine.

"Pour for me, philosopher." The young man didn't lift his hand from Jequilane's. Lord Allin poured each of them a cup and waited for his guest to choose one.

Lord Allin took the cup the young man didn't choose and sipped. A vintage from the south of Fhayden. He smiled and swirled his cup slightly.

"I have visited the vineyard that gave birth to this wine."

"Indeed, you are a well-travelled man then?" An odd expression crossed the young man's face.

"A man needs to know his domain." Lord Allin sipped again, but his stomach knotted at the open scowl on the young man.

"Tell me about this domain." The young man sipped his wine like water then slapped the cup on the table, splashing the maid's hand. "You have my permission to lick the drops."

Lord Allin talked about Fhayden, his attempts to make it a better home for everyone. He described the farms, the forests, the vineyards in the south. The young man sat enraptured.

When the wine had gone, he sighed and slouched back in his chair. "So my lovely, have you decided?"

"My lord," Jequilane whispered. "If I belonged to myself, I would not hesitate. Yet I belong to this man. He has sworn to keep my honour for my father. I cannot give what I do not own."

The young man pushed her hand away roughly. "You dare turn me down?" He jumped to his feet, knocking the chair over.

"My lord," the maid threw herself at his feet. "I am my lady's slave. If you must, I will go with you."

"How does a slave own a slave?" the man stared down at her as if his anger was forgotten.

"She does not own my body, but my heart." The maid stared up at him.

He lifted her to her feet, then kissed her. She curled her fingers in his hair to return the kiss.

"You are interesting." He held on to the maid's hand. "Come with me, all of you."

Lord Allin helped Jequilane out of her seat, as she still stared at her maid in wonder. The guards formed up around them, and they followed the young man. Men in different corners of the room stood and followed them. They walked through the streets to a door in a wall. It opened as the young man approached it, and he led them in without slowing. The guards stopped outside the door as it closed behind him.

The hall was long and echoed their footsteps. It had no decoration, no windows, no doors. Lord Allin lost count of the paces before they arrived at another door. This one too opened for them.

On the other side was a room of such luxury it left Lord Allin short of breath. The young man walked to a chair set against one wall, sat, and pulled the maid to sit on his knee.

"Tell your emperor, my dear, how does one come to own another's heart?"

She looked at Lord Allin, eyes wide in panic.

"It is all right." Lord Allin said to her. "Tell your story."

"My lord emperor," the maid's voice shook so badly Lord Allin could hardly understand her. The emperor lifted her to turn her to look at his face. He lifted her chin with a finger.

"Please?"

"I was born without a name," the maid talked as if only she and the emperor were in the room. "As I grew, my hair made me stand out, so the overseer sent me to the marques to be a servant. I was of an age with his daughter, so he gave me to her. I grew up serving her in everything. Yet she didn't treat me as a slave; she didn't abuse me, even apologized when she made me cry. She gave me a name – Magpie, because, she said, didn't I chatter like one." Her breath caught. "You are only the second to know that name."

"So, she treated you well, and you loved her?"

"My lord, it is more than that. I am a possession; she could dispose of me at any time, like a dress worn too many times. But she sees me, she sees a person, what I feel matters to her."

"I have many wives, but I own no one's heart. They compete for my attention, wanting favours for their fathers. It's boring. So, I walk in the city and look for those who will give themselves to me, not because I'm their emperor, but because they desire me. Your mistress is the first to refuse me. That is new, interesting. But you, you offered what you most fear on her behalf. No demands, no bargains." He kissed her again. "I want you to stay with me, teach me how to lose my heart or gain another's."

"My lord emperor," Magpie trembled, "I will obey any command you give me."

"I don't want you to obey my commands."

"My lord." Jequilane stepped forward and bowed. "If I may?"

When he didn't refuse, she stepped closer. "Dear Magpie, think. Does he have a name other than Lord Emperor? Or anyone to call him by that name? As you were given to me to be 'maid,' a toy to use or discard, he's been given to his people as emperor, so no one from least to greatest sees him as a man. Can you see that man? Can you help him to live? I will not give you an order, because friends, sisters don't order each other. I ask you, and whatever you say, I will accept."

Magpie leaned against the emperor. "I am so afraid. Can you hear my heart beating?" She put her hand on his chest. "See, yours beats too. I can promise nothing, I have nothing to give but this. I am willing to hear your name and keep it in my heart."

"For the sake of your mistress?" He pushed her upright so he could see her face.

"Yes, but for your sake, because you asked instead of taking. If the emperor of all Anca can bring himself to see me as worthy of asking, how can I not see him as worthy of being seen in turn?"

"The rest of you may leave. I will call for you tomorrow."

Lord Allin bowed and led Jequilane out the door. As they walked back along the hall, Jequilane wiped tears from her eyes. "It is like a story."

"I hope so."

***

The big man stirred on the ground in front of Robin. She heaved a sigh of relief.

He sat up and felt his head.

"Why din'ja kill me?" He asked.

"You aren't an enemy." Robin didn't move. "The land didn't want you dead."

The big man stood unsteadily but didn't fall again.

"What is your name?"

"They calls me Ham."

"Ham, you may return to your position. No need for you to be here as well."

"I will stand wit' ye." He clenched his fists and widened his stance. "Jus' feels right."

"Welcome then, Ham, it will be a pleasure to have company. My name is Robin."

Marshall raved at his troops.

"I have orders." He waved a paper in his hand.

"Ham, I'd like to see that paper."

"Yes, Lady Robin." Ham lumbered over to where Marshal ranted with his back to them and snatched the paper from his hand. "I be borrowin' this for the Lady."

Marshal drew his sword and swung at Ham, but the blade bounced off his armour. Ham gave the paper to Robin. Then turned to glare at Marshal, who stood, sword in hand, just out of reach.

The paper had the duke's wax seal on it, but it didn't feel right. She held it up to look at it closer and other writing appeared. The surface of the paper was smoother than it should be. The bit of paper with Sir Kenly's seal was the same.

"Why would the duke be reusing paper? This is the lord duke's signature."

"Of *course,* it is his signature." Marshal sneered at her. "Do you believe me now?"

"It has a date from three days ago. The handwriting doesn't look much like the signature."

"His secretary wrote it, and he signed it. You really think the duke writes his own letters?"

"The lord duke left Fhayden on a diplomatic mission to the empire a week or more ago," Robin said. "Sir James is in charge as the heir."

"Lord Paalip gave it to me in person." Marshal drew himself up.

"I figured that, since this letter was addressed to him before it was sanded and written over." She crumpled the paper and tossed it aside. "More to the point, Lord Paalip fled Fhayden as a traitor after setting empire assassins loose in the palace. Didn't you think it strange that you were given these orders, not Sir Kenly who is camped between here and the city? I'm willing to give you the benefit of the doubt and assume you are foolish enough to believe this forgery, not hungering for glory to match that braid, no matter the price."

She walked forward to address the army.

"I regret this, it is not your fault. If you stand down immediately, I will take no more action against you."

"Those are my troops." Marshal launched himself at her, sword ready to slash at her throat. Robin drew her sword and stepped back, bringing her blade around in a cut that made the air scream. It bit through his wrist. He stared at the bleeding stump in disbelief.

"The silk gloves do look good, but they don't do much to protect you." Robin wiped her sword with a cloth and inspected it before sheathing it. Marshal fell to the ground whimpering. She opened her satchel and bandaged up his stump.

"Why?" Marshal croaked.

"Why did I cut your hand off or why am I saving you?" Robin shrugged. "The answer is the same. Better to prune a tree than cut it down."

She stood up to see the army still watching her.

"Lady Robin, what are your orders? I am Dalvid, commander of a Hundred."

"What of your knight commander?"

"He fell sick and is at the eastern fort. So, your orders, my lady."

"Orders?" She looked around at the gathered army, all staring at her. "Okay, I guess. Two Hundreds will stay here. The others will do a sweep of the border; one to the mountains, the other to the sea. When they get back, I will decide what's next. Under no circumstances are you to cross the border, not even shoot arrows over the border. If there are empire soldiers in Fhayden, eliminate them."

"What if they surrender?"

"Carve an 'x' on their right arm and send them home. Anyone with a marked arm returns, you kill them as an oath breaker."

"What Hundreds do you want to go where?"

"I gave you my orders. The rest is up to you. You are the commanders. One of the Hundred that stays here can guard Marshal."

"Ham."

"Yes, Lady Robin." Ham loomed over her, but he looked uncertain. "I need to meet with the marshal's staff. Set it up, then get people watching the road. First sign of movement, you come get me. I don't care if I'm asleep or naked in the bath."

"Uh, yes, Lady Robin."

Everyone was moving purposefully, except for Robin. She picked up the crumpled paper to put in her satchel, then went looking for something to eat.

CHAPTER 18

The officious slave led Lord Allin and Jequilane through a maze of corridors. The man had his nose so far in the air it was a wonder he could see where he was going. Lord Allin had servants like that too, people who felt their lives were too large to fit in the small role they played. He knew nobles too, so it wasn't a matter of station, but attitude.

Jequilane clung to Nan, as if missing Magpie meant her whole world was upset. Perhaps it was; they had been together most of their lives.

Their guide opened a door and let them into a long room. The emperor sat on a throne at the far end. Magpie sat at his feet. Today the emperor wore a robe woven in intricate patterns, the ruby hung on his chest. He touched Magpie and she jumped to her feet to run to Jequilane. They hugged tightly and both had eyes glistening with unshed tears. Lord Allin left them to their reunion and continued forward to the throne.

"My lord emperor," Lord Allin bowed deeply. Gasps and murmurs ran through the room, the first Lord Allin knew that other people were present.

"Lord Duke Allin, welcome brother." The emperor nodded his head and winked at Lord Allin. The gasps and mutters were louder this time.

"Lord Emperor, we are at war with this duke." A person in gold-plated armour knelt to address their ruler.

"I am well aware, General. I signed the papers authorizing the invasion." The emperor lifted his hand. "But being at war is no excuse for being rude."

The general moved back without standing.

"General, please bring a chair for my brother. It is unseemly to keep him standing. He is near my equal in his own country."

The intricate helmet the General wore didn't let Lord Allin see their expression, but the sound of grinding teeth was unmistakable. Something was off here. Lord Allin's spine shivered. What he didn't know could kill them.

"I bring greetings from Fhayden." Lord Allin bowed again, then sat in the chair the general placed behind him, half expecting a knife in the cushions. "Must begin with an apology. I was bringing a gift for you, but it was stolen. Their master tried to recover it but was too late. The thieves were appropriately punished.

"Are you a spy?" The General rasped.

"I would be a very poor spy," Lord Allin's lips quirked, "to start by telling you I was such."

"Since you are here, I'm guessing their master was a wise man." The emperor tilted his head.

"He is, indeed, Lord Emperor. He sent a letter to you. The Marques Povost is Lady Jequilane's father." Duke Allin took the letter from his sleeve and held it out. A young boy in a plain tunic came and fetched it. He broke the seal and held it for the emperor to read, so the emperor never touched the paper.

"I see, Marques Povost has explained and admitted his negligence in allowing his own people to treat my guest in such a manner. He is offering his life and all his goods in atonement asking only that his daughter be spared." The emperor nodded at the boy, and he stepped over to a brazier and dropped the paper onto the coals. "Scribe."

A young girl ran over to kneel at his feet.

"This is what you will write. 'I, the emperor of Anca, have no need of the marques's life or his goods. I do need honest men who speak the truth without fear. I thank him for his aid to my brother. I will not insult him by offering gold, but he may keep this letter and bring it to me if he ever needs a boon from me.' When you are done, bring it back that I may put my seal on it."

The girl bowed to the floor then crawled backwards before jumping to run to a corner where she pulled out a piece of paper and set to writing.

"Brother, I am disappointed not to be able to honour your gift by receiving it. Will you tell me what it is you brought?"

"Certainly, Lord Emperor," Lord Allin breathed a sigh of relief for the marques. "I had four wagons of the best of the food and wine our country produces. One wagon of wheat for flour, one of such vegetables could make the journey, another of fruit preserved in wine or candied. Lastly, a wagon of dried and smoked meat as well as different cheeses."

The growl of upset that swept through the room made Lord Allin's skin crawl.

"And why would Fhayden think such a gift would be welcome?" The emperor looked at Lord Allin with fear in his eyes.

"My lord emperor, it is well known that your wealth is immense. What does someone who has gold coins like grains of sand need with more gold? It would be like gifting you a bag of sand. The wealth of Fhayden is the food we grow. So rather than trying to compete with your glory, we offer our humble work. I swear that I will send to my home to replace the gift down to the last grain of wheat."

"General." The Emperor slammed his fist on the arm of his chair. "You will take a hundred of your best men and escort Fhayden's gift to me. Scribe." A young man ran to kneel before the emperor. "Listen to my brother's will and write his words."

The young man moved to kneel beside Lord Allin. He didn't move as Lord Allin instructed his son to send four wagons and listed the contents of each. When the list was done, the young man ran to the corner and began writing furiously. The young woman returned to the emperor's side and held up the letter for him to read. He nodded once, then removed the ruby from his neck and touched it to the paper. The young woman, without looking at it, folded the letter in such a complicated fashion, Lord Allin was sure he couldn't match it.

"General, you will deliver this letter to the marques, then proceed to Fhayden to give them this letter."

"May I remind the lord emperor that we are at war with these people. We have no need of their gifts for we will soon own their whole land."

"What is given is different from what is taken. You have my orders."

"And if they will not let us across their borders?"

"Talk to them under the flag of truce. Your life depends on this. Take no action to dishonour me."

"Yes, my lord emperor." The general took the letter from the young woman and backed away. "I will go make preparations."

The emperor flipped a hand in dismissal.

The general marched out. Lord Allin wouldn't want to be the next person to annoy him. The young man returned with a sheaf of pages, the young woman beside him holding an ink well and a pen. Lord Allin carefully reviewed the letter, then wrote a short message to James and signed it. As he handed the pen to the young woman, the scribe folded his letter in a different manner.

"See that the general gets this letter. Put it in their own hand." The scribes bowed their heads to the floor then left.

Jequilane came and knelt beside Lord Allin. Magpie went to sit at the emperor's feet. She wore the same plan tunic as the scribes and the boy, but hers shimmered in the light. A red mark peeked out from the collar of her tunic. The emperor put his hand on her head as if not aware he was doing it.

"Now, Lord Allin, what do you know of the fae?" The emperor leaned forward as if this was the first time he cared about the conversation. "I received a report from two soldiers who returned from Fhayden and were compelled to travel all the way here to give me a message from the fae."

"May I meet these soldiers?" Lord Allin kept his voice level. The marques had mentioned similar rumours.

The emperor snapped his fingers, and two men in empire uniforms came to kneel where both Lord Allin and the emperor could see their faces.

They told about their encounter with the fae. She was physically small but inhumanly fast and strong. She'd defeated two of the elite without taking a scratch. They saw her as something other than human, as she didn't talk so much as growl like an animal. The younger man held out his arm so Lord Allin could see it.

"I had resigned myself to death when their leader ordered the fae to heal me. Though I was only partly conscious, I recall how she held my arm, then cut away the flesh. I awoke to find a bandage on my arm and a sign written in blood on my forehead." The man looked caught between fear and awe.

"We had been tied to trees," the older man took up the tale, "but not unkindly. Even if they had put no ropes on us, we would not have fled. The fae would have caught and devoured us. Not more than a day later, I woke from something dropping on my face. I could see nothing in the dark of night. A voice told me to take a message to the emperor. It spoke in the old formal tongue I'd only heard in the temples. The message was two words. 'Consider carefully.'"

"What did this fae look like?" Lord Allin asked.

"She was small and fair, with raven black hair. She might have been a child but for the armour she wore and the weapons she carried. Her sword dated from the era of the end of our last war with the Fhayde. Signs in blood covered her face and in green along her arms. I swear her arms glowed as she healed my companion. We'd been given our freedom to carry a message. We travelled without rest to bring the words to our emperor."

The emperor waved them away.

"What do you think, Lord Allin?" The emperor stared at him hopefully.

"I know no one who has met a fae." Lord Allin tried to buy himself time to think. "But we have plenty of stories of them. With your permission I will tell you one." When the emperor nodded, Lord Allin settled himself to relate the story he used to tell his children at bedtime.

"A farmer's third son decided to travel the land. He didn't want to be a priest or a soldier, but he wouldn't stay home and take from his brothers' inheritance. Wandering through the forest, he came on a bear in a pit…" Lord Allin forgot he was speaking to the emperor and told the story with different voices as James and Kaitlit had loved. "…and so the fae pointed in a direction and told him to walk until he met a woman carrying a large bundle of sticks. What he did from there was up to him. He helped the woman carry her bundle to where she worked, an immense farm that stretched in all directions as far as he could see. He met the lord's daughter, and they fell in love and wed. Since the lord had no other children, the third son inherited the noble's estates and land."

"Do animals truly speak in Fhayden?" The emperor's head tilted.

"I have never heard one, but in all the tales of the fae, animals speak like humans."

"That is all you know, stories for children?" The emperor slouched in his chair, and Magpie took his hand.

"My lord emperor, stories for children are all we have left of the fae, but be assured they were a real people, their blood runs in our blood. No one knows where they vanished to, but they left an entire land empty. They were the ones who taught our ancestors to farm the land without damaging the land's ability to grow food. We still farm with those methods."

"Could they return?"

"I cannot say, Lord Emperor, but there are stories which speak of the fae returning in times of great calamity."

"Such as a war?" The emperor sat up straight again.

"There have been many wars since then, and they haven't returned. It would have to be something more dire yet." Lord Allin danced on the brink of the precipice. He'd heard stories of the master sergeant's squire, how people described her as looking fae, who defeated everyone in her training group in one day, then fought the chief knight of the kingdom to a draw. She'd also been assigned to a squad in Fhayden at the right time.

"I heard one other report." The emperor broke into his thoughts. "An elite soldier came to report to her commander. A scourge was destroying all the units in the north of Fhayden. The commander sent his best squad of destroyers to find the scourge and kill it. They found many bodies of empire soldiers cut down and left for the scavengers. They found a group dressed in green to blend into the trees, and who moved so silently the birds sang as they passed.

"At night they attacked the people in green. The one who reported was an archer. She was ordered to watch, then report to the commander whatever she saw. The mages have a cream that allows soldiers to see in the dark, not well, but enough to give them an advantage. There are risks, but they knew them and chose to use the cream.

"The archer shot at a small soldier who kept watch. Though it was black night, and the soldier didn't have the mage's cream, she dodged the arrow, then ran to attack." The emperor leaned on one elbow. "Would you run to the attack in the dark when you couldn't see?"

"I would not. I would try to hold my position to give my companions a chance to flee."

"That's what the archer thought as well, until she watched this small figure cut down one soldier after another as if she could see and they could not. Eight of the best elite soldiers, and this one tiny person killed them all. The archer swore one of our soldiers stabbed the person in the face past her helmet, yet she continued as if nothing had happened. As the last fell, the archer fled straight north to return to her commander. She reported, then when she'd finished, collapsed in front of him, dead they discovered, though she had not a wound on her."

"I had been to visit my king, then put together the wagons and left immediately. I got no reports of battles in the northern forest. My son James might know more, I left him in charge as the duke apparent."

"I would like to meet this fae." The emperor's eyes glowed with something Lord Allin couldn't name.

“It would be hard for me to track her down in the middle of a war, but I will try and extend your invitation to her.”

“Not you.” The emperor frowned. “I require you here.”

“Perhaps a letter to my son?” Lord Allin tried to keep his voice even, though he hadn’t truly expected to be allowed to return home.

“My lord emperor,” Jequilane bowed her head to the floor. “A helpless woman may be able to accomplish what a general cannot. I would be no threat to this fae, and I would be willing to carry your word to her or perish in the attempt.”

“Very well, you will go as my emissary.” The emperor took the ruby from around his neck. “Come, stretch out your hand.”

Jequilane moved close enough to touch the emperor and kept her head lowered as she offered her hand. Magpie took her hand and steadied it. Jequilane gasped as the ruby touched her but didn’t move.

The emperor clapped his hands. “Prepare Lady Jequilane to be my Voice. She must be dressed properly for the role.”

Women bustled over and guided Jequilane away.

“I will allow you to say your farewells before she leaves with the General.”

“You are gracious, Lord Emperor.”

“Go, refresh yourself. You and I will see them off before sunset.”

***

Someone banged on the canvas of Robin’s tent. From the light, it was after sunrise.

"My lady, the watch has seen dust to the north. The enemy comes."

"Thank you."

Robin looked at her gear. The brown uniform was worn and stained. Her mail was dull. Even the breast plate and back plate were scratched and dented.

"They are soldiers, they will have to deal with it."

CHAPTER 19

Hob spent the better part of a day ordering the overseers to bring archers and their weapons forward to the front of the line. Then shield men went ahead of the archers to protect them. They shot ordinary arrows to get the range before retreating.

Flaming arrows were harder than the stories suggested. Several bows were damaged, and a few archers burned. More were killed by bows on the walls that shot huge arrows that went through armour like paper.

"The defenders on the wall don't like being shot with flaming arrows, but they don't burn like straw either."

"I can imagine." His master peered at the wall. "What about the gates?"

"Fill a wagon with oil, push it against the gates, and light it. I will supervise it myself."

"No, put one of your best Browns on it. We need to talk about what happens after we get through the wall."

"From what I saw the town is entirely stone. We will be able to raid it for supplies."

"The enemy is not going to leave anything behind for us." His master frowned.

"It will still be a chance to celebrate a victory."

She shrugged and turned away. "Do as you wish." An arrow struck her back. Hob shouted for shields. They helped his master away to safety. Hob threw overseers out of a wagon, and they set her carefully on her front. The arrow had punched through the plate and into her back. Blood leaked from the hole.

"Master, what do I do?" Hob's chest tightened until he could hardly breathe.

"Get all the other officers here. Count how many soldiers you have left. You are this army's only hope."

"Browns to me." Hob bellowed and his loyal group gathered. "Go with the overseers through the entire army, all the way to the end. The master orders that all officers and overseers gather here to take her orders."

"Yes, Hob." They saluted.

"One more thing." Hob clenched his fist. "Execute any who refuse. That will be one less coward to eat our food."

"Are you sure?"

"The master ordered it."

The group swept through the crowd for overseers and sent them to stand where they would able to hear the master.

"Master, I must deal with the gate. I will return." He ordered two overseers to watch his master and get her anything she needed. "If she dies, I will kill you all."

Hob stomped through the crowd. They had no camp, no tents, barely any food or weapons. He was going to destroy the straw men and save his master.

The wagon with the oil had one barrel on it. People had been pillaging it. He'd deal with it later for his master.

"If you can hear me, come."

A crowd gathered around, used to Hob relaying his master's orders.

"We are going to push this wagon up against the gates, jam the wheels, then set it to burning. Ten people to push, ten to hold shields to protect them. The rest of you find all the wagons you can, break them apart and make ladders with the wood. Get every person you pass to help. We will need the ladders before night ends. Before you push the wagon, fill it with anything that'll burn, someone objects put them in the wagon too. You have one candle."

Hob returned to the master.

"I hear the activity. You've done well, Hob. Now send everyone out of earshot. We must discuss the next part of the battle."

Hob shooed everyone away and set the overseers to maintaining the circle around the wagon.

"Master, I have done as you asked."

"Lie down beside me. It will be easier to talk."

Hob lay down, his mouth going dry at being so close to her.

"Listen, do not interrupt. When I am done, I will give you one last order." The steel still chilled her voice, but it was fragile.

"All this time, you have led the army. You must continue. No one else can do what needs to be done. If they could, they would be here doing it. This whole farce is a way of getting rid of people who are dangerous to those who gather about the emperor. Not one of us so-called officers is worth the steel we wear."

"But…" Hob bit his tongue; she'd said no interrupting.

"I have never commanded an army, never seen battle. That arrow punched through my armour because it is cheap, an imitation for show. The wrong person fell in love with me, when I refused him, I was sent here to die. I saw you in action and decided at that moment you would command the army for me. Think, however often we talked about what to do, not once did I give you a command different from your plan. I'm sorry. I used you." She put her head down.

"Master, I…" Hob tried to organize the thoughts fighting in his head. His eyes leaked tears. "Master, I would have served you anyway. I will still serve you to my dying breath."

"You don't know how happy that makes me." She turned her head to face him. "My name is Darah. Here is my order. You will kiss me, then call me by my name. You are the only person in this mess worthy to speak it. Then you will take this army and do what you will with it. I am giving it to you. I don't expect to live, but it would be nice if you came by to speak to me when you aren't busy.

Hob blinked until he could see, then stretched his neck until he could brush his lips against hers.

"Darah."

She sighed and dropped her head. Hob couldn't see her move, nor hear her breathe.

"I am a peasant, I have no idea what love is, but I think what I feel is love. Thank you for being my master."

Hob climbed to his feet and wiped his face, then set it like stone.

Faint roaring came from the crack in the stone. A woman in brown staggered out, eyes wide.

"Hob, they are rioting. Some think there is food here; others flee an attack."

"Move this wagon to the side. Guard it with your life. Spread the word, clear a way for what's coming. You are warriors, do not be moved. Spears and shields, anyone who comes out of that devil's lair must keep going until they are at the front. It is their turn to fight and die."

He jumped down from the wagon and a group formed to move it aside, where the master would be safe. *Darah,* he spoke her name in his thoughts.

A wild crowd poured out of the crack, they screamed and fought with each other but avoided the spears until they packed the space between the opening in the rock and the wall. The straw men on the wall shot arrows in swarms, but the crowd kept coming climbing on the bodies of those in front of them until they could reach the top of the wall. Smoke rose from the other side of the wall, then the night was lit by flames that reached to the sky.

The roaring stopped, replaced by wailing and moaning.

***

Jequilane had been dressed like one of the emperor's wives, if they wore jewel-encrusted armour. Now she rode in an open coach surrounded by the general's hundred best men. When she'd parted from Lord Allin, she put the tiny bit of paper Magpie gave her into his hand. She'd done her part; now it was up to him.

She hoped he survived, he had been kind to her, but the hollowness in her chest kept her from looking back.

***

Lord Allin read the paper Jequilane had slipped him, then dropped it into the brazier. The emperor was asking for his help. Far from being the omnipotent ruler of Anca, he was a prisoner in his own palace watched night and day by people who would kill him if he rebelled. The war was his generals looking for power in hopes they could rule in the daylight.

"Lord Duke, the emperor calls for you." The obnoxious slave was back. From the glitter in his eyes, he was one of the watchers. Lord Allin followed the man to the throne room where his chair waited for him.

"My lord emperor," Lord Allin bowed in greeting. "Now that we have set our business in motion, shall we pass the time with stories? I know many from my land. The first is called The Magpie and the Ruby."

"As you wish." The emperor waved a hand and sprawled in his throne and closed his eyes. Magpie held his hand and caressed it.

"Once there was a magpie…"

***

Robin stood in the middle of the road in the empty land between the fort guarding the road into Fhayden and the almost identical fort guarding the road to the empire. She could see individuals on horses at the head of the army.

"You sure they'll stop for the white flag?" Ham sounded nervous.

"Nothing we can do if they don't."

The empire's army stopped a bowshot from Robin and Ham. A man dismounted and walked to Robin, his hands spread wide. She lifted her empty hands and kicked Ham to remind him to copy her.

"I didn't expect to be welcomed to Fhayden by such a beautiful young girl." The empire soldier took his helmet off and held it under his arm.

"Are you the general of the Anca army?" Robin asked.

The man laughed. "Far from it, the generals' lair is in the emperor's city. They won't leave it for such a small thing as a war."

"I am Robin Fastheart."

"Is that your army behind you?"

"Some of them."

"I am sub-Commander Helius with the third vanguard. I'm here because I'm disposable if you plan treachery." He gave her a genuine smile. "Usually we walk over such a small force, but in respect for the white flag, I've been sent to ask if you wish to surrender."

Robin laughed in turn. "I won't ask you to surrender; I have no need of your army. But don't think I am weak as I appear."

A horn blew behind her, and Helius's face changed as he looked over her shoulder. "Are they yours too?"

"Perhaps, or maybe I am theirs." Robin shrugged. "You would do well to listen and carry my message to your commander."

"And what message would that be?" Helius's eyes grew hard and calculating.

"If you are thinking of breaking the truce with that knife in your helmet, you will not survive."

"I should be afraid of you?" A sneer crept into his voice.

"Very much so." Robin caught his eyes and peered into their depths. "Here is my message. Whichever army crosses this border to attack the other shall be utterly destroyed and their country will fall."

"We have invaded before and yet, here I am."

"I was not there to give warning. Now that the warning has been given, doom hangs over you. Good day, sub-Commander Helius. The truce ends when I cross out of the empty land." She turned her back on him and walked toward Sir Kenly who waited for her beside his horse. Ham followed close behind.

"You seem to have a thing about standing in the way of armies." Sir Kenly stared down at her. "I was informed you had taken command of the Northern Thousand after defeating the marshal in a single blow."

"True enough, you may ask him yourself, though I warn you he does little but complain about life not being fair."

"If it bothers you, tell him to be quiet or gag him. I've thought about that more than once."

"Perhaps he has the right to complain. Life is not fair." Robin looked up at him. "I will give you the same message I gave the sub-Commander of the third vanguard. Whichever army crosses the border to attack will not only doom themselves but the country they fight for."

"You expect armies to turn around and go home on your word?" Sir Kenly let an edge slip into his voice.

"It would be nice, but I expect you will fight each other, and one or the other will cross the border and bring doom down on themselves. And in case you're thinking you can let them cross to our side, take the doom, then chase them home, you may not let a single soldier enter the empire."

"What is this doom? How do you know this?" Sir Kenly stopped to yell at her.

"I haven't the foggiest." Robin shrugged. "You've been warned."

"A squire should not be addressing the chief knight in such a manner."

"Didn't you hear? I am Robin Fastheart, Shield Maiden of the Realm. Your orders no longer touch me." She scrubbed at her face. "I'll let Ham take you to the marshal, please let your men know to send the Sergeant Master to me in the fort when he arrives." Robin walked away before the grief in her heart sent her to her knees.

***

Sarge walked into the hall of the fort followed by Lencely and Rud. Robin waited for him with three chairs set out. The biggest soldier Sarge had ever seen in either world placed a table set for tea.

"Master Sergeant, welcome." Robin's voice trembled.

"Did you make it in time?" Sarge waved the boys to their seats and sat in the chair.

"I did, just."

"Why don't you just tell me what you don't want to tell me and get it over with?" Sarge rapped the stone floor with his cane. "This one isn't nearly as nice as the other one. Couldn't tell you why though."

Robin laughed, and the darkness in her eyes retreated.

"I have just told Sir Kenly that I am a shield maiden of the realm. His orders don't touch me." Robin took in a shuddering breath. "I don't mean that I ignore them to do what I want. It's hard to explain. They become just words, and too often the wrong words. I cannot swear fealty to the king. If I can't do that, I can't ever become a knight. I must withdraw from being your squire."

"I understand." Sarge sat and watched her struggle with her tears. "Happens I know a master sergeant in need of a post. You think a shield maiden could use the help of a cantankerous old man?"

"You'd put yourself under my command?" Robin's eyes widened.

"I spent most of my life serving people younger than me, and you're better than any of them. I'm a sergeant. I don't give orders; I pass 'em along and make my officer look good." He pointed to the patch on his shirt. The king said I could pass my colours to my heir. You're the closest thing to an heir I've ever had. I don't think it was a mistake them putting my stripes on a shield." He stood and saluted her, his heart full of something he hadn't felt in decades. "I will wear your colours with pride."

Robin stared at him with her mouth open. She tried to say something several times, but words didn't come out.

"Lady, the tea's ready. Ye want me to pour for you?"

Robin's laugh echoed in the hall, and Sarge thought he could see it shine in the light.

"Yes, Ham, please pour. Master Sergeant, I am honoured to have you with me."

Lencely and Rud jumped to their feet and put hands over their hearts. "We want to join you too."

"Welcome, friends. We'll enjoy our tea, then we'd better get to work. It isn't long until the end of the world, and I will stop it or die trying."

CHAPTER 20

"Find anyone who is alive, set them on wagons if we have any left." Hob choked out the order. If he had a sword, he'd put it through his heart. *What have I done?"*

"Hob." One of the Browns, Willow, knelt at his feet. "We only got part way to the end of the army, when we heard the sound of battle. The army was fighting itself. There was nothing we could do, so we tried to get people to move to safety, but they panicked…"

"I understand, it was not your fault." Hob steeled his heart. "They were my orders; the blood is on my head. Put together ten Browns, however many you can find. Got back along the crack and help anyone who is injured. Take your spears and shield, half of you stay armed. I don't want the fighting to overflow. Healthy people help you or come here. Anyone looting the dead, kill on sight. If they are still fighting, block the path the best you can, and leave sentries. Do not get drawn into the fight."

"Hob." The woman stood, tears on her cheeks. She looked like she wanted to say something else, but she saluted and turned to jog through the press calling for Browns.

"Master what should we do?" A man Hob didn't know stood wringing his hands.

"Hold on." Hob jumped on the wagon with Darah's body. "One brown to me." Someone in the crowd waved and headed his way.

Hob stayed on the wagon. The brown arrived, one of the first ones.

"Willow is organizing a search for survivors. You're going to pick people you can trust. Use some cloth to make arm bands. You will search for food and supplies. Bring it all to one place, but not here. Set a guard. Let Willow know about the arm bands. Anyone without one looting is to be killed on the spot. If someone you don't know is wearing an arm band, I leave it up to your judgement." He pointed to the man. "He's your first helper."

Through the night they worked by the macabre light of the burning town. When the fire began dying, Hob had people make torches and light the rescue work. Some overseers had thrown down their whips and were helping; others stood sullenly in a circle. Hob forced his way through the crowd to them.

"I don't have time to deal with you." Hob crossed his arms. "You have a choice: drop your whips and help or leave. I'd kill you, but there has been enough death tonight."

One of the overseers swung their whip at Hob. He ignored the lash and put all his grief and anger into a punch to the man's throat. The overseer dropped like a stone. The others dropped their whips.

"You are no longer overseers. You don't work for the officers. You don't work for the empire. You work for me, and I will not allow whips and blows to enforce my orders."

"We are your slaves," the overseers swore as they knelt.

"No, you are not my slaves." Hob had to restrain himself from kicking them. "There are no slaves here, no overseers, no officers, no nobles. We all work together, or we die."

The overseers stood and looked down.

"We don't know how," one said.

"You will learn." Hob pointed at him. "Treat everyone as your equal, not a master to be grovelled to, nor a slave to beat. I'm putting you in charge of the dead. We need the path through the crack cleared the best you can. Put bodies in any widened area but leave space for no less than three to walk through. If others will help, let them."

The overseers bowed and huddled to talk. Hob left them to it.

As the sky lightened, order returned to Hob's army. Men and women tended the best they could to the wounded. The report from Willow said that the far end of the camp was deserted. She had her crew salvaging what they could.

"Hob." One of the overseers came to him. "The overseers have a suggestion."

"Very well." Hob nodded.

"At the place where the path climbs up to the pass, the crack continues, we don't know how far, but it would be a place for the dead." He hung his head. "It isn't an honourable burial, but…"

"It is a good thought, and the dead don't care about honour. Get some rest, then find people to help you. Start at the far end and work this way. If you need anything, ask a brown."

Hob's strength was at an end. He crawled on the wagon beside Darah and lay down.

"I'm doing my best, Darah, but it is so hard. So much death and pain." He closed his eyes and rested.

He woke less tired but no less heavy with grief. His master had asked him to save the army.

"Hob." Ospen, one of the Browns, handed him a bowl of gruel. "We've started on your orders, but it will take days at least. Food is the biggest problem." She pointed at his bowl. "That's the last of it. We've fed everyone the same."

"Very good." Hob cleaned out the bowl and handed it back. "Work in shifts. Everyone needs rest as well as food."

"I've been guarding your sleep." Ospen stretched. "We know what needs to be done now."

"And it is my job to decide what comes next." Hob stretched and looked toward the wall. "I need a spear and rope, heavy enough to hold my weight, and the biggest piece of white cloth you can find me."

***

Hob stood on the wall. It looked strange with no straw men working. He peered back at his army. Someone waved, and he waved back. Over the other side of the wall, the fire had burned out, but the smoke was thick, making him cough. Someone watched from the other wall. Hob unrolled the white cloth and waved it until the person waved back and ran off. Another took their place. Hob tore a strip from the cloth and wound it around his face, then draped the rest over his back.

As he'd expected, the stairs were blocked. He put the spear through one of the spaces in the wall looking over his people, doubled checked the knot then tossed the rope over the other side of the wall. It was a scramble to get over the side, but once he'd made it, he could hold onto the rope as the straw man had shown him and slide down. His hands burned when he reached the bottom.

Hob started toward the other wall. The smoke filled his lungs making him cough, but all he needed was to survive long enough to talk to the straw men.

Men appeared out of the smoke.

"We're here to guide you."

Hob nodded; he couldn't speak without coughing.

They arrived at the other wall, the gate already open. A man came up to him.

"Hold still." He drew signs in the air and muttered under his breath, and suddenly Hob could take air into his lungs again. "You're lucky," the man said, "another quarter candle and you would be dead."

"Thanks. I must speak to Lord Huddroc."

"He is waiting for you." Someone who looked like a younger version of the lord stepped forward. "I will take you."

They walked through tents set up on green grass. Hob looked around; he'd forgotten what it was like to see anything other than rock. His guide pulled aside one corner of a tent. Hob ducked inside followed by the younger Lord.

Lord Huddroc waved him over.

"Have some food and water."

"No." Hob knelt on the grass and bowed his face to the ground. "I cannot eat while my people hunger, or drink while they are thirsty."

"Hob, stand up." Lord Huddroc put his hand on Hob's shoulder. "Say what you came to say."

Hob clambered to his feet.

"I surrender. You can use me as you wish. There will be dead on your side of the wall. But please." Pain ran through Hob and he fell to his knees. "Please save my people. I can't do it by myself."

Lord Huddroc nodded at the young man, and he left the tent already shouting orders.

"Come sit down and we'll talk." Lord Huddroc helped Hob into a chair. He dampened a cloth and wipe the soot and ash from Hob's face.

"We will help." Lord Huddroc said. "My son is already organizing a rescue effort. We were going to try to make it through to the wall to parley, but you beat us to it."

"Of course, you have people watching us."

"We do, and every single one who reported begged us to do something to help."

"What do you need from me?" Hob put his hands forward. "My life is yours."

"Very well," Lord Huddroc stood, "the first thing is to get you ready to help your people. You'll need to convince them we aren't the enemy."

"Yes, my lord."

A young man brought in a new brown uniform for Hob.

"This is your symbol of command, correct?"

"Yes, but…"

Lord Huddroc smiled. "I understand your confusion, but when an army surrenders the commanding officer is responsible for keeping it peaceful."

Hob changed into the new clothes, then transferred the arm band from the old to the new.

"We're ready, Father. The men are waiting at the gate. We have ropes and ladders." The son was back.

They walked quickly back through the gate and the burnt-out town. At the open space, wagons waited. Men and women with red arm bands and white coats stood by one.

"We will need to clear the gate on the other side." Hob's breath caught.

"Stairs are clear, no one's been on top." A man in brown reported.

"This is your part, Hob. Explain what is happening. We can't have any more deaths."

Hob climbed the steps, then stood in one of the openings.

"My people," his shout echoed in the space. "Hear my voice."

One by one people stopped to look up.

"The people who ordered this attack, they didn't want us to win, just to die. The people on this side of the wall are not our enemy. They did not send us to die. I have given my life to their lord. In return, he has help, food, what we need."

The people listening cheered. Hob put his hands up.

"Lay down your weapons, lay down your anger. If one of these people is harmed, my life is forfeit. There will be a time to pick up those weapons, to pick up that anger, and we will carry them to the people who are our true enemy."

The roar that came back in return echoed until Hob thought he stood in the mouth of a roaring dragon. When it subsided, he held up his hands again.

"The first task is to clear the gate. I know you've worked hard all night with little food and less rest, but the wounded need us to work again."

The overseers were the first to move, picking up bodies and carrying them aside. Others joined in until there was a space to the gate and room for the huge doors to open.

"The gate is clear!" Hob yelled down, then ran down the stairs. "I will walk ahead. I am your shield."

***

Robin stood on the road again, Ham, Sarge and the pages with her. She held a white flag.

Sub-Commander Helius appeared, followed by an older man and three others.

"Here we are again." Helius had put his pleasant face back on.

"Indeed." Robin didn't smile in return. "Did you give my message to your commander?"

"He did." The older man stepped forward and glared at her. "I have no reason to believe you."

"I don't expect you to," Robin said. "The Fhayden commander doesn't either. But it is my job to warn you."

"You're not the commander?"

"No, now that Sir Kenly is here, someone else will command. This the extend of my army now."

"We could destroy you now and get on with conquering your country." Helius sneered and put his hand on his swordbelt.

"Wait." The commander held up his hand and stared at her for several breaths. "Okay, Helius is so eager to draw his sword we'll allow it. Each of us sends a runner back to their army to say it's not treachery. When they return, you can have at it." He pointed at one of the men, and they took off running.

"Rud," Robin said. "If you would. Now, what are the rules?"

"Rules? This is war. It's over when one of us is dead." Helius sneer.

"Foolish, but if that is what you want." Robin shrugged. "I will send flowers for your grave. Is there one you fancy?"

"Nightshade."

Rud returned carrying Robin's sword and helmet.

She put the helmet on and set the sword on her hip.

The empire soldier returned puffing hard and handed a sword to Helius.

"Ham, Sarge, move back please with the boys. I don't want you getting hurt."

"How kind." Helius smiled.

"The winner allows the other party to return to their side unmolested."

"Agreed." The commander said and waved his people back.

"Any last words?" Helius grinned at her.

"I prefer daisies." Robin drew her sword and saluted.

Helius dropped his visor as he ran to attack, she side-stepped him without moving her sword.

"Quick." He tried another attack, this time she brushed the lunge aside. For an eighth of a candle, she defended.

"What's the problem, girl, never drawn blood before?"

"You're not bad," Robin said, "but you're more used to a stab in the back or having people's fear of who you are to weaken them."

Helius snarled and jumped to the attack again. At the last second, he pointed his left hand at her. Robin moved her head aside and the tiny dart stuck in her cheek instead of an eye. He leered at her then cut at her face. Robin pushed it aside and stepped back.

"I knew you for an assassin, you move like them, and your poison has the same odour."

"If you think you can last against the poison, let's see how long." He came on the attack again, but Robin defended easily.

"If you're waiting for your poison to work, I've faced it before. I came prepared for it. I think this has gone on long enough." Robin changed her stance. "I'm late for lunch." She plucked the dart from her cheek and tossed it at him. He batted it aside with his sword. Robin timed her lunge with his motion. Her sword caught his visor, and she flipped his helmet off his head, then used the knife she'd drawn with her left hand to stab through his cheek into his spine.

He collapsed like a rag doll, only his eyes held any life. Robin bent down and drew a sign on his forehead. "It will ease your passing." She turned and walked back to Fhayden.

***

In the morning, Rud woke her. "Fellow's out there with a white flag. He's carrying his sword, so you'll need yours."

"Thank you, Rud."

She walked out to meet the man in a grimy empire uniform. He leered at her.

"I'm going to kill you, then take..."

Robin darted forward, and he punched with his buckler. She caught it and swung on his arm. As he leaned forward, his sword jammed in the road. Robin jumped on his back and cut his throat.

"If you're going to wake me up early, you could at least be polite."

An arrow came from her left, and she swatted it with her buckler. The archer knelt away down the field, already drawing his second shot. She dodged it easily and jogged toward him. To give him credit, he nocked his third arrow and sent it at her. Robin slapped it aside and picked up her speed. His seventh arrow came at her face from only a few paces away. She expected it, and it shattered on her sword which she thrust through his left arm even as he reached for another arrow. A creak sounded to her right. She snatched the bow and a few of his arrows as she turned. This bow was much heavier than she was used to. She clenched her teeth and aimed her nocked arrow at a bowman who aimed at her. He flinched, and his arrow flew past her right shoulder. Crouched and ready for any other attacks, Robin scanned the line. The soldiers had their hands up.

The archer sat on the ground, her sword still through his arm. Robin went over to him.

"Do you wish to live or die?"

"L-live" he stammered.

"Finally, someone with sense. Hold still." Robin cut the sleeve away, then pulled the sword out. He shouted but didn't faint. She wrapped the cloth around the wound, then used his blood to draw a sigil. "It will heal without festering."

"Keep the bow." The man said. "You won it fair."

"Thank you then." Robin pointed to the wide-eyed army. "Help him to the surgeon." She picked up the bow and a few arrows then headed back to Fhayden, carrying her sword in the other hand.

"What the blazes are you playing at?" Sarge leaned on Lencely and Rud. "You're going to get yourself killed."

"If they want to die, doesn't being killed by a 'little girl' decrease their morale?"

"And if you die?"

"Everyone dies someday." Robin suddenly felt very tired.

"That may be true, but that doesn't mean to be spitting death in the face! You're our commander, you need to think about what that means." Sarge walked away.

"Having fun?" Sir Kenly glared at her coldly.

"It is not meant for fun, sir."

"That's what it looks like to the army, and you're teaching all your moves to the enemy. You aren't the only one who can read a pattern."

Robin looked at him. "I will think carefully on your words."

She walked through the ranks, men and women pulling away from her. On the back line of the army, Ham waved to her.

"Lady, let me walk with you. I won't bother you."

"Thank you, Ham." They walked into the forest, and Robin suddenly relaxed as if she'd been holding her breath all this time. She sat with her back to a tree and closed her eyes. For the first time in ages, she did the breathing Sarge had taught her. She'd given up on the sit-ups and push-ups too.

What am I doing? Sure, she was a shield maiden, but that didn't mean she was alone. Sarge, Ham and the boys counted on her. She wasn't under Sir Kenly's orders, but was she acting any better than Marshal with her antics? It would be a courtesy to talk to him.

Robin dropped her head on her knees. She wanted to weep.

Then weep and get it over with, then move forward. Gris's voice sounded in her head. Gris would have slapped her silly. Every time Robin jumped into the thick of things she got yelled at. If she got wounded or died, she'd weaken the squad. "Thank you, Gris." Robin held the amulet.

Angry voices sounded around her and then muffled thuds. Ham was taking care of it. Robin let the land sink into her soul. *I've work to do.*

Robin stood and dusted off her hands. "Thank you, Ham. If you would, bring Sarge and the pages here. I'd like to set up a camp in the forest."

"Yes, Lady. You going to be all right?" He dabbed at her face with a kerchief.

"I will, but I have to repair some bridges." Robin hugged him, then headed toward Sir Kenly.

"Sir Kenly," Robin said when he'd finished handing out orders. "As I told you, as a shield maiden, I must take orders only from the land. However, that shouldn't stop me from asking advice." She knelt. "I am sorry for my behaviour. In the future, I will discuss my actions with you first."

"It is easy to forget how young you are." Sir Kenly offered his hand and lifted her to her feet. "Life has laid a heavy burden on your shoulders. Don't try to carry it alone."

"Thank you." Robin bowed.

"As for advice, my first is that you attend the marshal's meetings, before breakfast and after supper. There are men from the sweeps you sent out wanting to report to their commander."

"I thought once you'd got here, you'd taken command back."

"Did you ask?" Sir Kenly put his hand on her shoulder. "A knight must, above all things, be aware of the needs of the people around them."

"I will never be a knight." The words sent a pang through her heart.

"Nonsense." Sir Kenly gave her a shake. "Being a knight isn't about the name. It's how you see the world. A shield maiden should have all the character of a knight and more."

"You're right." Robin shook herself. "I've been thinking I could die any day, so do what I can, but I should be thinking I could be a knight every day."

"Get at it then. I will see you at the commanders meeting. I'll send a page to collect you."

"I'm moving out of my room at the fort. We're setting up a tent in the forest. I need trees, not stone. We'll post the banner of the Northern Thousand so you can find us."

"Very good, carry on, Lady Robin. Bring your sergeant to the meeting if you can."

Taking the words as dismissal, Robin spun and ran back to where she'd asked Ham to set up. They weren't there yet. Suddenly a group of men stepped into the clearing.

"There you are, without that giant to protect you." The speaker stepped forward. "I'll not take orders from a little girl hardly out of diapers who leaves her unit out to hang in the wind."

"I wouldn't either." Robin leaned until she was almost nose to nose with the man. "What makes you think that a commander acting like a fool is an excuse for you to do the same? I need people like you to help me by telling me when I'm being stupid. I'm appointing you. The first thing you're going to do is gather the commanders of the Hundreds who are in camp. I want to meet with them here in a candle." Robin stepped back. "What's your name?"

"Temajim, lady."

"Thank you, Temajim. I will let it be known I've made you a sergeant."

"What the hell is a sergeant?"

"You've got a good start on it. Dismissed, Sergeant Temajim."

"Yes, lady." Temajim saluted with his hand over his heart. He gathered the other men with a tilt of his head.

"Robin." The master sergeant stood behind her leaning on his cane. "I see you have your head on straight now."

"I hope so, I'm working on keeping it that way."

"I like the looks of that man Temajim. You made a good choice with that one."

"I'm counting on you to help him." Robin hugged Sarge. "Thank you for being my master sergeant."

***

"Commanders," Robin stood in front of a semi-circle of frowning men and women. "I have been made aware that my command of the Thousand has been appalling. I can't blame you for being angry. It stops here. I have no idea how to be a marshal, yet Sir Kenly sees fit to leave you in my care. The only thing to do is ask you to train me to command the way you need. I expect honesty. Each evening you will speak to Sergeant Temajim here and let him know how I did that day. As the other Commanders arrive back, ask them to see me. Questions?"

"What kind of things do you expect to report on?" a woman asked.

"Sorry, name?"

"Betrice, lady."

"Commander Betrice, I expect you to comment on anything that will affect the life and morale of your soldiers."

"My lady." Betrice saluted and the others followed. "The soldiers would appreciate it if you stopped by the camp."

"I will do that after the marshal's meeting. Sergeant Temajim will guide me."

"Just what is a sergeant? Commander Franc -"

"Commander Franc, my sergeants will be a liaison between me and the people I command. They will be approachable, experienced, and they will take my, or your, commands and implement them with the soldiers."

"You plan on appointing more sergeants?"

"As I need to. If you have people who would be good in the position, give their names to me."

The commanders dispersed, and Sarge stepped from where he'd been listening. "Not bad, lass, not bad at all. No one likes a commander who makes excuses."

"Thank you, Master Sergeant." Robin smiled at him. "I am going to suggest that Lencely and Rud accompany you to strategy meetings. If you are too tired, send a message and I'd make do. I'm bringing Sergeant Temajim as my aide."

"What are you going to call Ham? He's not sergeant material."

"I'm not sure. Do you have any suggestions?"

"I'll think on it. Don't be overworking yourself."

"You neither. We call each other on pushing too hard."

"Deal." Sarge smiled.

CHAPTER 21

Lord Allin rubbed his eyes. He'd been telling stories all day, and his throat was sore. The captain and her guards remained close around him.

"I will go into the city for a while. I need a break from this place."

Two of the guard stepped forward, and Lord Allin nodded to them.

He meandered through the evening market with no goal in mind. The next day he did the same thing. On the third evening, a woman accosted him.

"You are the storyteller. I must buy you a cup of honeyed wine." She led him to a nook and ordered the drink. He picked his up and took the tiniest of sips. The honey almost covered the bitterness of the poison.

"Which of the emperor's wives are you?" Lord Allin put his cup in front of her. "Each time you lie, you will take a drink. The alternative is I have my men carry this back to the palace and ask the emperor why his wives are out to poison his storyteller."

The woman didn't move from her seat but reached for the wine. "And if the wine were to be spilled in the dust?"

"My men have already taken your man into custody."

She withdrew her hand.

"I am the emperor's third wife. I'm from the land farthest to the north. My people are being over-run, and he sends the legions south."

"Ah, what does the drug do?"

"It would allow me to plant a suggestion in your mind."

"Such as to slay the emperor?"

She nodded her head.

"How many of the wives are hostages?"

"All of us, though some choose not to believe it." She hung her head. "I've never seen him like he is with that slave of his."

"Jealous?"

"No… Yes." She sighed. "We women have our own battles trying to get close enough to influence the emperor. If one is successful, the others' lands will suffer."

"The emperor is as much a hostage as you." Lord Allin said. She stiffened but didn't move.

"Then all is lost."

"Not necessarily." Lord Allin tapped the cup. "We just need to change the direction of our plotting."

"I'm listening."

***

Hob knelt at Darah's grave. Lord Huddroc had her buried with honour. Hob's people were working with the people of Vilscape to rebuild. They sang as they worked. He'd never heard peasants sing, but they weren't peasants anymore. They'd named themselves the Free.

"Thought I'd find you here." Geoffroi stayed to the side so as not to cast a shadow on the grave. Hob stood and examined Geoffroi. He seemed like a good man.

"I'm curious, Hob." The woman with him was his intended, Jalliet. "What are you thinking when you stare at my betrothed?"

"I'm looking for signs of deceit. I've yet to find any. Sir Geoffroi is a good man."

"What do see in me?"

"You aren't happy here, but you put on an act for the people around you, because you know you belong here and so you're stuck."

Jalliet paled, then reddened. "I suppose I deserve that for asking the question."

"Lady Jalliet." Hob held up a hand. "I state what I see. It is not condemnation. You are strong and intend only good."

"What would you do if you were me?"

"I would start calling each other by your names." Hob bowed and left the couple alone. He was happy his people here were safe. Little more than one in five survived, but now they were free.

What would you have me do, Darah? People expected him to want revenge, but what would that do but pile up more bodies? Yet how else could he help his people still slaving under the whips of the overseers who were little more than slaves themselves?

Back at the hall he shared with the Browns, he slumped onto a bench. They'd been given new uniforms, a crest with a broken chain decorated each of them.

"You okay, Hob?" Willow sat beside him, like him, like Jalliet, she was caught in a prison of her own making.

"Just thinking."

"Still trying to think what your master would do?" She put a hand over his. "She'd look at you and say, 'what do you think?'"

"She would." Hob didn't move his hand like he normally did. "This is just another wall."

"Only you can't burn this one."

"I need to find the right kind of fire." His eyes widened.

"What?" Willow tightened her hand on his.

"I need to find the right kind of fire." He stood. "Assemble the Browns after supper."

"Yes, Hob."

***

He faced the assembled Browns, the people he was closest to, the people who would understand.

"I am going to leave the Free in your charge," Hob said as soon as the last entered. "I have other work I must do."

"Are you going alone?" Ospen asked.

"I can't take all of you with me. The Free need you. But I would be foolish to travel alone. I will let each of you decide. There is not a bigger task or a smaller one, just different. Bring me your answer tomorrow."

In the morning, the Browns lined up.

"We've decided." Willow stepped forward. "I and seven others will travel with you. Ospen has been chosen to lead the rest."

"Thank you," Hob bowed to them. "Willow, we need to speak to Lord Huddroc." They found him watching over the laying of the roof beams on a hall.

"Lord Huddroc, may we speak?"

"Of course." He led them to a quiet nook. "What do you wish to speak about?"

"I am leaving Ospen in charge. You have met him."

"Yes, a good man." Lord Huddroc peered at him. "You're too sensible to go after anything as foolish as revenge. I'm guessing you feel the needs of your people calling you."

"I do."

"Then whatever I may do, I will. I've already received permission to let the Free settled here with the people of Vilscape. My son, Vipal, has built a village on the other end of the pass. I will speak to Ospen about having some of the free give them a hand."

"I know nothing about travelling in the world."

"Duncan has been pestering Marshal Weston about being allowed to go with you. He has permission if you are willing."

"He is the one who climbed down to talk to me."

"That's him." Lord Huddroc smiled. "The marshal wasn't sure whether to praise him or punish."

"I know the feeling." Hob's lips curled up a bit. He was trying to smile more. Someday he might try laughing.

"Ah, there you are." Jalliet walked into the courtyard on Geoffroi's arm. "My lord, I know I have concerned you, but I took some advice and I hope to cease being a burden. Geoffroi and I have spoken about a date for our marriage. With the strife, few of the nobles will be able to come, so we thought making it a festival for everyone."

"A delightful idea, I will leave you and my Lady wife in charge."

Jalliet laughed and the sound made Hob shiver, she'd changed so much in a day.

"Still serious?" She winked at him.

"Lady Jalliet." Hob pointed to the band of cloth on his arm. "My master gave me this to remind me who I served. Darah would be happy to hear the Free sing. I would like to give my replacement something to guide him in his work."

"I have just the thing." Jalliet hugged Geoffroi's arms. "I will bring it when we come to see you off."

"You will want a ceremony of some kind to show the change in roles." Lord Huddroc rubbed his chin, "granting Ospen colours would be just the thing."

That afternoon, as many people as would fit lined the walls and the courtyard to watch them leave.

"My people." Hob stood on the wagon they'd be travelling with. "I am seeking an answer in the world. While

I am gone, Ospen will lead the Browns. Sing, laugh, and I will be stronger knowing the Free are happy."

Lady Jalliet walked over to Ospen.

"Hob has worn the colours of his master. Now as a symbol of our peace, I give Ospen the colours of Vilscape to wear."

The crowd roared their approval. Hob jumped down and walked over to Jalliet. He handed her Darah's band he'd worn for such a short time though it felt like years had passed. "Please put this on Darah's grave."

"I will, Hob."

Willow gave him a hand and hauled him up on the front of the wagon.

"Let's go."

***

Sir Garraik kept his mouth tight shut.

"Now that Vilscape is secure, we can bring reinforcements to Fhayden."

"Marshal Weston has sent a force to hold Kingstown. With Marshal Potter's Thousand and the King's Guard, we have fifteen hundred we can move."

"I am going with them." The king had no give in his face. They'd been arguing this since the army went west. Sir Garraik had lost the argument.

"Very well, sire."

"I have my plain plate. I will form a squad with my usual guard. As you have pointed out, wearing the fancy suit would be painting a target on my chest."

"Thank you, sire." Sir Garraik relaxed. "We leave before dawn.

***

A squad with one new recruit stomped onto a boat and found a corner.

"Rick, see if you can rustle up some water."

"Aye, Commander." The king jumped to his feet and repressed a grin. It would only work if they all played their roles. All the squires had come back from their tours with the Regulars changed. As if their feet were more solidly on the ground. The king, Rick, he reminded himself, hoped he would learn the same lessons. Maybe he'd see Robin there. All he knew was she'd gone south, collected the master sergeant and the pages then headed north again.

He found the line for the water barrel and put up with the teasing when he didn't have anything to carry the water in. They found him a bucket and warned him to bring it back. Water was heavier than he'd thought, but he got the bucket to his squad, then put up with another round of teasing.

They sailed to Fhayden. Sir Garraik went to report to Sir James as Rick and his squad marched north. He settled into his role as the one to take all the chump jobs. He'd never been just one person in the crowd. This is where everyone else started. He accepted his scratches and blisters as proof of his work.

The farther north they travelled the more Rick worried, not about his own safety, but that of the people around him.

***

The emperor's general pushed them harder the closer they got to the border. Jequilane no longer wished she could have ridden. Even the padded chair on her coach felt like stone with each jar of the wagon. He'd said they'd be there the next day. Her only comfort was the presence of Nan with the other servants.

"The one problem with being a general," he said riding beside her as he did when he wanted an excuse to hear his own voice, "is one doesn't get to be in the battle shedding blood."

The servants who'd been sent with her told her she had to be silent so as not to waste the emperor's words. Jequilane was soon glad of the need. It kept her from having to listen and reply to the horrible man.

She held in her heart what the emperor has asked of her. To find the fae and invite her north. The general never mentioned his duty to deliver Lord Allin's letter. When he wasn't talking about blood, he'd rant about the fae, licking his lips. As much as Jequilane wanted to succeed, she prayed the fae was far away from where they were going.

***

Robin sat with the marshals, mostly listening. They'd had a few skirmishes and learned the pikes worked the way the master sergeant said they would. One of Robin's Hundreds scoured the forest for trees to make replacement poles. The marshals from Caldera commanded the front line from one end to the other. The latest skirmish proved the weapons were just as effective on soldiers on foot.

"I have word reinforcements are coming from Caldera. They'll be here tomorrow." Sir Kenly waved a paper.

"They can hold back until we need them. It will give a nasty shock to the enemy," one marshal said.

"Are they pike men?" another asked. "We should bring them to the front to give our soldiers a break."

The argument went back and forth, opinion about evenly split.

"Lady Robin?" one of the older marshals asked. "What do you think?"

"The storm strikes tomorrow," Robin said. "Have the soldiers march as fast as they can without being exhausted to uselessness. When they arrive. they should have their weapons to hand and be dressed for battle." She shuddered. "The king is with them. I will have my Thousand form across the road. They'll split when the king arrives, and we'll support their flanks."

"Lady Robin?" Someone shook her and she started. The tent was empty, except for her, Temajim and Sir Kenly. "Drink." Sir Kenly put a goblet in her hand, and she drank it down. Herbs had been added to the water and they refreshed her.

"What happened?" Robin furrowed her brow. "Something about a storm." The words came back to her slowly.

"I've sent the orders as you said. The soldiers have been told it gets real tomorrow. They are resting except for the watch. If the king is in danger, should we arrange to protect him?

"The king is protected already. If we try to change it, we'll put him in danger. I will stand in the centre of my line and will be there when he needs me."

"I will leave him in your hands." Sir Kenly stepped back. "Get some sleep, Robin. That's advice." He smiled at her.

"I believe I will take your advice." Robin bowed and followed Temajim back to where her Thousand had gathered around her.

"Sergeant Temajim, please gather the commanders at my tent as soon as possible.

Sarge met her there.

"You okay, lass? You had the marshals more than a little upset with your speech."

"I don't think that was me talking." Robin sunk to the ground beside his chair. "If the land had a voice, that would be it."

"I thought as much. Sir Kenly's a sharp fellow, had them jumping before they could talk themselves into a corner. The Regulars will be ready."

"Thanks, Sarge." She leaned her head against the arm of his chair, and he put his hand on her head.

"All the battles going back to the fae have been over this border. What do you think is going on?

"If this land speaks through you, who will their land speak through?"

"You mean the lands are at war?"

"I think the lands made a truce, and the humans have been breaking it, at first because no one listened on their side, and then on our side."

"That makes sense of the warning. The lands are tired of war." Robin shifted as the sound of the gathering commanders sounded outside the tent. "Tomorrow, you will stay here while Lencely, Rud, and Ham guard you."

"Yes, my lady." Sarge nodded with a twinkle in his eyes. Robin hugged him, then went outside to give the orders for the morning.

***

The sky was grey when Robin woke.

"It's time." She jumped up and put her amour on. Lencely yawned as he helped her with the plate pieces.

"Be careful out there, Robin" He slapped her back after a final check, then went to crawl back into his bedroll.

Sergeant Temajim waited for her outside the tent.

"Ready, lady?"

"I am, thanks. I hope you got some sleep last night."

"Slept like a log. Set the young'uns to watch. They're disappointed to be out of the battle. Told them their watch let the rest of us sleep peaceful."

"Well done, sergeant,"

The camp buzzed with activity. The Thousand lined up in, each Hundred their own column of five across and twenty deep.

She walked out in front of them, Ham at her side.

"Ham, if you would let me stand on your shoulders. I want to feel like a giant this morning."

"Yes, lady." He grinned at her and lifted her like she was a toddler.

"Thousand of the North," Robin called out as Sarge had been teaching her, reinforcing her mother's lessons. Projecting not yelling, he called it. "You stand between victory and defeat today. You will feel left out, but the battle will come to you and you will stop it. When you least expect it, you'll hear a charge behind you. That will be your signal to split to either side. From there, I'm trusting you and your commanders. All of you know what needs to be done. All that is left is to make it happen." Robin jumped to the ground as the Thousand cheered.

"Go, Ham, you have your job to do."

"Yes, lady." He saluted and walked into the clearing.

They lined up across the gap between each forest, four deep. Robin took her place at the centre and they waited.

***

The third wife warned Lord Allin of the plot. With the general gone, others thought to profit from his absence. She'd placed people in key positions. They would use the attempt at a coup to free the emperor.

Lord Allin went into town as he had been accustomed to. In pairs and trios, his guard followed. No one paid attention, they were always polite and generous with their coin. The third wife's man was leading the assassins who were to kill Lord Allin so they could blame him later.

The street was busier than usual, probably half of the crowd were plotting for or against the coupe. Lord Allin sat at the wine bar and made his order. That was the signal. The assassins surged forward only to be met by a wave of people ready to stop them. The third wife had arranged for the seventh wife to learn of the assassination plot. Since the seventh wife was enamoured with Lord Allin's stories, it was easy to manipulate her into putting her own people in place. He slipped away in the chaos and walked toward the emperor's door. On the way, he flipped his cloak over and put a hat on.

No one disturbed him and he heard nothing on the way to the door. The captain waited for him.

"We got them all, but they took three with them. I'm disappointed. I thought they were supposed to be the best."

"What kept the emperor in line was their presence, not their skill."

She shrugged and the rest of her guard showed up. None looked like guards anymore. They'd left their heavy armour behind and wore mail under the clothes they had on.

"I will leave you then," the captain saluted. "The marques will be informed of these events."

"Tell him to be careful. It can only spread."

"I will, Lord Allin."

The door opened as she faded into the streets. The rumble from the fight grew louder.

"Ready." The emperor dropped his robe and put on the one Lord Allin's guard gave him. He pulled up the cowl to cover his face. Magpie put on a dress and tucked the hair she'd cut off into a bag.

"North then." The third wife stepped out the door already changed into a slave tunic. She handed the chain to the emperor. They slipped through the streets. The guards being loud and brash, people let them pass. The sky behind them had turned red.

When they turned back for a moment at the top of the hill to the north, the entire city was burning. The third wife shuddered, and the emperor put his arm around her. She looked at him in surprise.

Magpie took her other arm. "Thank you."

Guards switched outfits with the emperor, the third wife, and Magpie. They headed west to draw any pursuit who might have seen them at the door.

Lord Allin led the remaining guards and the others north. As they passed through the village in the night, the emperor dropped the ruby in the well.

"I am no longer the emperor. Call me Henry." He stood straighter as he spoke holding onto Magpie's hand. He offered his other arm to the third wife, and they walked away from the village.

CHAPTER 22

Rick checked the sword at his side yet again. No one laughed. They were doing the same thing. Orders had been a long march, four candles rest, then march again. With the tall trees on either side, they still marched through gloom.

"You stay behind us, Rick." The squad leader said. "No heroics."

"Yes." Rick concentrated on keeping time with the march. The north drew him as if a line on his chest was being pulled tight. He ignored the impulse to run and stayed with his squad.

***

Jequilane clutched at the chair thankful it was fastened securely to the open coach. The road was rougher, and the general was pushing the guard. All fifty of them had the same feral grin. Jequilane prayed the coach didn't overturn.

Up ahead, a line of black ran across the world. Soon she saw they were people, soldiers all looking the other way.

"Make way, make way." The general's voice thundered. The army ahead of them split to let the charging knights through. For a few seconds, she saw endless terrified faces. The other coaches had slowed to a stop, but her driver laughed like a madman and cracked his whip harder.

The fifty knights had formed into a wedge and broke into a gallop, shouting war cries and holding the lances they'd carried the whole way.

"Sorry, Father." Jequilane forced herself to keep her eyes open. She would not die a coward.

Another line blocked their path. It would be impossible for them to stop the knights. Then long spears lifted from the ground all along the line. The morning sun glinted off the steel points.

"Stop!" Jequilane screamed though she knew it was useless. The knights crashed into the line, and the spears stopped the first few knights, but the others rode over their enemy and companions alike. The wall of spears shattered as the general and his thirty remaining knights rode soldiers down.

The coach hit the pile of horses and men and flipped, launching Jequilane into the air.

***

"Hold!" Robin shouted. "We have to break their charge." She fired arrow after arrow, but even she couldn't hit the tiny slots in their visors. The other archers matched her speed, but the Ancan knights rode through the arrows like a spring rain.

Hands grabbed Robin's shoulder, and she was pulled back into the line as her soldiers lifted their own pikes. She was tossed unceremoniously out the back of the line as the knights crashed into the pikes.

"Squeeze." Someone shouted and the line compressed, doubling the number of pikes.

Robin drew her sword and knife and stood back on the sloping road ready to jump in to support her soldiers. The charging knights crashed into the pikes. The crash shook the ground, but the line held. The roar of battle grew as the Ancans advanced. Empire soldiers flooded through the break in the broken main pike wall, like blood from a wound.

"Hold the line!" commanders bellowed, and the soldiers pushed forward. The Ancan foot soldiers hit, making the line shudder along its length. The foot soldiers couldn't get past the pikes, but when they pushed forward the line couldn't hold against the mass of men. A knight in gold armour bellowed and set his horse into a charge, bowling through the line. They set their lance at Robin and charged.

From behind her, another roared sounded, and the knight's lance wavered. Robin ran forward on his right side and jumped on his lance like it was the branch of a tree. Then she leapt up, driving the point into the ground. The jar pushed the knight halfway out of his seat as he twisted to avoid the lance. He couldn't avoid Robin's boots as they hit solidly on his shoulders. The ground hit, and Robin rolled away, losing her grip on her sword. The knight pushed himself to his feet between her and the sword.

"Leave them, hit the line." The order came from behind her. Soldiers ran past on either side of her and the knight. He hefted his sword and shouted something rude, at least they were Ancan words she hadn't been taught as a trainee.

A hand shoved a spear at her. She grabbed it one-handed, sheathed her knife, and had barely enough time to brace herself. She didn't try to stop him but jabbed at his helmet. He snatched at the spear, but not fast enough. They circled each other. Robin kept her focus on him, her sword as good as lost.

Fight with the weapon you have. She let the memory of spear training flow into her. The first sight of Sarge had been when she held a spear. Strength flowed into her from the wood as if the tree it had been made from was supporting her.

He charged, trying to get inside her spear. Robin danced back, then poked at his head. For all the decoration, his armour was the best she'd seen. *Breathe.* Robin fell into the pattern of her breathing. as she'd expected he didn't have an easily read pattern. He was a bit like the elite soldiers, a bit like the assassin, but also something else she'd never seen. She kept her distance and waited for her chance, but he wasn't giving her any. He wasn't going to let her climb on his back either.

He has to think he's won. Working that without actually letting him win would be tough. The soldiers had all passed, pushing the Ancans back foot by foot.

The knight caught her spear and threw it to the side.

There. Robin's body moved before she could think, her left hand went back to get her knife as he charged exactly as Hal and Sir Garraik had. His sword caught her left arm and pinned it to the ground as he landed on her.

He flipped his visor open. "I'm going to enjoy this."

"Good." Robin slammed the knife in her right hand into his eye. To her horror, he didn't die but grabbed her throat, and even through the mail and gorget, she felt him cutting off her air. Then something clanged into his helmet and his hand loosened. He rolled off to the side and lay still.

"You were taking too long." Sergeant Temajim grinned at her as he offered his hand.

Her knife was jammed in the knight's skull, and her left arm was telling her it was done for the day. She picked up the knight's sword. "A bit on the showy side, but it's better than nothing. Sergeant, be my shield."

"Yes, lady."

She looked over the battle. A squad had been isolated and they fought desperately back-to-back.

"Get me over there." She pointed with the sword.

***

Rick tripped over a sword, picking it up as the squad leader hauled him to his feet. He hoped Robin could use the spear he shoved at her. A girl in gold amour stumbled through the battle.

"I don't know who she is, but she needs help."

"Not a good idea, Rick," his leader said.

"That's King Rick. I can't explain, but she's important."

"Yes, sire."

His guard formed a ring around him and pushed into the melee. The Fhayden soldiers made way as the leaders bellowed. Ancan soldiers who thought they'd broken through the line were knocked to the ground. His guard wielded their swords like battle hammers and forced their way to the girl. Rick pulled her into the circle, but they'd lost their momentum. His guard held back the Ancan soldiers while he stood beside her and stopped any thrusts that made it through. The girl bumped into him, so he held her up with his left arm.

"This isn't what the emperor wants." The girl said. She closed her eyes as the next words flowed from her like waves in the ocean, knocking the soldiers back. "STOP, IN THE EMPERORS' NAME."

They looked at her as if she'd just appeared in their midst, then dropped to their knees.

"Hold!" Rick shouted. The Fhayden army stepped back as the circle of kneeling Ancans widened.

"Return to Anca." The girl pointed north.

"Let them pass!" Rick shouted, and a loud voice behind him took up the order. The armies backed away from each other. The girl slumped so Rick picked her up. "Where's the surgeon's tent?"

"I'll guide you, sire." Robin grinned at him. She was covered with blood and dirt. She'd never looked better.

"I'd hug you, but…" Rick lifted the girl.

"Later then." Robin wound her way through the press until they arrived at a white tent. Moaning soldiers filled the space as surgeons moved to help as many as they could. "Put her on the bed over there. I've got work to do.

Much later, Sir Kenly came to where Rick kept watch over the girl. He'd learned her name was Jequilane. "A delegation from the Ancans is here."

"I have work to do." Rick brushed her hair off her face. "Rest here. You're safe. I will be back."

"I have a message for the lord duke's son."

"Okay, he's not here, but I will get you to him." He bowed to her. "Two of you stay with her."

"Yes, sire."

He followed Sir Kenly to where a group of Ancans stood with empty hands under a white flag.

"I am King Rick of Caldera." Rick looked at the Ancans who appeared more worried than angry. "What do you wish to talk about?"

"We understand you are holding the Emperor's Voice prisoner. We came to ask you to release her."

"I think I know who you mean; come with me. Sir Kenly, if you could arrange to bring her outside, maybe a chair for her."

"Yes, sire."

By the time Rick had led the Ancans to the surgeon's tent, Jequilane was installed like royalty, Sir Kenly and his two guards standing behind her at attention completed the effect. The Ancan delegation knelt at her feet.

"Voice, we need your help in our camp. We're in chaos."

"I have work to do here," Jequilane said, but she looked torn.

"How about we go for a walk and at least let your people see you?"

"I don't know that I can walk."

"We can carry you in the chair."

"No!" Jequilane held her hands up. "Anything but that." She pushed herself to her feet, and Rick caught her as she almost fell.

He put an arm around her waist and helped her along to the road and walked out in between the armies.

"People of Anca." Rick raised his hand. "We heard you were worried about the Emperor's Voice and wished to reassure you. She is safe and not a prisoner but must rest before she completes the task the emperor set her. Will you trust us with her? You may send four men to be an honour guard, but they may carry no weapons. If the Voice has attendants, they may come as well.

A soldier came out of the fort with a chair, and Rick helped her sit.

The Ancans knelt, and Rick held her hand as she wept.

***

"Where's the king? Sarge leaned on his cane as soldiers repaired the damage to the camp.

"Being kingly." Robin smiled. "I think he may be smitten with the girl."

"You're okay with that?"

"Of course." Robin rolled her eyes. "He's the king."

"And you aren't staying around, are you?"

"How do you know that?"

"You keep looking north." Sarge put his hand on her shoulder. "We will go with you."

"Thank you. It will be dangerous."

"And this wasn't?" Sarge waved his hand at the camp. "Rud thought to run and alert the soldiers left to watch their camp when he spotted the Ancans coming this way. Ham and Lencely held them off, then Rud led the charge to hit their rear. The Ancans folded."

"They did well."

"They did."

"Lady Robin, the king calls for you." The young soldier looked at her wide-eyed though he was probably older than her.

"Lead on," Robin said. "Master Sergeant, let Sergeant Temajim know where I am. He may join me if he thinks it necessary."

"Yes, lady." Sarge saluted her.

***

A group of weeping Ancans knelt at the girl's feet, and she looked overwhelmed.

"Sire." Robin saluted.

"I heard from Sir Kenly about the warning you gave both sides." Rick looked pale. "The Ancans just received a messenger. The Imperial city has burnt to the ground and the emperor is missing."

"I have to ask the fae for help." The girl whispered.

"Jequilane, I told you the fae are all gone." He put an arm around her shoulder.

"Not quite," Robin said. "They intermarried with the humans, so we are part fae."

"I've been hearing stories." Rick lifted an eyebrow. "Would you go north for me? I don't want to see the empire collapse into civil war."

"The empire is done." Robin shook her head.

"But could you help shape what comes next?" Jequilane took her hand.

"I happen to be going north. I will do what I can."

"When are you leaving?"

"First thing in the morning."

***

Robin looked at the column of soldiers behind her.

"I'm told you can't follow my orders, so I ordered your Thousand to follow you. I will not have you tramping around a country on the edge of civil war without someone to keep you safe. Besides, they have wagons of food. Travel under the white flag." The king scowled at her.

"Very well," Robin sighed. "It will be nice to have some company."

"From what you said, there is no problem with the doom unless they attack. Jequilane has given you her blessing, and you'll have some of the Ancans with you to help explain things."

"I feel you are right; the land is asking for my help. I don't think it will mind if I bring a few friends." Robin slapped her satchel. "I have your letter to your father Jequilane. I promise to deliver it."

"People of Fhayden, of Caldera, of Anca. Greet Lady Robin Fastheart, Shield Maiden and friend of the crown." Rick pinned something on her uniform, then saluted her.

She grinned and hugged him "I'll back for the wedding, sire." Robin said in his ear. Rick turned red. "Now I'm not the only one to look like a tomato. Take care of each other."

She walked over to the wagon and Ham hauled her up beside him.

"Let's get going before the king makes any more speeches."

"Yes, lady." Ham set the horse in motion. "I thought you'd get to rest after stopping the war."

"I wish." Robin stretched and looked north. "We're just getting started."

Other books by Alex

Series:

Calliope Books
Calliope and the Sea Serpent
Calliope and the Royal Engineers
The Third Prince and the Enemy's Daughter
Calliope and the Kershian Empire

Spruce Bay Books
Wendigo Whispers
Cry of the White Moose
Disputed Rock

The Belandria Tarot
The Devil Reversed
The Regent's Reign
The Empire Unbalanced
The World Widens
The Fury Unleashed

Blue in Kamloops
Tranquille Dark
Columbia Smoke

STAND ALONE BOOKS:

Leedles and the Golden Tree
Generation Gap
The Gods Above
Tales of Light and Dark
Like Mushrooms (poetry and photography)
The Heronmaster
Blood and Sparkles, and other stories
Princess of Boring
By the Book
Sarcasm is My Superpower
Playing on Yggdrasil
The Unenchanted Princess

Read short stories and excerpts from his novels at alexmcgilvery.com

CPSIA information can be obtained
at www.ICGtesting.com
Printed in the USA
BVHW081924240721
612087BV00001B/24